Allan,

Finding Max

Thanks for the
Support!

Warren M Jorgensen

Finding Max

By Darren M. Jorgensen

Creators Publishing
Hermosa Beach, CA

Cover art by Peter Kaminski

CREATORS PUBLISHING
737 3rd St
Hermosa Beach, CA 90254
310-337-7003

Library of Congress Control Number: 2017955992
ISBN (print): 978-1-945630-68-2
ISBN (e-book): 978-1-945630-67-5

First Edition

Printed in the United States of America
1 3 5 7 9 10 8 6 4 2

DEDICATION

I know many people who deserve to have a book dedicated to them for courageous feats of the heart, great leaps of faith, strengthening exercises of endurance—so very many different reasons. But this is not that book. Or, shall I say, this is not their book.

This book belongs to one woman only, the only woman who exemplifies all the above qualities in spades and to an extraordinary degree. Her laughter sets the birds a-clattering, while her sorrows cause the very air around her to sigh. She is forever inventive and always gung ho to try out my latest brainchildren. She reads like a trouper, and I love watching her gears going when something I've written has set her mind twisting and turning aflame. Then, suddenly, she is bouncing with ideas about where I might go next with my keyboard and tablet.

She is a veritable fountain of enthusiasm, and the sun that radiates from within her is almost enough to break apart my darkest of skies. Her gentle stroke of hand through my hair is enough to dispel tears from continuing their rapid descent. The sound of her calming voice is enough to dissipate even the darkest pits of my anxiety.

For ten extraordinary, fun-filled and, at times, surprising years, this woman has shared her life with me, laughed at my stupid jokes, cried when my own tears wouldn't stop, tried new foods with me, gone on adventures with me, been through hell with me, sold soap with me and basically done everything it took to simply come along for the ride and love me for it.

Ginette Law, this book is dedicated to you. I love you with all my strength.

CONTENTS

CHAPTER ONE

The cat was almost dead. And it was all his fault.

He hadn't meant to kill the cat, but who would believe him? Certainly not Gary, who would taunt him about how the cat must have felt in its last moments; the terror it felt being chased as it darted across the park; the screech of the tires, like nails on a blackboard; the agonizing *Riiip!* as its back legs tore apart from its torso; the sound of it clawing at the road, trying to drag itself home. And then Gary would run home to tell their mother.

She wouldn't believe him either. In her afternoon haze, she would totter on the couch and demand he tell the truth. Was he teasing the cat? Was he tormenting the cat? Why did he chase it into traffic? Then he'd get a beating, and then she'd exile him to bed.

He sat on the cement curb. The cat was no longer screeching loud snarls but rather lapsing into soft, small cries. He tried not to look at its abdomen and the gore smeared across the pavement where its legs should have been, but his eyes kept travelling there, curious and clinical. The cat's blood was bright red in the afternoon sun. It left a brilliant crimson streak where the tire had scraped the cat along the road. And now, a pool of it was creeping all around the dying animal.

Maximilian held his knees to his chest, wrapping his arms around them and pulling them tight. He was trying to keep it together, but he felt that he might not be able to for long. He felt as though he shared something with this dying cat, some kind of connection, like a secret to be told in hushed tones under the bedsheet. But he was also disconnected from it, as though he were floating above himself and looking down. Both sensations coursed through him, making his legs feel like jelly.

He wanted to kick the cat, give it one good boot to send it soaring to the other side of the road. He wanted it out of his sight, out of his mind, out of his memory. But he couldn't do that. He couldn't bear to bring more misery to the poor animal, whose breathing now sounded like a choking motor with water in its lines.

Suddenly it stretched out, all its remaining muscles tensing. A cry escaped from its mouth, a feeble cry that ended on a simple exhale as it finally relaxed.

The cat was dead.

Maximilian began to rock in place on the cement curb, gripping one wrist with the other hand until they were both bone white. He felt a stinging behind his eyes as tears gathered. He was on the street at the far end of the soccer field. He hadn't realized how far he had run.

How could he have done this? *Why* had he done this? He'd seen the cat scampering across the road toward the park, where he and Gary were playing on the monkey bars. Well, Gary was playing on the monkey bars, but Maximilian was still too small to be able to pull himself up. He was standing to the side of them, pleading with Gary to push him on the swings. But he wasn't listening.

It wasn't like he thought about running toward the cat. He just did. He and Gary didn't have any pets. Their mother wouldn't allow it. "You won't look after it," she'd say any time they begged for a dog. And they knew instinctively not to push her. It wasn't safe; her moods were mercurial, brooding and dark. And her wooden spoon came out far too quickly.

How much trouble do you think you'll be in? he thought, though he could have sworn he'd heard the voice out loud. But he ran nevertheless, leaving Gary behind on the monkey bars. Gary didn't even notice that he was gone.

The cat had reached the playground side of the road by the time it saw Maximillian hurtling toward it across the dry, brown grass. It froze, sensing danger in its path. Then, as suddenly as it had stopped, it turned and ran back down the block toward the alley it had crept from, the alley that offered shelter, hiding places and the stink of days-old garbage bags piled up against brick walls.

"Hey! I won't hurt you," Maximilian called after the cat as it streaked toward the road. But it didn't care what he said.

"I won't hurt you! I promise," he said. And it was true. All he wanted to do was sit and stroke the cat in the late August sunshine, watch it roll over on its back like Mrs. Crabtree's cat next door. He put on a burst of speed and ran as fast as his little legs could carry him. Still, the cat ran.

Maximilian's shouting woke Gary out of whatever reverie he had been in, and he saw his five-year-old brother at the other end of the soccer field, beyond the limits of the playground, beyond where he was supposed to be. And if their mother were to find out that Gary wasn't watching Maximilian properly, there would be hell to pay.

"Hey, Maximilian! Get over here! You know you're supposed to stick by me. You can't leave the playground. Wait until I tell Mom," Gary said.

He let go of the monkey bars and plopped to the ground. The landing hurt his feet more than he'd expected. Maximilian was running down the sidewalk now, so far away, and Gary felt a knot in his gut. He was too close to the road, and if he were to run into it, there'd be no way for Gary to reach him in time. There wasn't much traffic but enough to seriously hurt him, or even kill him. It would only take one car. . . . He began to jog after his brother.

The playground was set in the middle of a long stretch of dead grass and bushes that were only barely kept up by their small city. The soccer field, dotted with potato chip packages and candy bar wrappers and other assorted litter, flanked the playground on one end, a tall chain-link fence separating the two. On the other side of the playground was a baseball diamond, also separated by a chain-link fence. Two sets of bleachers stood forlornly in the green, one to the side of the baseball diamond and one beside the soccer field. They would give you splinters if you slid your bum across the seats. Gary found this out one day while he and Maximilian were climbing them.

And then Maximilian was out of his view, having disappeared behind the bleachers just as a silver-grey car tore down the length of the road toward him. Terror gripped Gary's heart like a fist.

This was it: This was the day Maximilian would die. And it would be all his fault for not watching him. Playing on the monkey bars . . . how could he have been so stupid?

The cat ran right into the road and under the car's tires. Gary heard a short screech and then saw the car speed out from the other side of the bleachers. *Phew, it didn't hit him*, Gary thought. He relaxed slightly, but it was hard for him to breathe. He slowed his pace a little so he could catch his breath, but it wasn't enough. He stopped, leaned over, put his hands on his knees and hung his head down until he could see between his legs. The fear and adrenaline was making him dizzy.

From this vantage point, he saw something very strange. The same car had turned right and ambled down the road in his direction, appearing upside down just in his right periphery. At the stop sign, it turned right again, crossing behind him. He straightened up and turned around to his left. He watched the car turn right yet again, and then right once more, past the alley. Its pace slowed to a crawl, and then it disappeared behind the bleachers.

Gary felt some kind of realization, some kind of understanding struggling to rise to the surface of his thoughts. But try as he might, he couldn't quite grasp it, couldn't quite read the signs around him. Out of his view, the car stopped, and its window rolled down. Maximilian was there, not here beside him. Gary knew not to talk to strangers, and Maximilian knew it, too. But Maximilian also knew not to leave his brother's side when they went to the playground, and he hadn't much followed that rule today. But what could really happen from talking to a stranger on a sunny afternoon at the park? Surely they weren't going to do anything bad to his little brother . . . the brother he was supposed to be watching; the brother he was supposed to protect; the brother who looked up to him. Fear buzzed in his ears, and he began to run. By the time he reached the bleachers, the car was speeding away.

Maximilian was gone.

CHAPTER TWO

The subway car hurtled down the track toward the next stop, Spring Street Station. Even at this time of day, there were no open seats, and Gary was left to sway back and forth, back and forth while holding on to the bar overhead. Below him, a grossly obese man sat hugging a weathered briefcase made of soft brown leather. One strap looked ready to tear in half. Next to him sat a very thin Asian woman who looked about twenty-one or twenty-two. She was dressed in a short, black dress and wore a deep-red lipstick. Her nails looked like they could shred moose hide. Her eyeliner was crooked on one side, but Gary was hardly going to be the one to tell her. As they approached the stop, she stood up and almost fell into him face first.

"Sorry," she muttered in the way only New Yorkers can apologize: with fire in her eyes. And if he were a typical New Yorker, he might just retort and bite her head off. But he wasn't.

First of all, he wasn't born or raised in New York, so the sarcasm, brevity and forcefulness with which they all seemed to speak didn't come naturally to him. Second of all, and maybe most tellingly, he was more than willing to give up his subway seat to someone who needed it more. Part of this may have been due to growing up in Albany, where people tended to be kinder and less truthful and to move decidedly slower.

He was a kind man but a hard one, too. He was a man's man in some ways but not in others. He was silent at most times, keeping his thoughts to himself. He liked watching football on Sunday afternoons. And a part of him still felt that he needed a good woman to complete his life, though he hadn't found one yet. This was partly due to his shyness, a trait that most people didn't discern because he trained himself in school to be the forward one when talking to his clients. He had to be; it was his job. And part of him still liked to cook for company, though it had been a long time since he'd been able to do this, primarily because he had no friends. It wasn't that he didn't want friends. He just hadn't found anyone who met his three discerning requirements.

Number one: Know your place. He didn't like friends who were brash or overwhelming, or took up too much space. He liked social situations where everyone had a place and no one would hijack the conversation. He liked to be able to contribute to the conversation somewhat, and he knew that other people did, too.

Number two: Don't come over unannounced. This didn't seem to be as much of a problem in New York City as it was in Michigan, where he went to school. He didn't like surprises, like people catching him unawares in the shower or when the house was unclean.

Number three: Keep your problems to yourself. He didn't much care for having to work overtime, but when friends were complaining about their issues, Gary felt like he had to slip into social-worker mode and counsel them, make them feel better or fix them somehow.

His life experiences during his short twenty-five years had already hardened him somewhat. But he was cool in a crisis and demanded that others be that way, too. And when they weren't, he could always be counted on to stand up and maintain his demeanour. Whereas his work colleague Saundra was more prone to panic in difficult moments, Gary was the one who calmed the room down. She was prone to losing her head, while he was prone to keeping his.

His eyes were creased despite his age, with tiny crow's-feet spidering outward toward his hairline. His dark-brown hair was already speckled with grey, and when it was longer, it would stick up in crazy angles. No amount of gel would keep it in place. He'd given up the fight long ago while still an undergrad and kept it cut short since so he at least looked presentable.

"Presentable" was a good word to describe him in both appearance and demeanour. He was the man who a woman would not fear bringing home to her parents, though none had done so. At the ripe age of twenty-five, he'd had remarkably few lovers. And the few relationships he'd been in occurred during his undergrad years at the University of Michigan. He hated that university, the only redeeming aspect being the excellent School of Social Work that he attended. It was rated number one in its field by all the reports that mattered. He'd decided he wanted to go there when he was researching colleges during high school. He was living with foster parents at the time, and they encouraged him to visit the school before making a decision. So he did, with them kindly footing the bill.

He abhorred the midwestern attitudes that he encountered. It was a huge school, and he hoped that the town of Ann Arbor would have its fair share of open minds and forward-thinking residents. But instead, it prided itself on its completely boring lifestyle and its general malaise about everything worldly. So he tucked his head in and down and scrutinized his books and handouts rather than the people around him. He hated the university and the town with a passion, but he loved the pathways of learning.

With the seat next to him now vacant, the porker with the beat-up briefcase readjusted himself, oozing onto her seat. She scooted around him and stood at the door, swaying as the subway car came to a stop. The doors opened. Gary followed her out onto the platform and up the steps to the street, where he finally lost sight of her. He was sure he'd seen her before, probably on the same train and at the same stop. That was his best guess.

It was about ten degrees cooler on the street than it was in the subway car. At least it felt that way. That was one of the things he really hated about New York: the weather in July and August. He loved almost everything else. It was the morning of August 17, and he'd heard on the radio that it would get up to ninety-three degrees. *How are human beings supposed to live in this heat? They just aren't equipped*, he thought. Or at least *he* wasn't equipped. During the summer last year, his first year living in New York, he frequently came home with a frightening heat rash between his legs, under his arms and on his feet. No amount of ointment seemed to help. He was unlike himself, taciturn, angry and out of sorts as he tried—and failed—to manage his body temperature by sucking on ice cubes, drinking bottles of fizzy soda and stopping at the Stuyvesant Town pool every afternoon before work, where the water was always cool.

He walked the length of the block, turned right and walked several more blocks past shop after shop that seemed to have no purpose but to just to be there; past shops that were locked up tight with darkened windows and metal panels; past a shop that sold phone cards and plumbing repair goods, though it looked like it was in need of a repair itself; past bars that stunk of stale beer, sawdust and curdled vomit. By the third one, he felt like vomiting himself. Luckily, he turned down the block and arrived at work.

He always loved this walk. It gave him time to think about the Mets, about the unfailing cruelty of crushing poverty, about the injustice of America's health care system. He wondered often whether his feeble meticulousness had any bearing on any of it. None of his choices had any effect on the Mets, he knew that for certain. He also knew that the problem of America's health care state was beyond his control. The Bowery Mission shelter had doctors who volunteered their services to clients, but that was the extent of it. Yet he hoped that he might somehow be alleviating the pulverizing effects of poverty on his clients.

He would often think about years past and wonder whether he'd made the right choices. Becoming a social worker was chief among them. While all his friends at Michigan were studying history and political science, getting ready to take the LSAT or enrolling in organic chemistry in preparation for med school, he was learning the ways of a clinician. While some of them had been bucking the system and shucking their footwear for shoeless walks through campus during their four years there—whether as a statement of personal preference or political idealism he knew not—he was striving to understand the aberrant human brain, the intersections of class and race and poverty, and the numerical classifications in the Diagnostic and Statistical Manual of Mental Disorders.

Sometimes he wondered where Maximilian had ended up, what untimely end his brother might have met. But these thoughts he quickly pushed away. They were just too damned painful.

He wanted to do more. He wanted to find a way to end the relentless poverty that his clients lived under and that lived within them. He wanted to alleviate their pain. If he could find buckets and buckets of money to distribute evenly, he would, though he knew that was only a short-term solution to their problems. They ran deeper than that, as did his own, and a panacea of gifted cash would still never supplant their grief or their nightmares. He knew this deep inside, and he also knew that relieving their tears would never quell the rivers that flowed behind their eyes. Rather, education and jobs, cleanliness and health care were some of the keys to their eventual success. But to facilitate all that, Gary would have to cut his wrists and bleed, bleed dark red into their waiting, hungry mouths, and they would consume all that he could offer. And offer himself he did, as much as he could, as much as they could individually consume. One by one he worked with the the ones who were ready and able to suck his lifeblood dry. But he could only offer so much before the evening shift's end, and he would pack himself up in his briefcase to return another day. He wanted so much to give, but there was only so much of himself he could slay. Some gossiped that he was a workaholic. He believed he was there to work, so work he did until the hard-won day was gone and he was dog-tired. Tomorrow he would come back. Tomorrow he would bleed himself dry again all in the name of Maximilian, so he could make up for that day in the park so very long ago when he should have been watching but wasn't.

The red door of The Mission was set into a beautifully kept brick wall. Gary could almost feel the sweat licking his neck, and he couldn't wait to get to the cool, dry air on the other side. He walked through and waited for the woman behind the front window to buzz him through the second door, a safety precaution to keep out the inebriated, the stoned and the other undesirables. This space was just as hot as it was outside, as the air conditioning did not flow out to it, and his hand was already on the doorknob in anticipation when she let him through.

As he walked down the length of the hall past the gated entrance and a gathering of administrative offices, he could hear the sounds of dinner preparation, pots and pans clanging against one another and cupboards closing with a bang behind some laughing volunteer. Volunteers staffed most of the programs at The Mission, but others like him were on payroll. Every person who sat at one of the desks behind the administrative doors was on payroll. When he arrived at his office, which he shared with Saundra, he knocked on the door and waited. The metal plate on the door was simply inscribed with the words "Social Worker."

He had been a professional social worker for over a year now, having landed this job right out of grad school. He always wanted to work with indigent populations, the homeless and the otherwise distraught. He wanted it so badly that he pursued an internship with The Mission while still an undergrad, which was renewed every summer during school. He would travel to New York City, a city that was more his speed, with worldly attitudes and bagel stores everywhere. He'd secure temporary housing with other students whose roommate was gone for the summer. It wasn't such a surprise to him that he landed a full-time job there after grad school, since he had already clocked so much time. It was really the only place he had ever worked, and he loved his work, despite the consistent level of stress.

The stress came from the impossibility of ever really changing anyone's life while attempting so hard to do so. He worked hard, always lending an ear to a client in times of need. And he tried his best to funnel them into The Mission programs: the Short-Term Housing Program, the Long-Term Housing Program, the Good Foods Program, the Clean-Living Program or the Life Skills Program, the last of which they were probably best known for in the industry. But no matter how hard he tried, there were always those who were going to disdain the Good Foods Program or stay addicted to whatever substances they loved. Trying to help but being unable: That was the worst part of his job.

"Come in," sang Saundra. She was sitting at their desk. She wore a pair of black pants and a bright-pink blouse with ruffles on the end of the short sleeves. Her faded red hair was speckled with grey, and she sported deep crow's-feet in the corners of her eyes. She'd only just reached her midthirties, but she appeared to be about forty-five or forty-six. In a chair beside the desk sat a rather short man with golden hair. His back was turned to Gary.

"Oh, hi," she said. She gestured to the man. "This is David, a newcomer at The Mission. We're just discussing Life Skills classes that I'd like to see him get into. We've also been talking about short-term housing solutions that are available to him."

"Congratulations, David, for deciding to take the Life Skills Program," Gary said as he walked up to the desk to face him. "It's a very good program, and lots of our clients have benefited from the classes."

The first thing Gary noticed about him was the fear in his eyes. He looked like a scared rabbit might look. No, not a rabbit—more like a scared wolverine, if there ever were such a thing. He was probably in his early to midtwenties, but Gary knew from experience that many of The Mission's clients often looked older than they were. Living on the streets was hard. He had a strong jawline, a tan face and dark-blue eyes. His downy golden hair lay in curls that could use a cutting. Gary thought about how stunning this young man's looks would be once he was bathed clean and smelling like soap. His arms were a rich tawny, no doubt from the hours spent uncovered in his ripped and dirty T-shirt. They were covered in a fine, almost translucent down that was long and rather thick. He needed a shower, clean clothes and something to get rid of the sour smell that accompanied him from living on the streets. The black sweatpants he wore looked like they could stand up on their own. They probably smelled like it, too.

Gary got a distinct impression that he had met this man before.

"Have you stayed with us before, David?" he asked.

"Never."

"Where have you been sleeping? If you don't mind my asking."

"Here and there. Mostly under an overpass in the Bronx. At least lately. Before that on the Upper West Side, near Harlem and the 120s. And lots of other places before that. I keep on the move."

He had a cautious air about him. He seemed a bit shy, a trait not often seen in other clients. But at the same time, he seemed unashamed and unreserved, completely able to stand up for himself and claim his place in a room full of strangers. It was a curious mix that only heightened Gary's desire to know the man further.

"Have you spent much time in the East Village?"

"Not much. Why? Does that matter?"

"Not at all. I just have the feeling we've crossed each other's paths before. But I could be mistaken. Where do you hail from?"

"What?"

"Where do you come from? You say you like to keep on the move, but where were you born?"

"North of the city. Look, if this is going to be too much of a problem, I can just leave."

"I'm sorry, but I'm not trying to be rude; just passing small talk."

"It's not just small talk if you think you've seen me before. It's more like you're digging for information. I don't like digging the past up, and I don't like anyone else digging it up either. Who are you, anyway?" His eyes narrowed.

"David," said Saundra in her most placating voice possible, "this is our evening-shift social worker, and he's just passing the time with you. He's a bit early for work." She gave Gary a pointed look that clearly said, 'Get out.'

"I was just about to go get coffee from the Sneaky Bean. Either of you two want something? My treat," Gary said as he put his briefcase down on the floor along the edge of the wall.

"I'm coffeed out for the day. But you, David?"

"I'll take one. Six sugars and some cream."

"I'll be back in a flash," said Gary, closing the door behind him.

As he walked the two short blocks to the coffee shop, he couldn't shake the feeling that somehow, somewhere he'd met David before. But where? If it wasn't through The Mission, then how? None of his friends were likely to know this young man. Not that Gary had any friends here in this city, or many friends at all, for that matter. And from the sound of it, David didn't either. If he liked to keep on the move like he said, then he was unlikely to forge ties with other people.

In his experience, there were two primary kinds of homeless people: those who banded together with others for companionship and safety, and those who were loners, who kept to themselves and moved easily from one point to another, slipping between the cracks of society like a sharp edge through silk. The loners never developed lasting friendships and never left a trace of themselves behind. They were the easily forgotten ones, whom even the other homeless didn't remember after a short time. They were the ones who kept to the shadows and only came out at night, their days spent sleeping fitfully in nooks and crannies and alleyways where they were unlikely to be discovered. They were the ones who were usually hiding from something, whether the past, the future or themselves. David seemed to be one of them.

Gary arrived at the Sneaky Bean while his mind was still troubled with thoughts of David. The coffee shop was mostly empty. A group of high school girls in their green tartan skirts and white short-sleeved shirts sat at a table near the back of the room. On closer inspection, he noticed that one of them was actually a boy with longish, dark hair and black, square glasses. He obviously wasn't in uniform. *Probably their token homosexual*, thought Gary. A blond wooden counter ran the length of the plate-glass window facing the street. Standing there was a balding middle-aged man.

He wore small, square reading glasses and was deeply engrossed in a book. Gary tilted his head to read the cover from where he stood in line: Alice Munro's *Friend of My Youth*. Another young man, who looked remarkably how Gary imagined a vampire would look—brooding and taciturn, scowling at passersby while he sat hunched over his coffee mug and stirred it relentlessly.

"Can I help you?" a voice said.

Gary's head spun forward, and he was struck dumb for a moment.

So this is where I know her from, he thought.

Before him, asking for his order, was the Asian woman with the crooked eyeliner from the subway. All thoughts of David were banished from his mind in an instant. She was stunningly beautiful, with a heart-shaped face that held black eyes that curved up slightly at the edges. It was a sad beauty reminiscent of autumn days and thunderstorms that wasn't apparent in that hot, uncomfortable, filthy subway car earlier that day. He'd been so bothered by the heat that he hadn't even noticed how a deep mystery oozed from her very pores. She seemed to be floating above the ground, her movements graceful and almost hypnotic to watch. Gary was mesmerized. She must have been only five feet tall, if that. And when she smiled, Gary could read a weariness, as though she were carrying the weight of countless slights upon her shoulders. Her smile was devoid of comfort. He wondered how someone so young could have lived through such lonely days and remained so intact. But appearances, as he knew, were deceiving. *Now this is a woman I could sink my teeth into*, he thought.

"Can I help you, sir?" She was clearly annoyed with him for holding up the line.

"Two medium coffees, please. One black, the other with six sugars and cream."

"Six?" she asked incredulously.

"Yes, six." He he felt slightly embarrassed. "The one with the sugar isn't for me. It's for a client."

She began to pour the coffees. "A client? What kind of client takes six sugars? A starving one?" She laughed like a neighing horse.

"Yes, actually. I work at the homeless shelter down the street. The Mission. And most of our clients are starving for food and nutrition."

"Sugar doesn't give you much nutrition." She set the coffees on the counter before him as he dug out his wallet.

"No, but it gives a false sense of it to someone who hasn't eaten in days."

Jean stared at him, a little dumbfounded. She wasn't expecting such an answer. Of course, it rang of truth. But it was still hard to swallow.

"That'll be four bucks, please." Gary rifled through his wallet for a five but found four singles instead. He handed them across the counter.

"What's your name?" he asked before he could stop himself. He could feel the blood rising to his cheeks. "It's just that I come in here all the time and I don't even know your name. It's so much more personal when you deal with someone day in and day out and know their name, even in New York. But I'm not from New York originally. I'm from Albany, and people there tend to be friendlier than here. So I guess I'm asking because—"

"I'm Jean." She cocked her head to the right and smiled a smile that committed to nothing. "And you're cute, especially when you blush."

"I . . . well . . . thanks," he said more sheepishly than he'd intended. And with all the bravado having left him, he turned and walked quickly out of the coffee shop, his shoes slapping hollowly against the tiles.

All the short way back to The Mission, his mind was occupied with thoughts of Jean: the line of her jaw, her almond-shaped eyes, her bright-red lipstick and razor-sharp nails. And that short, black dress that gave a man a good view of her very skinny legs. He could see the muscles there, her strong calves and even stronger thighs. But something seemed a little off about her, and it wasn't just the uneven eyeliner. He couldn't quite put his finger on it. Then again, this was New York, the place where damaged people congregated from all four points on the compass. There was something wrong with everyone he'd met here so far, some fragment missing from their otherwise perfect armature. They were like handmade oriental carpets: beautiful in appearance but flawed in their design up close. Nobody was perfectly balanced here, because everyone who came to this city came because of their flaws. New York was a place that could hide you. It was a place that could either minimize or exaggerate your flaws. It was a city that absorbed the worst of humanity as well as the best, and he knew that if Jean were actually able to hide her flaws, it was only with studied practice. With a start, he realized that she didn't ask him his name. She did tell him he was cute, though that could have just been a bit of charm to increase the tips in her jar.

When he got back to the office, Saundra and David were just finishing up.

"I thought you'd never get back with the coffee," joked David, obviously more at ease than when Gary had left him.

"Here you go. I had to fight through angry mobs of Arab cabbies and off-duty policemen to get to the front of the line. Six sugars and cream, as directed."

"Thanks much."

"I'm very sorry about earlier. I didn't mean to offend you with my questions. It's just that in our line of work, we are used to asking questions—many of them—to understand the range of services that we might be able to offer. Peace?"

"I'm just not used to talking much about myself. No one asks, and I usually don't speak. Peace." Gary still sensed that he was not one of David's favourite people in the world.

David turned to Saundra. "Are we finished yet? I could use a smoke."

"Yes, we're about done. There's no smoking on the grounds or within fifty feet of the doorway. Most of our clients smoke in the alleyway. We keep a space cleared away for them, so you'll find others to talk to there before dinner is ready. That is unless you want to help out preparing dinner, but I think we already have enough volunteers tonight."

"I'd rather not, but I'll head to the alleyway. How do I know when it's time for dinner?"

"Everyone in the alleyway will start lining up to get back in. That'll be your cue. But you might want to head down to the housing office to put your name on the roster for a bed for tonight. If you want one, that is. It's down the hall and around the corner, the one with the big window facing the hall. There's probably already a line."

"Thanks. I'll do that," he said as he closed the door behind him.

When it was clear that David was gone, Saundra said, "Well, I think we can safely assume he doesn't like you, Gary."

"You got that, too?" he said with a chuckle. "I usually don't make such a good impression so quickly."

"It may just be that he doesn't like other men. He seemed almost frightened when he was talking to you, like he was scared you'd see through him. And he certainly seems to have enough walls and barriers. But who's to say with a short meeting like that? And I suspect you earned some Brownie points by getting him the coffee."

"How easily you see through me, oh, ancient one."

"Are you calling me old?"

"No, just wise. Now clear out of my chair. I've got to get ready to solve the problems of the masses in one short evening shift."

"I already did that during my one short day shift. Cheers!" she called back over her shoulder as she walked out the door and left it open behind her.

Gary sat down, logged into the computer and began to catch up on new developments with his clients since last night. Samuel had gotten into a fight with another homeless man and come out the worse. Thankfully, the fight wasn't on the premises, though it seemed to be about some kind of territorial rights to a sleeping spot he had outside The Mission. There were eighteen stitches where a broken glass bottle had sliced a gash in his cheek. He'd arrived at The Mission covered in his own blood. It was dry by then, but his cut was filthy and raw. Samuel was one of his clients who wasn't really ready to enter the Long-Term Housing Program.

Donovan needed some new clothing. He'd shown up without pants, wearing only underwear and the striped green shirt he was so attached to. He accepted a new pair of pants, brown khakis, but did not accept a couple of new shirts. Instead, he asked whether his shirt could be laundered in the Mission facilities. He insisted on staying in the laundry room to wait for his shirt to come out of the dryer, rather than spending his time shirtless outside. If Gary remembered correctly, Donovan was rather shy.

Knock knock knock.

Gary looked up from the computer screen and glanced at the doorway. David was there again. He looked like he'd forgotten something. As they made eye contact, Gary felt his whole world converge instantaneously. He was slammed with a whirlwind of images and an onslaught of memories. He thought he heard the wind rushing past him, but he realized that it was his pulse pounding in his ears. For a moment, his vision was blurred and he was thrust backward in time to a day long ago, another hot day like this one, when he was running across the brown grass, running away from the monkey bars toward his brother, who would be long gone and never return.

Gary started to stand.

"Maximilian?" he said.

His brother turned and bolted toward the front door.

CHAPTER THREE

Gary's chair toppled over from the force of his backward push. He couldn't let his brother get away. He wasn't quite sure how he'd recognized Maximilian. It had been seventeen years since that awful day, that day that changed his life forever.

Why wasn't Maximilian dead? Everyone thought he was. He was abducted so many years ago. If he had been freed and he were still alive, then why hadn't he contacted his family in the years since? Or done something to acknowledge his survival? Something to let them know he was alive? Something to try to reclaim his life, which had been ripped from his very hands at the age of five? And how exactly had Gary recognized him after all these years? He was taken so many years ago that Gary sometimes had trouble recalling his face. He was more of a mirage, a dreamlike image that teased Gary with its instability and fragility.

Was it the telltale golden curls that still framed his face? Was it his deep, reticent, dark-blue eyes? Was it the curve of his mouth, the corners that slanted downward as though he were perpetually frowning? Maybe it was those age-progression pictures that had been drawn up by the Albany police force upon his request two years ago. They garnered no new leads in Maximilian's case, though they looked remarkably like the man presenting himself as David, the brother he might have had if it hadn't been for that fateful day that remained shrouded in mystery, a larger-than-life puzzle missing crucial pieces.

After the abduction, after Gary ran home with his tongue dried up in his mouth from fear, he spent countless hours in the black of night rethinking his actions on that day. If only he'd been watching Maximilian more closely. If only he hadn't been having so much fun on the monkey bars. If only he hadn't been hanging by his knees with his arms swaying back and forth, back and forth, and his hair standing on end. And if only there hadn't been that car, that evil car with its evil occupant and evil intentions that ensnared their small family in its grip. From that day on, they'd lived in their own private hell.

Their mother's fate had been her own. She was incarcerated for a murder she didn't commit. And afterward, Gary became a ward of the state, shunted from foster home to foster home, too old to be adopted but too young to live on his own. He immersed himself in school during that time and was drawn to subjects like social studies and English and humanities. He sweat out all the pain, the loneliness, the anguish and the tears, striving for grades instead of memories because there was nothing left in him to strive for. He no longer carried his identity of "big brother to Maximilian," so he strove for another identity: the "good boy." And he garnered those good-boy grades, every one of them hard-won. At night in his bedroom, he worked tirelessly on essays and assignments and exam preparation. It didn't matter where he was living or which foster home had taken him in; he still worked to become something he'd never been before, something bigger and better. It was his way of turning inward, and it helped to stem the flow of his tears. When asked, "How are you feeling today?" by his revolving world of foster parents, he simply replied, "I'm fine." He never let anyone in. He never let anyone see the depth of his sadness. Rather, he walked through life with his head hanging low, trying to avoid trouble at school and at the homes he was shuttled between.

Eventually, he turned eighteen and was no longer a ward of the state or a child. With much determination, he applied to the best colleges. But Michigan had an excellent School of Social Work that was ranked best in the country by U.S. News & World Report. He wanted so badly to make up for what he had done—for what he hadn't done, actually. He had not watched over Maximilian that day. He had failed to protect his little brother when he needed him most. He had failed to protect him from the world. There was so much he had not done. He needed to make up for it now by becoming a social worker and saving all the little brothers he had the power to save.

Gary often wondered whether Maximilian had ever forgiven him for that day. He also wondered whether he would ever be freed from blame. But he never deserved forgiveness. He deserved to suffer, to live with the guilt of losing Maximilian forever. He deserved what he got: a string of foster homes and ulcers by the age of fifteen, and a constant dread that set in every morning he woke still alive. Perhaps he once hoped there would be a future without guilt, or that he'd be able to share it with someone else. But now, at the age of twenty-five, he believed he was cursed with a private guilt that was his burden and his alone to carry upon his shoulders, on his back and in his shattered heart forever. "Keep a close eye on your brother, Gary," their drunken mother demanded that day. And he didn't. Climbing the monkey bars was much more fun.

But he was only eight years old then. He came to that realization many years later, after many counselling sessions during which he cried his eyes out over his laziness and stupidity. Eight. What eight-year-old boy could be blamed for forces beyond his control? An eight-year-old was no match for a silver-grey station wagon and the monster behind the wheel. And where was their mother? Why didn't she come along that day? She was drinking alone in the living room of their low-income flat, too busy to supervise her own two sons. *Well, she certainly paid for that choice,* Gary often thought. And there was no dad in the picture; he had been cut down years before by a knife-wielding opponent in a bar fight across town. How was an eight-year-old boy to protect his five-year-old brother from the evil in the world? Even now, he still didn't have an answer. Why? Because there was no way he could have protected him. Evil pulsed like a purple vein, part of the lifeblood of a chaotic world.

Even though everyone thought Maximilian was dead and had thought so for years (despite his body having never been found), Gary kept him as alive as he dared through his constant contact with the Albany police force, his urging—no, pestering—the officers to continue looking through their meagre file for any possible new leads. But to them, the case was closed after their mother's trial. Only Officer Downing continued to humour him. Gary would call their mother every year on Maximilian's birthday and try to coax good memories of her youngest son to the front of her mind. In some way, these calls were cruel. He never called her during the rest of the year. Some of his foster parents offered to take him to visit, but he always refused—and not necessarily politely either. He remembered Maximilian as alive, as a living, breathing mass of flesh, blood and bone. He had to. He remembered Maximilian as though he'd just seen him yesterday or the day before, or had just spoken to him on the phone at length. The computerized drawing helped him imagine his brother as more than a young boy, as an attractive young man. He doggedly pestered the New York City precincts with the image and obsessively tried to get them to begin their own searches. But to his knowledge, none of them had. Maximilian had been gone far too long to grace any milk cartons.

And just recently, Officer Downing had suggested, as though he were tiptoeing on shattered glass, that it was time for Gary to abandon his search.

"Don't you think, Gary, that if Maximilian were still alive and able to contact you, he would have by now? He'd be twenty-two years old. That's plenty of time spent missing you and your mother. If he somehow turns up in the future, it'll be a miracle. More likely, though, he won't. Let him rest, son."

Gary knew in the depths of his heart that Downing was right, but that didn't mean giving up the search felt right. Maximilian had always needed him, and maybe he needed him more than ever right now, all these years later. What if he couldn't remember their last name? He was only five years old when he'd been abducted, after all. What if he couldn't remember the name of their city? What if he couldn't remember their address and phone number (though neither would help him now)? Their childhood home was just a distant memory for Gary, so it would be even more so for Maximilian, he surmised. And Gary moved to New York after college without looking back, so Maximilian would have no idea where to even begin looking for him—if he even wanted to.

Gary ran as fast as his legs could carry him, as quickly as the crowd lining up for the cafeteria would let him. Maximilian's blond hair was bobbing in and out of sight as he weaved through the crowd. Gary's mind was a blur, though one thought screamed above all others: He just couldn't lose his brother a second time, especially not here in this city of millions, where he could hide in countless nooks and crannies and shadows. If he were to lose him now, he would be truly lost again, probably for the last time.

His heart sank as the inside entrance door opened to a stream of bright sunlight and then slammed again. But he caught another glimpse of his brother and breathed a quick sigh of relief.

"Maximilian! Don't run! There's nothing to be afraid of!" Gary said. But he kept running, desperately knocking people out of his way to break free of the crowd. Someone not far ahead fell to the ground.

"Maximilian! It's me, G—" The door opened again. His world spun sideways as he watched Maximilian flee through outer door and into the big world on the other side.

"No! Please!" he screamed as he sank toward the ground. But with a Herculean effort, he righted himself and kept on running. He threw open first the inner door and then the outer door, missed the top step and toppled down to the pavement below. The door slammed shut behind him.

After the initial shock of landing on the pavement had left him, he got to his knees and looked around. A crowd had begun to gather and form a loose circle around him, most of them smokers emerging from the alleyway. But Maximilian was nowhere to be seen.

Gary could almost hear his heart shattering.

Why did he run? What had terrorized him? Why didn't he recognize Gary, his own brother? It occurred to Gary that Saundra never formally introduced him to the interloper who called himself David, so he'd never heard Gary's name. To Maximilian, Gary was just another social worker doing another job, one who saw through his constructed illusions. Maybe knowing each other's names—real names—beforehand would have helped them recognize each other sooner and avoid all of this.

"Hey, Gary. Are you okay? You're bleeding pretty bad," Donovan said. Gary barely heard the words, but he accepted Donovan's hand and was helped to his feet. Suddenly the chatter of an excited crowd burned through the pounding in his ears. Drama. Always drama at The Mission. And the little group around him had just been fed its daily dose.

"You should go in to the doctor, man, and have him look at your arm. Maybe your face, too," Donovan said. Others murmured in agreement.

"I'm fine, thanks. I haven't been hurt badly," Gary said. But as he brushed the tickling away from his forearm, his hand came away dripping crimson. He looked down and was shocked to see the long, jagged gash that desperately needed attention.

"Well, maybe my arm is a bit banged up, but I'm sure it isn't bad." He took one last longing look around knowing already that he wasn't going to see Maximilian's head amongst the others. But the weight of years of searching for his brother was hard to banish so quickly, and he couldn't help feeling pangs of fruitless hope. He turned his back on the crowd, climbed the stairs and re-entered The Mission. Maybe he had better see the doctor.

Thirteen stitches and a flimsy excuse later, Gary headed back to his office and sank into his chair. There was no one at his door, and there likely wouldn't be until after dinner was over. A hungry tummy took precedence over life in turmoil for most of The Mission's clients. Gary felt sick to his stomach. It could've been the heat of the day. It could've been the coffee that now gurgled inside his stomach, threatening to make him retch. Or maybe it was because for a brief moment, the briefest of moments, he watched his innermost dreams come true, only to have them broken upon a rocky shore like the cold, cruel waves of the sea. Most likely it was a result of all three.

His mind began to stir obsessively, playing questions upon questions on loop. What had terrified his brother when he called his name? Gary just couldn't figure it out. He picked up the desk phone and dialled Saundra's cell phone. She probably wasn't going to appreciate a call that wasn't an emergency, but he had to try.

"Hello?" she answered on the third ring.

"It's Gary. Are you home yet?"

"Just walked in the door. What's up?"

"That client, David. What do you know about him?"

"What's he done?"

"Nothing. Nothing at all. I just want to try to track him down."

"Has he left? I thought he'd be staying the night."

"Something came up for him."

"And you're trying to track him down? What's so important that it can't wait until tomorrow? I'm at home now." Gary could hear the annoyance in her voice.

"This is important, Saundra. I really need to know everything I can about him."

"Couldn't you have just looked in my notes? Everything I know about him is there."

"Your personal impressions aren't."

Gary heard an exasperated exhale through the phone. She was obviously very annoyed at his intrusion.

"Well, I found him very guarded, very frightened," she said. "But he's very strong, too. He looks fragile, feels fragile, but has a strength that belies his complexion. And he's like a chameleon. I got the sense that he mirrors back at you whatever he thinks you're looking for. Is that what you want?"

"I suppose so. Anything else?"

"Not sure. Like I said, he's a mirror. I couldn't get a straight answer out of him no matter how hard I tried. Everything was just smoke and mirrors. I got the feeling that he's running from something. Or someone. You know; you talked with him."

"Thanks, Saundra. It's not much to go on, but it helps. Sorry to bother you after hours."

"Uh-huh. See you tomorrow." And the line went dead. Gary held on to the receiver for a minute, the dial tone sounding in his ear as he processed the conversation.

»

The dinner bell sounded just as Gary closed and locked his office door behind him. He pushed past the milling crowd, excusing himself repeatedly as he walked toward the cafeteria and got into the serving lineup behind the kitchen counter. He usually liked serving. He would pass plates of food through the window and across the counter to hungry, impatient clients and exchange a few pleasantries. Tonight they were serving spaghetti with red sauce, bread and bowls of thin soup. But his heart wasn't in it, so he was silent and taciturn for the duration of the serving. At last, he gathered his own meal together and sat at the end of a table amongst a group of chatty clients.

"What happened to your arm, Gary?" asked Samuel.

"I fell outside. Missed the top step."

"That was you?" Word got around The Mission fast. "How many stitches?"

Gary forced himself to pay attention to the conversation, but he couldn't shake the deep sadness that had washed over him. After so many years of hoping, after so many years of pestering the police and blaming himself, after so many years, why had this happened? The shortest ray of blazing light was shined into his darkened world and then snuffed out like a lit wooden match dropped into the raging sea. . . . He should have waited. He should have approached his brother carefully. Who knew what demons might be torturing this young man? He certainly didn't. Gary surmised that David was frightened—terrified, even. But of what? And why did he bolt the moment Gary called him by his real name? Gary couldn't make sense of any of it, except that he must be running. But running from what, or whom? What happened to his brother that instiled such palpable fear inside of him? What scarred him so badly as to register a torrent of terror in his eyes?

Imaginings crept up in Gary's mind. He could only think that whomever had taken Maximilian had kept him alive all these years for a reason. But he could only guess at the meaning that underscored such thoughts. Why had he been taken, if not for the simple pleasure of murdering him? Why hadn't his body been found days later in a dumpster, like so many other abductees? He'd been kept alive for some purpose, some devil's reason that Gary was frightened to think of. Just what had Maximilian endured all these years? Gary could only guess at what his life had been like on the streets. He knew about that life from his work with The Mission and the countless conversations he'd had with clients. But what about his life before, from the moment he was stolen to his years on the streets? Gary could only imagine, and what he imagined made him sick. He couldn't eat his supper and gave most of it to Donovan.

At the worst of times, Gary was a clinical man. "When things get rough, the tough get clinical" was something he liked to say to himself. He was even like that as a child. On the stand during their mother's trial, he didn't cry. He talked in that cold, detached manner that always served him so well. Without emotion, he told the truth of what happened that day in the park. He knew now that his demeanour might have been one of the reasons the jury never believed him. Instead, they believed that he was afraid of their mother and the rage that would ensue upon their return home if she were set free. But they never did return home. Gary exited one door and their mother another.

By the time he finished his shift, The Mission had grown mostly quiet. As he turned the key in his office door and locked it, he wondered again whether he would ever see his brother alive. Though he'd always nurtured the hope in his heart, now he had no hope. He knew that if Maximilian wanted to hide from him, he would surely succeed. Their meeting today was only by capricious chance. And he knew that his brother was adept at hiding. A loner like him was always adept at living in the shadows, keeping his nose to the ground and sniffing out danger. That was how they survived, those broken street souls. Sometimes The Mission would conduct searches for clients who had disappeared without a trace, but it was rare to succeed at finding them, much less coaxing them back. Besides, they hardly had the manpower to conduct these search-and-rescue missions, so they only attempted them for their more promising clients. But the staff knew that if someone wanted to hide, then they were adept at staying hidden.

The heat slapped Gary in the face when he opened the front door and stepped out onto the pavement. Under the streetlamp's glare, he could see his blood on the sidewalk where he had hit the ground only hours before. His arm was throbbing now that the anesthetic for the stitches had worn off. He stepped past the small pool of dry blood and walked slowly toward the subway entrance. The beginnings of a dull headache descended upon him. Tension had gathered in his neck and shoulders throughout the day. A dreadful ache squeezed at his heart. There were so many thoughts in his mind that his head felt like it was going to burst open on the sidewalk. Why had he been given a glimpse of hope only to have it snatched away at a moment's notice? How could the world around him be so immensely cruel that it snatched Maximilian away from him not once but twice?

He arrived at the subway entrance in no time. The platform was mostly empty at this time of night; only a few late-night stragglers waited to be carried toward Midtown and the Upper East Side. Most of them looked like they could have been Mission clients, though Gary was too absorbed in his thoughts to recognize any of them. When the train arrived, he walked disconsolately climbed into the car and sat down. He heard someone call out to hold the doors but couldn't tell from where he was sitting whether anyone did. As the train rattled out of the station, he caught a glimpse of the empty platform sliding by. *Sliding by like my life*, he thought as he settled into his seat.

And the train rattled onward, crawling through the dark tunnels beneath the city streets.

CHAPTER FOUR

"Howdy, stranger," Jean said.

Gary replied, "Hi, Jean. How's the world treating you these days?"

"Peachy. What can I get you?"

"Medium black coffee, please."

"Where have you been?"

"I was sick for a few days." It was kind of true. He had difficulty getting rid of that pounding headache that came the day of Maximilian's return. But it only plagued him for the better part of the next day and then disappeared. He took two days off simply because he couldn't face the empty room, the cluttered desk, the heads constantly poking in to ask him questions and request services. He did call Saundra each day, ostensibly to get updates on his clients. He was really calling to ask her in as many roundabout ways as possible whether his brother had returned. He hadn't.

It was strange . . . even though Maximilian was his brother, his own flesh and blood, he was reluctant to tell Saundra. He would have thought another social worker would be the ideal person to confide in, but he got a sick feeling in the pit of his gut every time he thought about doing so. Given the severity of Maximilian's reaction, Gary felt it best not to divulge his true identity to anyone. If the young man wanted so desperately to hide from the world, maybe he had his reasons. Who was Gary to break his anonymity without permission? If his brother wanted to confide in Saundra, then he would have already, regardless of Gary recognizing him. The fact that he hadn't returned since validated even more so that he was right in his assumptions. This way, if Maximilian were to return to The Mission, Gary could truthfully assert that he had not divulged their secret, and that The Mission was a safe place. Besides, if he were to tell Saundra about Maximilian, then he'd have to relive that awful day in the park and his culpability in Maximilian's disappearance. This was a conversation Gary had with few people, and certainly no one at work.

The events of that day so long ago were a private matter. He had travelled through life keeping it hidden, pressing it down, smiling meagre smiles through the pain. It was no one else's business. Even through his years of study at the University of Michigan, he lived in his own private hell. Though he and all the other students were encouraged to out their demons through writing assignments and personal essays so they could more effectively help their clients down the road, he never divulged the circumstances surrounding Maximilian's abduction or their mother's incarceration. He used these moments in life as fodder for his university entrance essays, but that's how you got into the better schools. You were expected to divulge your innermost monsters in these essays, for that was how they determined your level of maturity. Or so they said. He wanted into Michigan so badly he could almost taste it, and he wasn't going to let anything stand in his way, even his own guilt. So he swallowed it along with his anxiety and hunkered down, obsessing over every little detail included in the essays.

"Sir, your coffee," said Jean, handing him the cup. "That'll be two bucks, please. Um . . . I don't know your name yet, but you already know mine. Not fair."

"I'm Gary," he said, passing her the money. She smiled, warmly this time, and cocked her head to the side, a gesture he suspected she used often.

"I'm Jean. Well, you knew that. So, Gary. Where are we going on our first date?" She cocked her head to the side and smiled up at him sideways.

He swallowed hard, unable to break his gaze from hers. "I didn't know we have one."

This is going to take some getting used to, he thought. "But let's see. How about dinner and a movie?"

"Boring. Can't you do any better than that? Put a little thrust behind it. Put a little motion into it. Put a little slide into it."

His face turned the colour of an aubergine. "Let me think about it, and I'll tell you tomorrow." He wondered if his voice betrayed how he felt, but Jean seemed not to notice.

"Okay." She laughed her horsey laugh. "But you better show up, not like the past few days."

He smiled to himself on the way out the door, blushing without a care.

The door to his office was closed when he arrived, meaning that Saundra was in with a client. Usually he wouldn't mind just knocking to see whether he could come in, but this time a niggling voice in the back of his mind told him to wait, so he decided to pass the time chatting with some of the clients in the hall. Five minutes hadn't passed before he heard rustling coming from within, indicating that Saundra was finishing up. Finally, he knocked.

"Come in," sounded Saundra's sing-song voice. He opened the door and almost dropped his coffee. Standing in front of him was Maximilian, who was obviously about to leave.

"David . . ." It was all he could manage as a greeting. A hot rush flooded over his body, from the tip of his head to his toes. His fully grown baby brother was in front of him, in the flesh, once again. It was surreal. An instinctive impulse kicked in, and he wanted to reach out and grab hold of him so he couldn't run again.

"Hi, again." They stared at each other. Maximilian seemed deeply curious about Gary, but not curious enough to blow his cover. There was trepidation in his eyes, yet he was back.

Couldn't resist a little adventure to spice up your night, right? Gary thought.

Beyond that he could sense Maximilian's bravado. Not many people would chance coming back to the place where the fear originated. And the way he looked at him with his intense blue eyes. . . . Maximilian had those eyes even as a child. He had this way of looking at you that told you he was sizing you up, determining who you were and making decisions based on those determinations.

"I'm sorry about the last time we met. I didn't mean to chase you out the door. I thought you were someone I used to know a very long time ago."

"And I thought maybe you were someone who'd been looking for me."

"Maybe I am."

"Maybe you are." He angled his body as if preparing to push past him.

Saundra scooted her chair back, stood up and said, "I've got to run and pick a seven-year-old up from her after-school program. David, I hope you'll stay for dinner. Gary can help you get set up with a bed for the night." She looked from David to Gary. "Would you mind?"

"No problem. I'm sure we can handle it between us." Saundra slipped past Gary and disappeared into the crowd.

"I should go, too," said David.

"Please. Stay, so we can talk," Gary pleaded. "I mean, stay and have dinner, and I'll help you with the bed. And I can introduce you to some of our other clients, so you'll have some familiar faces. There's a lot more going at The Mission than just food and shelter."

"Saundra was telling me, but I'm not sure I should stay. I'm just getting over the last time I was here." He glanced at the door, as if to say how badly he wanted to bolt through it as soon as possible. But instead, he turned and sat down in the chair.

Gary walked around the desk, set down his briefcase and settled into his chair, all the while wondering how to proceed with this man. It wasn't often that he was at a loss for how to proceed with a client, because most of them presented clearly defined needs: meals, shelter, beds, practical skills, etc. But he decided that Maximilian needed him to meet him head on, that they should address issues that were far beyond the scope of The Mission, issues that stemmed from that day when Maximilian had been abducted. To his surprise, Maximilian spoke first.

"Why did you call me that the other day? That name, Maximilian."

So he remembered the name! Gary had called it out once, maybe twice, and this young man still remembered it. Why would he remember such an uncommon name having only heard it from Gary? And why would it give him cause to run if it weren't somehow meaningful to him? If David was truly his name, why hadn't he simply corrected Gary with a frown on his face? Why was he panicked and not just offended?

Gary breathed deeply and chose his next words carefully, knowing he was about to lean far out on a dangerous ledge. "Because I believe it's your true name."

Maximilian looked down. Gary could see his eyes narrow and his mouth contract into a thin, bloodless line as he picked at a hangnail. He couldn't help but notice how dirty the man's hands were. Then again, they were predictable for someone without access to a sink and running water, let alone a shower and some soap.

"Who are you really?" Maximilian asked plaintively as he slowly looked up. "Did Cameron send you?" His eyes were bright and shining, but he blinked several times and the tears disappeared.

"Look," Gary said, leaning toward him, "I don't know any Cameron. I don't know who you're running from. I'm not trying to hurt you."

"I said, who are you?"

"Don't you know who I am?"

"I have no idea. I only came back because I thought that if you were one of his men, you wouldn't be posing as a social worker in a homeless shelter. That would be a good front . . . but there's something I've learned through all these years: You never can tell what the next one's going to look like."

"Didn't you hear me call out my name as you were running away the other day?"

"Like I said, I have *no* idea who you are. Who are you?!" Anger riddled his voice.

There were two ways Gary could manage this moment: He could tell Maximilian everything he knew about his life in Albany leading up to his abduction. Or he could tell him about himself. He chose the route he felt was the safest to take and hoped it was the right one. Everything depended on it. He could feel sweat accumulating at the small of his back and running down his temples. He knew deep in his heart that if he were to overstep the wrong boundaries, this was the last time in his life he would see his brother.

"My name is Gary Aldertree. I grew up in Albany with my mother and my brother, who was three years younger. One day, he and I went to play in the park. He was five years old at the time. He wanted to play with a stray cat, and as he ran after it, it was run over by a car. He was sitting on the side of the road next to the cat when the car came back around the block and grabbed him and sped away. It was a silver-grey station wagon. He was abducted that day. We never saw him again."

Gary paused. What would he would do if he were wrong? He would've exposed that part of his life to a client. He would relive the embarrassment of what he did and didn't do the day Maximilian was taken.

Max's shuffling feet brought Gary back to the moment. He continued.

"You know, I've spent my whole life trying to find him, trying to keep the case open and convince the police that he was still alive and waiting to be found. My brother's name was Maximilian. And my brother . . ." He had trouble seeing the young man through the tears that had filled his eyes, the young man who had so filled his thoughts since he first saw him and had so transfixed Gary since first meeting him. Finally, he went ahead and said, "And my brother . . . is you."

The room was quiet, save for muffled chatter coming through the door and the usual sounds of Manhattan beyond . . . sirens, cars backfiring, mufflers gone bad, shouting. But he felt that the whole world outside of this room was deadened. None of that noise meant anything to him. None of that noise phased him. The only sound he was aware of was the buzzing in his ears and the *drip, drip, drip* of his tears. Finally, Maximilian let out a deep exhale.

"Aldertree," was all Maximilian said, his voice cracking and raspy. It carried in it years of hurting, years beyond his age.

Gary waited on the edge of his seat. He wondered whether he'd ever breathe again because now it sure didn't feel like it.

Maximilian continued. "I've never known my last name. Well, I think I did in the beginning, but over the years, it was forgotten like so much else. All I knew was the men."

What did he mean by that? Gary wanted clarification but didn't press for any information. It was enough that Maximilian hadn't run from the office screaming and tearing his hair out. It was enough that his baby brother was only three feet away, and that their feet were almost touching on the floor below them. It was enough that Maximilian was staring at the wall across from him, lost in thought, remembering. This was all that he needed to know that he was right, that this David, this stranger who walked into The Mission on a hot summer day like any other in Manhattan, was his Maximilian. He was finally found, and Gary knew he must save him.

But save him from what? Gary had no idea what, or whom, Maximilian was running from. He had no idea what he was up against. What kind of help did he need? Certainly the Life Skills classes would be helpful. They taught clients how to manage their money; how to put together a nutritious grocery list and stick to it; how to apply for a lease on an apartment; how to keep that apartment by paying rent on time and being a good tenant; and a host of other helpful task-oriented skills. But what else would he need? He had learned how to survive on the streets, which was no easy feat. All kinds of dangers and presented themselves on streets: knife-wielding assailants, territorial feuds, food scarcity which left him begging for money, lurking near bagel stores and asking for handouts, or dumpster diving through restaurant garbage bins. There was no Lonely Planet travel guide that would help him navigate those streets. So he was obviously resourceful enough to keep his head out of trouble.

When Gary emerged from his reverie, he noticed that Maximilian looked shrunken and defeated.

"What's happening, Maximilian? What's going through your mind right now?"

"Can you call me Max? I don't like the name Maximilian."

"That's the name our mother gave you. It was our father's name."

"I don't like it. I have my reasons. Call me Max or David."

"Well, I'm not sure I can think of you as David. But Max is fine. I'll call you that if that's your wish."

"It is."

"What else is on your mind? You look like a fish in a net."

"That's kind of how I feel," he said with a laugh. "It's hard to have your whole world come crashing down around you in five minutes."

"I'm so sorry if I've upset you. I just couldn't bear to see you walk out of this office again without us having connected." Gary sat back in his chair and assumed his social-worker pose, with his hands neatly folded in his lap and his head slightly hung. Hee used it with all his clients to indicate that he was there to talk, to listen and to help.

"Now, what do you think you need to help you get back on your feet? I mean off the streets, into a job, into an apartment of your own, and living a safe and productive life," Gary asked.

"I'm not sure I'm meant to have any of that."

"What do you mean?"

"I think I'm meant to be a wanderer. I'm meant to live a broken man's life, to live the life of the hunted."

"Maybe that's how you feel now, but feelings aren't always fact," he said as gently as he could. He wondered how Max had gotten through this much of life feeling as he did.

Max looked at him with a level gaze. As he spoke, his voice carried scores of hurt, untold anger and immense pain. "The hunted are never free, Gary."

"What do you mean by feeling hunted?"

"Oh, nothing really." Max wasn't as good a liar as Gary thought, but he decided not to press the point.

"Okay then. Immediate needs. You're living on the streets right now and, I'm assuming, sleeping there, too. Right?"

Max nodded.

"And you've got no employment, no reliable way of feeding yourself or addressing your basic needs?"

"Not exactly. I hook sometimes, when I can get cleaned up enough to be presentable. No one wants to fuck a street person with filthy clothes that stink. You've got to look like you're not."

Gary was dumbfounded. It's not like he hadn't come across other young men through his work who prostituted for a living. But in all the years of wondering whether Max had survived childhood, it had never crossed his mind that hooking would be key to his survival. His heart felt like it could break. His baby brother, the one not watched so long ago. . . . Gary struggled to ensure that Maximilian had no idea of his internal thoughts, no idea of his reaction to the words being spoken.

"So, prostitution brings in some money for you, but it's not a consistent income?" His mouth garbled the words; he couldn't get his tongue up and around the vowels, and he sounded listless, flat, monotone.

"With my looks, I can usually bring in five or six hundred a night. But like I said, I can only do it when I can clean myself up enough. And that's not often. Money tends to slide through my fingers, so I'm usually broke pretty quickly after."

"So most immediately, you need dinner tonight, a shower and a place to sleep."

"I can still sleep where I've been sleeping if there are no beds available. I've got a pretty sweet spot behind a gym in the East Village."

"I thought you told me that you hadn't spent much time in the East Village?"

"I didn't lie. I haven't spent much time there. It's a new spot. I keep on the move."

"Got it. Well, you can get a meal here that'll fill you up. And we could fix you up with a bed. But I've got another proposition." He held his breath and waited for a reaction. Max raised his eyebrows and stared at him with those piercing blue eyes.

"You can come and spend the night with me in my apartment. I don't have two bedrooms, but I do have a futon that pulls out to a bed, and it's pretty comfortable. Please take me up on it. I'd love for you to come."

"Are you serious? You don't even know me. I could be anyone. I could rob you blind or kill you in your sleep or . . . I don't know . . . turn your cat into a tea cosy."

"Yes, that's true. But you're my brother, and I've been looking for you all my life. I want you to come stay with me."

Max twiddled his fingers. "I'm not sure. I like to keep on the move."

"I'm not taking that from you. Please, Max. Please hear me out. Let's say it's only for the one night. And if it works out, we'll talk about you staying another night. We'll keep it low-key with no strings attached. I promise. Please . . ." He noticed the pleading in his voice but was unable to reign it in.

"One night?"

"Yes. Only one night, and we'll see how that goes."

"Could I think about it over dinner?"

"Of course, but you'll have to decide by the time dinner's over, so you'll still have a chance to take a bed here if you want."

"And no expectations? I don't have to do your dishes or take out the trash? I don't mind taking out the trash, but I don't want you to expect that—or anything—from me just because I'm staying on your futon."

"No expectations. And Max?" he added. "I don't own a cat."

They both laughed.

»

They sat with Samuel, Donovan and a few others at dinner. The cafeteria was always too packed to find a seat alone. You were almost forced to be social. You could certainly sit among a group of clients and keep your head down, but it was hard. Throughout the meal, Gary partly chatted with the others about this and that, but he was mostly preoccupied observing his brother, who was sitting opposite him. His every nuanced movement . . . the shadow of his hollow cheek . . . the way his eyelashes brushed his lower lids . . . Gary was taking him all in.

Max kept his eyes on his plate, as though he were afraid of someone snatching it out from under his watchful gaze. In fact, most of the eyes around them were on Max, probably because most of the clients knew one another, either from sharing common ground on the streets or passing within The Mission's walls. All the smokers knew one another, or at least could recognize one another from the alleyway. But Max was a new face, an unknown face, a fresh face. Gary knew the stares would not be welcome.

Max was clearly a young man who liked to blend in with his surroundings, a difficult feat for someone so attractive. Many of the women across the room had already noticed him, as had some of the gay men. It would certainly be hard for him to blend in here. Gary wondered whether he was aware of the stares he was collecting. He was pretty sure that Max knew precisely the effect he had on people. Despite his general dishevelment and the scent of darkened nights, back-alley wanderings and stale sweat that drifted off him with every footstep, Max had the ability to turn heads. Gary watched as he tried to shrink into his chair. If he could have, he would have even slid under the table.

Max was a beautiful child, Gary remembered, though he didn't realize it back then. He always had those looks . . . that golden hair that shined like gossamer, those striking deep-blue eyes that he held steady even in the face of an oncoming beating, and those strong cheekbones set high on his face. When the wind blew, the wispy curls in his hair swirled around his head like a tiny swarm of swallows. Yes, he was a beautiful child, but now he was a gorgeous man—no, drop-dead gorgeous.

His tan skin set off the downy hair on his arms. It was long, thick and so white it was almost translucent. His eyebrows were almost the same colour; they were thick and strong and pronounced, though they never became bushy. Rather, they looked as though some gentle hand had lovingly shaped them into a perfect arch. All in all, he was the kind of man who caused passersby to lose their train of thought midsentence. But while the eyes are normally the window into the soul, there was no entryway into Max's. His eyes were guarded, locked tight against prying intrusions.

At the end of the dinner service, they carried their plates and silverware to the appropriate bins and headed toward Gary's office.

While walking, Max turned to Gary and said, "Okay."

"Okay what?" Gary asked, though he was sure he knew what Max was referring to.

"Okay, I'll come and stay with you tonight. But you cannot tell anyone that I am, or even that you found me. I'll turn and run again if I catch wind that you have. And you cannot support me. I have ways of supporting myself."

"Fair enough." Gary couldn't help but grin.

"Why are you smiling so big?"

"Don't you realize that this is my dream come true? I've been longing for this day since I was eight years old."

"In some ways, I have, too. But after awhile I lost hope it would come true." Maximilian's anxiety gripped his gut and refused to let go.

"Then why the look of fear?"

"It's complicated."

"What could be so complicated? Now you're here beside me. And with a bit of work on both our parts, you'll be able to build a life for yourself. Look, I know what living on the streets is about. I've had enough clients walk through my door to have heard everything. Your story, though it's seems unique because you're the one living it, is no different from anyone else's who you just had dinner with. If you really want to apply yourself, I'll move mountains to help you get back on your feet."

He paused a moment, letting his commitment sink in, and then added, "But you'll have to do your part, too."

"If only it were just a problem of moving mountains. Moving mountains I can handle. But I'm treading water with my feet encased in cement. I'm scared."

"What are you talking about, Max?"

"Just don't get your hopes up with me, okay? Don't hope for too much. There are things even you can't handle with your fancy degrees."

"What do you know about my degrees?"

"I saw those diplomas on your wall. A bachelor's and a master's in social work, both from the University of Michigan. They can't have taught you how to save me. Sometimes the only way to save a bird with a broken wing is to break its bloody neck."

"What are you talking about?" Gary asked him. What Max was saying sounded so down, so defeated. Just what had his brother lived through to break his spirits so?

"I'm saying that the only thing that will save me is my own broken neck—only my own death will get me out of the life I live."

»»

When Gary's shift was done, he locked up his office. He had sent Max to the basement to pick out some new clothes. The Mission received donations from stores that were both suitable and appropriate, and with a slip from one of the social workers on duty, clients could go down and pick out new items to replace their torn, filthy rags. Max needed badly to replace what he was wearing. Though Gary was familiar with the smell of homelessness by now, it could still turn his stomach. He made Max promise not to change into his new clothes until they got back to the apartment and he had bathed, so as not to sully them.

After work was finished, they headed for home. At the 14th Street-Union Square Station they transferred to the L train and headed toward Brooklyn, disembarking at the 1st Avenue stop just before the train sped along the tunnel and across the river. Gary ushered Max into the twenty-four-hour grocery store that he passed every evening on his way home. As they perused the aisles, he eventually coaxed the names of some foods Max liked, including orange mangos, sweet green grapes, frozen hamburgers and buns and fixings, and strawberry-rhubarb jam—the kind that had extra fruit and minimal sugar. Gary knew his pantry was already stocked with brick cheese, sliced cheese, whole-wheat bread, tomatoes, good Colombian coffee and enough sugar to keep even Max happy. It was certainly enough to get through one late-night snack, one breakfast and one solid lunch, but not too much to suggest that he expected Max to stay for more than one night.

When they passed the frozen-food aisle, Gary picked out a tub of vanilla ice cream and dropped it in the cart. He was hoping that a late-night snack might elicit a sense of brotherhood and camaraderie between them. Somehow he remembered that Max wasn't fond of chocolate ice cream, and he hoped that was still the case. If not, too bad. Vanilla it is. And they could warm up the jam and drizzle it on top, like a glaze.

After paying the cashier, Gary led the way out the store and directed Max toward the apartment buildings of Stuyvesant Town, where he had been lucky enough to buy an apartment in foreclosure last year. The money from their grandparents' estate had helped him immensely with that purchase; he never would have been able to afford it without such a financial blessing, even at its reduced price. When the elevator door closed behind them, Gary pushed the button for the 17th floor, leaned against the mirrored back wall and breathed a deep sigh of exhaustion.

He noticed that Max had been very quiet throughout the trip, and that he kept his head down as they walked. Perhaps he was just tired. But he was constantly looking from side to side, sometimes glancing at the street ahead, sometimes turning to look behind him. Why was he constantly looking around, watching and waiting as though he were expecting someone to jump out from the crowd? What was Max waiting for? Who was he waiting for? Or was he running from something, or someone?

So much mystery surrounded Max, and Gary had almost nothing to go on. A shroud of fear whispered around him, growing louder when the day descended into night. His eyes registered unspoken anxieties that were compounded by the fact that he had kept alive by someone for some unknown reason. He was like a treasure chest waiting to be unlocked by a rustic key wielded by some unknown entity who knew how to coax him out, how to caress him and heal him in a way Gary couldn't. How would he ever penetrate through Max's layers upon layers of self-constructed armour? After all these years of searching, he'd finally found him. But how would he ever save him? And would he ever *truly* find him? Could the Max who was buried deep inside, the brother Gary knew must be in there somewhere, ever be led to the light? To a new way of living? A new way of loving?

Bing. Floor seventeen.

Gary led the way down the corridor, past the hallway lights that stood out like sentinels marching up and down the length of the hall, to apartment number 1734 all the way at the end. He pulled out his key, let them in, closed the door behind them with an unintended slam and chained the door. This was home. It was home for both him and his long-lost brother, at least for one night. A tickling sensation crept up behind his eyes. He banished the tears before they fell, and before Max could see his weakness. But it wasn't really weakness; it was more a sense of strength that he felt. He knew deep down that if either of them were going to make it through the next few days, it would require courage in the face of fear. It was that courage that threatened to make him cry now. Just as he stepped over the threshold of his one-bedroom apartment in Stuyvesant Town, it suddenly dawned on him that despite his own dark memories, and the hurts and fears and anxieties borne from his past, he had so many advantages over Max.

Max held his hand over his mouth in awe himself and dropping it to his side. Here he was looking around at the sheer wealth that ownership of an apartment in Stuyvesant Town represented. He knew deep in his own heart that his older brother had been blessed with so much more than he had ever known. The disparity was overwhelming. He pushed the feeling down and walked around the room courageously.

CHAPTER FIVE

"Did you eat enough for dinner?" Gary asked.

"Yeah, thanks."

"Because I could fix up a couple of hamburgers if you're still hungry."

"No. Thanks anyway," said Max as he looked around at the original artwork hanging on the walls.

Gary noticed his eyes wandering. "None of those are worth much," he said. "They're local artists, friends from school and friends of friends. Stuff I like. Maybe they'll be worth something one day, but probably not. And if so, then only long after I'm dead."

Max stood up from the futon he has sat down on when they first arrived to take a closer look at the artwork on the walls. He stopped in front of one particular piece and said, "There's some nice stuff here. I don't know much about artwork, but I know when something speaks to me."

"I took some art history classes at school. My contemporary art class was one of my favourites. Learned bunches and developed a real appreciation for the period. You know, happenings, events, conceptual art—stuff like that."

"No, I don't. You're speaking to the unwashed masses when it comes to my contemporary art knowledge. But this one is nice. Subject matter aside, I just like it for some reason."

He was standing in front of a photograph—an image rather, that was composed of two photographs superimposed on top of each other. One was of the Flatiron Building, that triangular structure just a few blocks down the road. The other was of a beautiful young man who was probably about fifteen or sixteen years old, though he could have passed for eighteen if the artist were challenged in a court of law. He was buck naked and holding two tires, one on either side of himself, and his penis—a rather large one at that—was rock-hard, standing almost perpendicular to his upright body.

"Striking, isn't it?" Gary said. Max looked at him with his eyebrows raised, and they both burst out laughing. "I'm not really sure why I bought it. Maybe for the shock appeal."

"It certainly has that," Max said.

"Okay. Speaking of the unwashed masses, time to hit the shower." Gary pulled out a fresh bath towel and facecloth, both of which he'd only recently picked up from Bed, Bath & Beyond; a bar of soap; a toothbrush; and a scrub brush that Max could use on his fingernails. He searched through the vanity for his spare pair of nail nippers.

"Here you go, bro—everything you need to transform into a brand-new man," he said as he handed Max the toiletries.

"Thanks, Gary. I really appreciate this . . . more than you know."

"I know you do. I see it in your eyes." He smiled warmly. "The soap is handmade. I buy it at the farmers market on the weekend. This couple makes it in their home and sells it. And it's really gentle and healing. The shea butter they use—and they use a lot of it—is supposed to heal nicks and abrasions on the skin faster. I'm a firm believer in it. Whenever I get scratches on my legs or chest, it seems to speed up the process. Is the scent okay?"

Max sniffed the soap, breathing in its woody, spicy, masculine aroma. He had no idea what it was supposed to smell like, but it smelled great.

"I like it."

"Good. Enjoy. And take as long as you want in the shower. I've got lots of hot water. The scrub brush is for your nails, cuticles and feet. I haven't seen your feet, but most of my clients who live on the street have lots of problems. How are yours?"

"I'm no different," said Max, looking sheepishly toward his feet.

"We should look at them later to see how bad they are, and maybe get you to a podiatrist if they're bad enough. Okay, bathroom's down the hall. I'll fix us up a bedtime snack." He crossed through the living room toward the kitchen.

"Podiatrist?" Max said, trailing after him.

"A foot doctor," Gary replied.

"Oh. Got it."

Max headed down the hall and closed the bathroom door behind him.

As Gary heated up some strawberry-rhubarb jam in the microwave, he wondered whether Max was gay. He certainly liked that piece of art, maybe enough to betray his preferred sexuality. On the other hand, he himself liked that image, too, and he wasn't gay. In this day and age, liking an image of a naked man didn't mean you're gay. Even though he knew this, it was hard to keep in mind, especially when he was trying so desperately to figure out just who his brother really was.

When the microwave beeped, Gary reached in and grabbed the jar. It was scalding. He released his grip and yanked his hand away and cursed to himself. He ran his fingertips under cold water. *How could I have been so stupid?* he thought. He wasn't paying attention. He was so transfixed by the enigma under the spray of water in his bathroom that it didn't occur to him to use a potholder. He dried his fingers carefully with the kitchen towel and then properly removed the jar from the microwave. Max would be out of the shower soon, and Gary wanted to surprise him with this treat, the same treat that their mother used to make for them on hot summer days.

As Gary finished his preparation, Max was scrubbing shampoo into his scalp for the third time. He needed this so badly. He hadn't showered in about four months. The water coursing down his shoulders and back was a welcome reprieve. After the abduction, Cameron and Quinn kept him very clean, almost obsessively. He needed to be clean—scrupulously clean—in order to be attractive enough. No one wanted a boy who smelled, or had filth behind his ears, or hadn't had an enema. He was given so many of those as a child that he actually felt unclean without one, and he wished he could have asked Gary to purchase him a couple, so he could be clean inside and out. But that was somewhere he would not go with Gary. There were things that Gary needn't ever know, like what his life was like living under Cameron's rule, and the desperation he felt as he longed to escape from the basement. Like what it was like to live his days never feeling the warm rays of the sun upon his face. Like what it was like to run from Cameron and Quinn and keep running. No, Gary needn't ever know these things about him.

He had lived in that cursed basement from the day he was abducted until the day Cameron ordered Quinn to kill him at the age of thirteen. He lived longer than most of the boys; they were usually killed at age eleven, just when they were hitting puberty. He survived because he was a favourite of most of the clients, and they were willing to look past his developing features for a time. They were paying for boys, not adolescent almost-men with hair growing in new places. When the boys were abducted, none of them had any idea what their short lives had in store for them, and they desperately hoped to be set free from the basement after they learned. But Max was different. He sensed what his life was amounting to that first night, when Quinn had him on his back. And he accepted his fate with a calmness, if not a resignation that made him valuable in Cameron's eyes. Here was a boy who they didn't have to beat senseless to get him to acquiesce to his fate. Here was a boy who never even cried.

Max leaned forward, dousing his hair in the steaming water. The shampoo tickled as it coursed down his back, between his butt cheeks and down his legs. He twirled the woody, spicy soap around in the facecloth and used it to wash the rest of his body yet again.

Living on the streets left you with the feeling that you'd never be clean again. No matter how many times he rung his grime out of the facecloth and loaded it up with fresh suds, he couldn't shake the feeling that the only way to clean himself properly was to wash a full layer or two of skin down the drain. That might be the worst of it. For someone who'd been raised scrupulously clean, receiving sometimes two or three baths per day, it felt like the stink of the dumpsters just wouldn't leave him.

He knew he was taking an exceptionally long time in the shower, but Gary had told him to take as long as he wanted. Gary seemed nice enough, even if he was trying too hard. The one problem with Gary that Max could see was that he didn't know how to save Max, or that Max couldn't be saved. But that was because of Max, because he hadn't told Gary the whole story;

because he wouldn't let Gary in—no, *couldn't* let him in—for both their sakes. He would know way too much. Too much about his past, too much about his present and too much about the bleak future that he was condemned to live. Telling him would be dangerous, much too dangerous for both of them. Max just couldn't endanger his brother's life like that. This was the very reason he had never tried to contact his family. He didn't know his own last name, so he couldn't have found them if he'd wanted to. But now that he'd found his brother, he wasn't going to hurt him like this. He already felt he was a disservice to Gary for staying with him this one night, but he was so curious about his brother. He so desperately wanted to know him, and so desperately just wanted to love him, that he'd gone back to The Mission after three days' absence and agreed to spend the evening with him.

Maybe it was foolhardy. Maybe it was a huge mistake. What if Cameron were to get wind of him spending the night in Gary's home? Quinn was still out there . . . always searching, always watching, always seeking him out. Maybe he'd be safe with Quinn knowing. Maybe not. Just because he got one reprieve from Quinn's hands, even if it was a huge and crucial reprieve, didn't mean he'd get a second one. For all he knew, Cameron had a new lackey by now, though he didn't think so, because the kind of relationship that had developed between them over the years was based on fear, loyalty and a mutual decision to save each other's asses. Yes, Max had gotten that one reprieve nine years ago because of Quinn's sentimentality, but that didn't mean he'd get a second one, especially so many years later. More than likely he wouldn't. No, he definitely wouldn't. No doubt Cameron had punished Quinn for his lapse in judgement and Quinn had been searching for him to appease Cameron's wrath. For all these reasons, for all these mistakes on all their parts, staying with Gary was more dangerous for both of them than it ever should have been.

By the time Max emerged from the bathroom, clouds of steam were ready to emerge as well. The mirror was dripping condensation. Max wiped it down with the towel so he could comb his hair and brush his teeth. *God, that felt good*, he thought. How long it had been since he'd brushed his teeth? Who knew? He noticed that Gary had set a clean robe on the toilet seat for him to wear, since he had no pajamas and no robe of his own. *He's a nice guy.*

"Up for some ice cream with strawberry-rhubarb glaze?" asked Gary as Max walked into the kitchen. He handed him a bowl.

"Remember when Mom used to make this for us when we were little? But she used to use raspberry jam, I think because it was the one flavour we could all agree on. Do you remember that?"

"I don't remember much about Mom. Except the beatings; I remember those. She used to lose her temper over the smallest things and beat the living shit out of us."

Gary stopped eating and moved to sit on the futon. Max followed, wondering why his comment stopped the conversation in its tracks.

"Where is she now, our mother? Is she still alive?" he asked.

"Yes, she's alive," Gary answered, scooping ice cream onto his spoon and letting it fall back into his bowl. It was beginning to soften.

"Why so morose? Did I say something wrong?"

Gary put the spoon down in the bowl and looked out toward the balcony and the night sky beyond. He ran one hand through his hair and then placed it on his knee.

"Mom's upstate," he said.

"Still in Albany?"

"Just outside. In a penitentiary."

"What? What for? What did she do?" Max asked incredulously. He waited for Gary to answer.

"For your murder, Max. She's in prison for your murder. She has been since just after you disappeared."

"But I was never murdered! I was abducted! You had to have told the police that . . ."

"I did, but they didn't believe my story. And no one actually saw you get pulled into the car that day. None of the people who lived in those houses surrounding the park were looking out their windows at the right time. None of them even saw us playing on the playground. And our neighbour Mrs. Crabtree had a lot to weigh in on during the trial. She testified to hearing us screaming all the time during the beatings. And I guess the jury went one step further in their minds and decided that mom stepped over the line that day. They decided that she beat you to death and got rid of your body somehow, so no one would ever find it. They convicted on circumstantial evidence and without a body. I guess they felt the need to do that, since it was a case concerning a child and they wanted to wrap the trial up quickly. As for my testimony, they just decided that I was frightened of what she would do to me if I didn't lie for her on the stand.

"So there you have it: a terrified eight-year-old, a mean-spirited, nosy old neighbour and no witnesses to the truth. The jury came back with a verdict in less than an hour."

"Which means . . ." Gary glanced at him across the futon. Something was dawning in his consciousness. He whispered, "Which means that the case was closed. No wonder . . ."

"No wonder what?" He didn't dare look away.

Max's eyes met his, and he said, "No wonder no one came looking for me. All those years while Cameron kept me; all those years while I played Dress-Up Dolly for his clients; all those years I spent lying in bed waiting for the next one, and the next one, and the next one, dreaming that I could remember a different time— not a perfect time but some other time than the hell I was living; all those years I used to tell myself they were looking for me, that they'd find me and take me away to a place where this wouldn't happen again . . . All those years I waited. But no one was going to take me away, because they weren't even looking."

The sounds of traffic stole through the balcony window and seeped into the room. Gary felt his heartbeat hammering away inside his chest. *What does it feel like when a heart breaks?* he wondered.

"Max, after our mother's incarceration, almost no one looked for you. Officer Trent Downing of the Albany Police did. And I did, when I grew older. I went back to that park time after time, just trying to see if there was something else I could remember, something that would help us find you. Our mother gave up, mostly because there wasn't much she could do from within a prison cell. I think she eventually gave up on herself, too."

"When was that?" asked Max with rancour creeping along the edge of his voice.

"About the time she began proceedings to declare you legally dead."

Max looked down into his melted ice cream. He'd lost interest in it several minutes before, about the time he realized there was a reason no one had come looking for him; about the time he realized why no one had saved him from his private hell. How could they have done this to him? How could they have just left him there to rot in the basement of a house creeping with insanity? How did they just forget about him, cover him up like some old dog turd in the yard? And how would he ever learn to live with this, this understanding, this knowledge that he'd been worth no more than yesterday's newsprint? Living on the streets without this knowledge was bad enough; living on the streets with this knowledge would be another kind of torment.

"Gary?" Max asked as he looked down at his bowl and stirred the melted muck.

"Yes?"

"Why did you keep looking when everyone else stopped? What kept you going?"

"I knew the truth. I saw that car arrive and drive away with you in it. I couldn't let that knowledge die. And there was something else . . ." Max waited, but with Gary's prolonged silence, it became clear that he wasn't going to speak again.

"C'mon, Gary. Please tell me."

"Yes, I knew the truth, and the truth is that you had gotten into a silver-grey station wagon on the edge of that park. But that's not all. I knew I was right, dammit, and I wasn't going to have anyone—any law enforcement agency, any nosy neighbour, anyone at all—tell me I was mistaken," Gary said with grim determination. "One thing you don't know about me yet, well, because you don't know me at all, is that I don't like to be told I'm mistaken. I don't like to be proven wrong."

»

Gary pulled out some extra bedding and helped Max dress up the futon. Luckily, he also had an extra pillow in the back of the linen closet. After rinsing the dishes and putting them in the dishwasher, he bade Max goodnight and closed his bedroom door behind him. He thought it would take him a long time to fall asleep, for his mind was stirring. But he was exhausted and slept within moments, drifting into thoughts of all the intervening years when Max was absent.

That night, he had troubled dreams, dreams filled with faceless figures and shadows that clung to the edges of things. He slept fitfully, sensing his brother's presence in the living room. He wasn't used to having someone in his apartment, and even though Max was his brother, his dream come true, he was still a stranger.

Sometime in the night, his ears filled with screams, and he sprang upright in bed. Were they real? Were they his? Had he cried out into the dark of night? Most importantly, had he woken Max? Still disoriented, he got out of bed as quietly as he could, crossed the room and put on the housecoat that hung from a hook on his bedroom door. He opened the door quietly, cursing the squeaking sound it always made, and closed it behind him. He walked down the short hallway to the edge of the living room.

By this time, his eyes were adjusted to the darkened room, and he could tell that there was no movement under the covers on the futon. *Whew, I didn't wake him up.* A quick glance around the room told him that all was in order—except two things. First, the balcony door was wide open. Strange, since the air conditioning was on. Maybe Max opened it. Maybe, having lived on the street for who knows how long, the sounds of the traffic calmed him, sang him softly to sleep. That must be it. But the second thing amiss was even stranger, and even more troubling. Gary looked back at the futon and squinted. It dawned on him that there was no movement under the blankets because there was no one under the blankets.

Max was gone.

Gary pulled the thin blanket up off the futon. Max had disappeared like a ghost troubling the night air around itself. Or fled. Or simply vanished out the apartment door, down the elevator, out of sight. Was it all just too much for him to take? Was this all getting to be too much for Gary to take? *How much more of this disappearing act can I handle?* He tossed the blanket down and stood in silence, his hands hanging by his side.

What was that sound? It was like a child's muffled, anguished cry. He turned his head this way and that, and then walked slowly around the room. Was he imagining it? Where was it coming from?

Across the hall, he was sure of it. But he didn't think there were any children living there. And the apartment beside him was completely empty, since it was up for sale.

Gary stepped gingerly toward the front door, still listening intently. As he neared it, he noticed he'd left the closet door slightly open, and he pushed it closed as he stepped by. The cry immediately got quieter. Gary stopped in his tracks. He placed his hand on the closet door handle, turned it and slowly slid the door open. Inside, crouched on the floor, was Max, wiping tears from his cheeks with the back of one hand. Clutched in the other was a deadly looking switchblade that seemed about six inches long. He was making little stabbing motions at the air in front of him. His eyes looked out and into another world. He saw dark figure after dark figure pass before his eyes, fearing each and trembling before each, but not crying out. With each stab, a puff of air escaped his mouth.

"Max?" Gary said softly. "Max, can you hear me? Max, give me the knife," he said as he reached down toward the blade. Max redoubled his desperate efforts to stab the demons in his mind.

"Max, please. Give me the knife. It's Gary," he said, sounding desperate. "I won't hurt you. Please hand me the knife. Please, Max."

Max slowly lowered the blade and let it fall on his knees. Gary reached down and gently took the knife, putting it into his robe pocket. He knelt down, pushed some pairs of boots aside and sat beside him in the closet, just like he used to do after their mother beat Max. He put his arm around his little brother, his hand resting on his shoulder. The number of times he had comforted his little brother in this way he didn't know, but he knew one thing for certain: For Max, the closet was a place where his mother didn't follow. For Gary, it was a place where he knew he could keep his brother safe. It was his place, a place where he had power. It was a space where he could hold his brother and be reminded of their order in this world, where Gary was the big brother who helped Max, who held Max, who kept the demons at bay. They would sit crouched together, two brothers cloaking themselves from their cursing mother, who was lying on the sofa exhausted after her expenditure of cruelty. He used to keep a few books in there, to read to Max, to calm him. But those days were long past, and there were no books to be read in this one.

Gary was thinking of a moment in time, a fragment of his memory, when Max was lying on the floor and their mother was sitting on top of him. He had done god knows what to enrage her, some inconsequential infraction that caused her grief and insecurity to bubble over. She had caught him running from her outstretched arms, and now she had him pinned. She was grasping him by the hair, his golden-white curls, and using them to slam his head into the floor over and over again as she screamed, "Why'd you do it, you little fuck? Why'd you do it, Maximilian?"

And Gary was standing over her, screaming as loud as he could to try to break through her rage and reach some semblance of sanity. "You're going to kill him, Mom! You're going to kill him! Leave him alone, please! Leave him alone!"

But she kept on banging, not even hearing Gary's pleas, until Gary was able to pull her off of him, her anger and fury finally abating. Gary didn't know about concussions back then, but if he had, he would have insisted that Max be taken to the nearest hospital. As it was, Max never displayed any leftover signs of a beating, except the emotional scars that Gary tried to assuage in the closet for hours afterward.

Although Gary had forgotten most of the books he read, he remembered in this moment that the book he read that day was called *Goodnight Moon*.

Max's mind travelled back to the day when Quinn took him away from the basement for good. He thought it was his last ride, his ride to death, like all the other kids who had gone before him. He knew they were dead—Cameron made sure of that—and he knew that his own time must come soon. He was thirteen by now (by his best calculations), much older than most of them. Once the first hairs grew under their arms and on their groin, they were slated for execution.

Quinn had taken it upon himself to shave Max's pubic hair down to the skin so they wouldn't notice. And if they did, they could still keep their illusions about how young he was in their mind. When he started to grow taller and couldn't fit into the Dress-Up Dolly clothes, that's when the axe fell. And so, Quinn took him on that ride to his end. But he set him free under a Queens overpass and told him to hide himself from Cameron. Quinn took a chance with his own life that day, for Cameron possessed a frightful desire for revenge and he had disobeyed a direct order.

But now it came to this: Quinn knew where he was, and he no longer felt safe.

They sat in silence for a long time. Gary repressed his urge to lapse into social worker mode and get at the problem through questions and prodding. Finally, Max spoke.

"Here, Gary. He was here. He was here, Gary." He turned his head viciously this way and that, looking around the closet at images only he could see.

"Who, Max? Who was here?"

"He was here. Quinn! Right here! In the living room, standing by the futon. I woke up, and he was touching me. I was sleeping naked, and he pulled the covers back and he was touching me, just like he used to before. He . . . he . . ." The rest was lost in the cacophony of Max's sobs.

"He couldn't have been here, Max. We're seventeen floors above ground. How could he have possibly gotten in? He certainly didn't scale the wall, and he didn't come in through the front door, because it's locked. I always lock my doors. The chain is probably still on it."

"But he *was* here! He was here, and he was . . ." He swallowed hard and said, "He was touching me, just like he used to before . . . before . . ."

"Before what, Max? He'd fondle you and then do what?" But Max had lapsed into an almost-drunken stupor. He looked so lost, so forlorn and dejected. Gary couldn't help but wonder what he was reliving in his mind. Just what visions was he seeing in this darkened closet? It broke his heart to see his brother like this. He was both saddened and appalled.

"Come on, Max. Let's get up off this floor and turn on some lights and look at what happened tonight with rational minds." Gary helped him to his feet and guided him with his hand on his shoulder to the kitchen table, thinking that maybe the futon wasn't the best place for him right now. Then he walked around the apartment and turned on as many lights as possible in order to dispel the darkness and banish any shadows that might look like this Quinn. He produced some chamomile tea from a cupboard and made a strong pot of it. After pouring two cups, he returned to the table and placed one before Max.

"So, Max. Who is Quinn?"

With his head hanging low, Max replied, "He's Cameron's right-hand man, Cameron's best friend—if he's even capable of having friends. He does all of Cameron's dirty work, and he's paid very well for it."

"Cameron pays him?"

"Quinn gets the pick of the litter. Whenever he wants it, however he wants it, he gets his way."

"And who is Cameron?"

"Cameron is the one who abducted me that day at the park. He's the one in charge, the leader of the pack, the one who chooses, the one who determines when you're too old. He's the one who decides."

"Who decides what?"

"Everything. No one has any say but Cameron. Cameron says who comes in, and Cameron says who goes out—and how they go out: by knife, by fire or by gunshot. Cameron must be pleased, or else you're out. If Cameron's not happy, then you're in trouble. If you do something wrong, he gets back at you, because it's Cameron who decides. He decides who to take. He decides who to keep. He decides when you're too old to live anymore."

"What do you mean when you're too old to live anymore?" Gary asked, his breath catching in his chest.

"When you've outlived your stay and you're too old to please him or his customers—eleven or twelve—he sends you off with Quinn, and when the deed is done, Quinn comes back with your head to prove that you're dead. Whenever he brought one back, all of us kids were paraded up to the upper floor in single file and told to sit at the dining room table while the covered head was brought in on a platter. The platter would be set down on the table before us and uncovered. We were told that that would happen to us if we weren't good and didn't do what was asked of us. Then, each of us was taken back downstairs and told to lie still and quiet and think about what we had been told. And then life went on."

Gary felt he might choke from the rage that was erupting inside him. How could anyone do something like that? To children, no less. And to his brother! What kind of man intimidates children, scares them half to death with severed heads on platters and warnings that the same will happen to them? How had Max endured?

"My God, Max. Have you been to the police with this?"

"Of course not."

"Why?"

"Because I want to live."

"How come you're alive if you're past the, uh, age that Cameron likes? How is that possible?"

"Quinn always had a soft spot for me. I looked good, and I knew how to please him in ways the other boys didn't. When he'd talk, I'd listen. The other boys would just cry. I never cried. He almost loved me. Maybe he really did. I don't know. Regardless, when he was told to bring back my head, instead he let me go."

"But Quinn couldn't have been here. No. It must have been a nightmare."

"It was him. Quinn found me again. I don't know how. Look, you can see he left the balcony door open when he ran away."

"You must have opened it before you went to sleep, Max," Gary said as he got up and walked to the door. He opened it wide to show Max that the balcony was empty. But in that moment, he noticed that the balcony of the apartment next to his, the one for sale, was close enough for someone to traverse easily. This was one of the things about his apartment that he'd never liked—the close proximity to his neighbors. But he wasn't going to mention this to Max. Not now, though he seemed to be slowly calming down. He hoped the chamomile tea was helping. He closed the door, turned and walked back to the table.

"God, I'm going to draw you into my mess, my mess of a life. And you'll be tangled with me in Cameron's eyes. He'll kill you, too, you know. I can't let that happen," he said, his voice quickening and rising with angst. "I can't let him kill you, Gary. He'll do it. He has no conscience."

"Max, it's the middle of the night, and you've been scared by a nightmare. Let's get some sleep. It'll all look better in the light of day. We can figure out what to do in the morning."

"It wasn't a nightmare, Gary. You have to believe me. I know this man. I've known him my whole life. You've known him, too, Gary. He's the one you were after all these years. He was behind the wheel of the silver-grey station wagon. And he *will* kill you."

"Would you feel better if you slept in my room with me? In my bed?"

Gary waited for Max to reply. Seconds that felt like long minutes passed. He wondered whether he'd gone too far, whether Max would believe that he was strangely misunderstanding his needs. Finally, he said, "Yes, I'd feel safer. Thank you."

And so, they finished their tea, grabbed Max's pillow and headed for Gary's bedroom. Max went to use the toilet. In his minute of solitude, Gary took time to stretch. He reached his arms far and wide, bent his neck side to side until it cracked and then bent down to touch his toes. All the anger and fear and curiosity that he had felt during the course of the night had made his muscles tense up and cramp. And sitting on the floor of the compact closet hadn't helped either. He hoped they could get through this night without further hitches.

His brother was damaged. That was clear. But who were these men that he was so afraid of? Were they even real, or were they the figments of a sickened mind, a mind rattled with mental illness, an illness that turned shapes and shadows and imaginings into a reality only he could see? He didn't know. But he was determined to get to the bottom of it. He would not abandon his brother, no matter how sick he might be. He would help purge the memories that infested his mind, that threatened to unbalance this beautiful, tortured soul.

»»

In the morning, Gary couldn't help noticing the black bags underneath Max's eyes. How could he live like this? Gary knew that many homeless people suffered from mental illnesses, schizophrenia and Tourette's syndrome being predominant, but Max didn't present classic symptoms of either. He made a note to have a chat with Saundra about her opinion of their new client in this regard. God knows those diseases were more frequently found in the American population than most people realized.

They had woken late, and Gary needed to get to work soon. After coffee and lunch, they both dressed and headed out the door, locking it behind them. As they got to the elevator, it was opening, and two of the building workmen emerged. Gary recognized both of them, since they had been in his own apartment to fix things on various occasions. Gary pushed the lobby button, and they began to descend.

"Damn. I forgot something," Gary lied to Max. "Do you mind waiting in the lobby while I run back upstairs? No disappearing act, please. You'll break my heart if you take off," he said with a smile.

"I'll stay put," he responded with a wan smile.

Gary rode the elevator back up to the seventeenth floor. He turned down the hallway in the direction he'd seen the workmen go—toward his own apartment. He found them at the apartment next door.

"Hey, what's up, guys? What brings you up to heaven on the seventeenth floor?"

"Ah, some idiot broke the lock on this apartment last night," one of them said. "I have no idea why anyone would even want to break in. There's nothin' in here." He shrugged.

I bet I know why, thought Gary. *Quinn.* Then he shook his head. Were Max's delusions getting a foothold in his mind?

Gary walked slowly back toward the elevator. He didn't know what to say to Max, or whether he should tell him anything. Someone had broken into the apartment next to his last night—the night Max insisted he'd been woken by this mysterious Quinn. Gary tried not to believe in coincidences, but here was one staring him in the face. He felt fear's fist gripping his throat like a steel-banded glove, tightening and closing off his breath. Wouldn't telling him reinforce his ideations of the ghosts of Quinn and Cameron? Most certainly. He decided not to tell him.

CHAPTER SIX

Friday, Gary thought. The weekend was almost upon them. As he and Max approached the Sneaky Bean to get coffee, he remembered that he was supposed to have come up with a date idea to entice Jean out with him. How could he even think about going on a date with her with everything that was going on? On the other hand, some normalcy like a date might be just the thing to inject some rationality into his suddenly irrational world. *Yeah, as if dating were a normal occurrence for me!*

Dating opportunities didn't arise very often for Gary. He had a shyness about him that rose to the fore when it came to asking women out on dates. Though he was a strong man in so many ways, he was also a man who didn't like to be embarrassed or ridiculed, and putting himself out there in the open to ask a woman out wasn't something he felt capable of doing very often. But with Jean, things were different. He didn't have to be vulnerable here, because Jean was the one putting herself on the line, not him. That was one of the main reasons he felt capable of dating her.

"So, a regular coffee again? Or do you want something else, like a cappuccino or latte?" Gary asked.

"I'm fine with a regular coffee. And I'll pay for mine, thanks," replied Max.

"You should keep your money for important things, like food and toiletries and bus fare."

"Now that I'm cleaned up, I can get some good money pretty quickly," Max said quietly. They moved to stand in the lineup.

"I'd rather you not hook, if you can help it," said Gary. He thought about all the dangers that awaited Max out there on the streets when he was selling his body to men he didn't know. STDs. Violence. Murder. He was sure that Max could take care of himself, but his brotherly love still caused him to fear for Max's safety.

"I have no other skills," Max said matter-of-factly. "I don't even have an education. Who's going to hire someone like me?"

"Lots of our clients haven't finished high school, if that's the problem. We have volunteers who help them with that and coach them to get their GED."

"No, Gary. You're not getting it. It's not that I don't have my GED. It's that I've never been to school at all."

Gary stopped in his tracks.

"You've never been to school? At all? Ever?"

"Ever. Not even first grade. Cameron wasn't too concerned about my future, you know, because in his eyes I didn't have one. The customers liked to talk to me; and I learned a lot from them. But I lived in a basement with other boys rotating in and out until Quinn set me free. Since then, I've lived on the streets. I don't even know my ABCs. Well, I know some of 'em. But I can't read. I don't know which letters are which. I can't even count out my own change. Now, which of your volunteers will want to open a can of worms like that?"

Gary was both shocked and angry. He was shocked because his lost brother was finally before him, and in all the years he had dreamed of this day, he had never considered that Max would be so far behind everyone around him. And he was so angry that he could barely see straight. He was livid with Quinn and Cameron for having ravaged his brother's life with their own desires and illegal acts. Gary wondered how to overcome this latest revelation of Max's. How could they ever educate him? How would they ever teach Max everything he needed to know?

"To be honest, I don't know, Max. But I'm sure we can find someone to teach you. You can't go through life without knowing how to count change."

"I've always just trusted the person to be honest, but I have no idea if they are. I just smile, put the change in my pocket and walk away."

"C'mon. Let's get some coffee, and we'll work this one out. I promise."

Today, Gary and Max were the only ones in line. Jean greeted Gary with a huge smile. "You came back. Didn't know if you would after I was so forward with you."

"Why were you so forward anyway?" Gary asked. Jean called one of her coworkers to the register to replace her and then walked to the end of the pickup counter with their coffees. Gary and Max followed.

"Because a girl has to be strong and forward in this town, or life just leaves her behind. Besides, I know what I want and when I want it." She handed Gary his coffee.

"I guess I'm the lucky one," said Gary, feeling rather excited by her attention toward him. Max, however, was beginning to feel like a third wheel to their private moment.

Jean turned to Max. "Is this coffee for you?"

"Yes."

"So you're the one with the nutritional deficiencies. I've never served a coffee with six sugars before," she giggled.

"There's a first time for everything," Max replied.

"What's your name?"

"David," he lied.

"David, this is Jean," announced Gary.

"Nice to make your acquaintance, David." She turned to Gary again. "And you? Have you come armed with an amazing idea for a first date?"

Gary fumbled around with the keys in his pocket. "I was thinking. . . . Have you ever been to the Abingdon Square market on Hudson? They have more nutritious food than a sugar-loaded coffee."

"Can't say that I have," she said slowly, intrigued.

"How about coming with me tomorrow morning? I know it doesn't sound romantic, but it's lots of fun."

"Sounds like a good time. And you are the lucky one: I took a class in preventative medicine, which was mostly about food choices, actually. I could teach you. I love teaching."

Gary's eyes widened. "You actually took a class in preventative medicine? Wow. I'm impressed. For what kind of program?"

"It was an elective."

Gary smiled broadly, wondering at his good fortune.

Jean had loved teaching since she was little. She was the one who was caught on the playground telling the other kids which flowers were which and what their mothers meant when they said a child was "precocious." She even shared her knowledge of why the sky was blue, and not green or purple or yellow. This garnered her a reputation of being a snob, a reputation that had followed her through life, mainly because most people don't like those who know more than they. Jean was a repository of loose assortments of otherwise-useless facts, figures and wanton ideas.

But her love of teaching had never abandoned her. It was her shroud of armour when she was caught in uncomfortable social settings, as most were for her. She decided early on in life that there was no vocation more noble, no job more honourable, no life better than a life spent teaching. In times of stress, Jean lapsed into her role as a natural-born teacher as easily as a fire-eater breathes flames. And she loved children, which helped a lot. They were hungry for information, desiring truths and greedy for facts about their surrounding world. She couldn't wait to have children of her own, and she secretly harboured a keen desire to homeschool them when the time arose.

"Well, it certainly is a unique first date," answered Jean, her thoughtful face indicating that she was genuinely warming to the idea.

"Okay, I'll meet you at the the corner of Hudson and West 12th then, at ten a.m. When it comes to farmers markets, the early bird gets the fishcakes. You know where that is?"

"Fishcakes?" Her eyes twinkled at his attempt at humour. *I wonder if he's nervous*, she thought. *That's kind of endearing.* "But the market—yes, I've walked by it before. I'll meet you there."

"Okay. Tomorrow morning. Ten o'clock," Gary confirmed as he walked backward toward the door. He spilled hot coffee down his hands but tried hard not to show his discomfort.

Once they were outside, Gary felt calmer; the anxiety that had devoured him since leaving home that morning was diminishing, and he felt more and more at peace the further he got from the apartment. He hadn't had many first dates, which meant that he didn't have many second or third dates. In fact, he hadn't had a date since his undergraduate graduation.

He'd had a few short, unfortunate relationships during those years. The longest was his third and last girlfriend, who he so affectionately named The Cuisinart. They dated during his last undergraduate year, and she broke up with him by telling him that he was too obsessed with his studies and complaining that he just wasn't into her. He argued that he was into her, that he even loved her in his own way. But that love just wasn't enough for her. He also said that his studies were important to him because he wanted to enter graduate school straight away, but that wasn't what she wanted to hear either, and she told him so in no uncertain terms. He left that relationship with four deep gashes down the left side of his face, and she with what he suspected was copious amounts of his epidermis under her nails. He graduated with a 4.0. "Good riddance," he said to himself, realizing in the nick of time that he didn't love her at all. He'd actually been with her just to satisfy his needs—needs that were powerful at the ripe age of twenty-two. But no amount of sex was worth nail tracks down his face. Maybe his back, but not his face. Now, three years later, those needs were still clamouring for attention, and obsessive masturbation just wasn't enough. But other needs seemed to be surfacing, like the need to be loved, which he'd never really felt before, but was certainly tearing at him inside, as though The Cuisinart had somehow cut at his heart. He hadn't dated at all since her.

Though it was eleven-thirty in the morning, the day was already hot, the kind of hot that wears you down and sucks out every last drop of moisture from your skin. With each step toward The Mission, Gary could feel the sweat dripping down the small of his back and soaking the back of his pants.

"You didn't tell me about Jean," Max teased with a sidelong stare, his lips curving into a smirk. "She's really pretty but a bit too thin for my taste."

"So she's not your type?"

"Not really. I do like Asian women though."

"So you're not gay?"

"No, not at all. You'd think I would be, since all my experiences have been with men. But I'm not. Why did you think that?"

"Max, there are no studies that indicate conclusively that a boy who's sexually abused by an older male will turn out gay. There is no reason to think that what happened to you should have made you gay."

The heat was wearing into Gary. Each step brought new beads of sweat to his forehead, his underarms, the small of his back. The very buildings seemed to almost sag under the weight of the heat as they reflected the blazing rays of the sun onto the pavement. It was unbearable.

"You can never tell if someone is gay in New York," said Gary. He thought about Max's past and wondered how anyone could live through that abuse and have any sense of healthy sexuality intact. But instead, he said, "Anyone could be into anything here, Max. And remember, I don't really know you from Adam. You could be straight. You could be gay. You could be bisexual. You could be into dogs, for all I know. And in New York, you *could* be into dogs. This city seems to attract all kinds of sexual deviants. You're *not* into dogs, are you?"

Max didn't acknowledge the question. "New Jersey attracts them, too."

"What do you know about New Jersey?"

"That's where I was raised—in Newark."

"Where all those deviant New Yorkers can travel without going far," mused Gary.

Max changed the subject. "So, you'll want me out of the apartment tomorrow for your date, right? I know a place where I can sleep."

"No, you can sleep on the sofa. In case you didn't hear, it's our first date. And for our first date, we will be perusing all that rural

New York state has to offer, not licking each other's butts," said Gary playfully.

"To each his own sexual deviance, I suppose."

"Seriously, I have no plans to bring her back to the apartment for sex tomorrow."

"It could happen. What if that's what she's after?"

"But that's not what I'm after. And I have a say in the matter, too. Look, you'll be perfectly safe from Jean's forward advances. I might invite her back for dinner, but that's it. You can even benefit from the dinner I'm going to cook us with the food we pick up at the market."

"You still need a chaperone at age twenty-five?"

"Technically, the date will have finished by that time. I hope you'll join us, but if you don't want to, you can always grab dinner at The Mission. You might even make some friends."

"I doubt I'll be making friends at The Mission. I can't put anyone else in danger."

"The Mission's probably one of the safest places for you to be right now. There's always a crowd. There's no way for Quinn to get you alone."

Max stopped walking, just yards from The Mission entrance.

"What's wrong? What did I say?" Gary asked. He looked at Max imploringly. Sweat continued to roll down the small of his back. He longed to get inside to his air-conditioned office and the cool spaces beyond.

"It's just that . . ."

"Just that what?"

"Just that last night, when we were talking, you didn't seem like you believed me." Then Max was looking past Gary, staring back into his own memories again. There was a glimmer of something in his eye, as though he had just latched onto something that gave him hope.

"And?"

"And now it sounds like you do."

Gary took a sip of his coffee, but it was still too hot to drink comfortably.

"What happened? Why do you believe me now?"

"Max, I'm giving you the benefit of the doubt. Part of me has to believe you, because if I don't, then there's no trust between us. And if we're going to get through this, if we're going to build any kind of relationship, then we've got to trust each other. But . . ." His voice trailed off as he searched for the right words. "I don't know. . . . Another part of me finds this whole story so far-fetched. It's frightening in a way I have trouble describing. It's a stretch of my imagination to believe that a person—let alone two—could be so evil."

"Thank you, Gary, for believing me at least in part." Max understood how difficult it was to fully believe his story, so that was enough for now. Gary would eventually come to believe him fully if they were around each other enough. Max felt sure of it.

"It's not so much that I believe you as it is I believe in you."

"You don't realize, Gary, that no one has ever believed my story before. I haven't told many people, because I've always been so afraid of Cameron, but the few people I have trusted in the past never ever believed me."

Gary felt that same sting in his eyes that he had become so familiar with these past few days. He held the tears back with great effort.

"I'm so sorry to hear that, Max. It hurts to hear everything you've been through. Sometimes I don't even know what to say."

"You don't have to say anything, Gary. Sometimes there is nothing to say. But hey, cheer up. Maybe those days are coming to an end. I mean, here you are, and you believe parts of the story, and hopefully you'll grow to believe it all one day and learn that I'm not exaggerating or lying. So that's something to look forward to, isn't it? I would never lie to you, Gary."

"It sounds like you're going to stay with me again tonight. Is that right?"

"That's what I was thinking. I agree with you: If we're going to build any kind of relationship, then we have to get to know each other. And the best way is for me to stay with you for however long it works. I mean, if you don't want me to stay, I won't. I know you said it was for one night only. But I . . . I want to stay, at least until the welcome wears out. Or before that. If you get tired of me, then please tell me.

"Besides," he added, a smile upon his face, "the soap was nice."

Gary smiled. "It is nice soap, isn't it?"

»

"David! You're back," exclaimed Saundra as Gary and Max entered the office. "Where did you find this stranger, Gary?"

"Out in the alleyway, smoking with the rest of them," Gary lied. "I thought I'd set him up with the Life Skills Program. Do you know how much material they're supposed to read for that program?"

"There's some, but not much. Most of it is aural training. Just some papers that recap what the instructor is teaching. Why? Is reading a challenge for you, David?" she asked, turning to Max.

"Uhh, yes."

"But I could help you by reading the text to you after class each day," said Gary.

"Oh, no . . . you don't have to do that," intoned Max, but disappointment registered in his voice.

"It would be no bother."

Saundra began shuffling papers on her desk. "It's what we're here for, David," she added. "Gary works the evening shift, so he'd be available to work with you when your classes finish. Most of them run during the afternoon."

"What are Life Skills classes anyway?" Max asked.

Saundra glanced down at her watch. "I'll leave you two alone to discuss this, if you don't mind, David. Got to pick up the seven-year-old from her after-school program. But I think I told you that the other day." She gave up organizing the paperwork and simply threw everything together into one big stack.

"Cheers," she said candidly as she backed out the door carrying her briefcase and papers in one hand, and her purse in the other. She closed the door behind her.

Gary turned to Max. The yellowed wall of Gary's office behind him framed his eager face that was intent on what Gary was about to say.

"Life skills are the skills that most of us take for granted as we go through life: nutritional knowledge, grocery lists and shopping, budgeting money, cooking, managing a home, making and keeping appointments, maintaining a calendar, basic math, managing your bills . . ." Gary said, counting the skills on his fingers.

"There's also learning social skills, such as interpersonal relationships, avoiding neighbour disputes and other problems, and developing self-confidence while building a network of friends and acquaintances. There's actually a lot to it, and the program runs about six months. We run them on a rotating basis to accommodate as many people as we can. Most of the clients who come around for a period of time are encouraged to do it. It's one of the best in the city."

"Wow. I don't need all of that."

"You may need more than you realize, Max. Many clients have an unrealistic understanding of how lacking they are in some of these skills. For example, do you know how to negotiate a lease with a landlord?"

"But I don't need that skill. I'll never be signing a lease, not with Quinn out there, and Cameron calling the shots and countering my every move."

"Okay, true. But there may come a day when you're free of Cameron's directives, and then you'll want to settle down and have your own apartment, don't you think?"

"I can't imagine a day without running from them."

"What if they're caught? They can't go on abducting and murdering children forever. Somehow, someday, someone's going to squeal. And then you'll be free."

"I've prayed for that day since I was five years old, and it still hasn't happened. Seventeen years later he still comes out on top."

"Why do you think that is?"

"He's careful. He grabs kids far away from Newark. He found me in Albany. The police have no idea where to look for him. They have no idea what he looks like. He's a phantom. The day he picked me up, he was sporting a fake moustache and a long red wig. I never saw that silver-grey station wagon again. The few times I was taken out of the basement and driven to another location, we always rode in a different car. And let's face it: The only people who know what he's doing are his clients, and they wouldn't say anything. They get too much out of it. A hot, young boy was more than they could ever want."

Max paused in thought. There was that dreamy, distant look in his eyes. Finally, he continued.

"I'll tell you what more they want: They want not to be caught themselves. They can't satisfy their need for young boys easily. There's not many stores that sell it. The closest thing is child porn, but that doesn't even compare to the real thing, the real sensation of being with their heart's desire. Cameron supplies their own brand of heroin. And they're not likely to tattle to the police on someone who provides their drug fix. I know this from watching them return and return and return again. These boys are their addiction, the heroin they inject into their souls. And it blackens them; it rots them from the inside out, but they still come back for more. I know. I was Quinn's favourite. I was the one he always asked for. I was the one he couldn't get enough of. I was Quinn's undoing. He would have done anything for Cameron to ensure continued access to my body. And he did. Cameron had him hooked, and I was the bait."

Max looked down at his fingers twisting in his lap. A single tear coursed down his cheek. Then he said, "Can we get registered for the program now?"

"Sure. Whatever you need."

Gary led his brother down the hall to an office with a metal plate affixed to its door that read "Programs." The door was open, but Gary knocked anyway.

"Gary! How are you?"

"Hi, Zachary. I'm fine. You?"

"Just great. What can I do for you?" Zachary was a huge man. He overflowed the chair in which he sat. His black hair curled tightly against his scalp and shone with some brand of product that Gary could smell from the doorway. It was a pleasant smell, even if rather strong, that reminded him of honey and ginger and sunshine. His brown skin shone, too, but with a glistening of sweat. He wore a green and yellow shirt with horizontal stripes, which did nothing for any attempt he might have been making to call away from his size. His pants were pulled taut across his huge waist, the button straining against its closure. His white sneakers were scuffed and dirty, almost as dirty as some of Gary's clients', which didn't surprise him, since Zachary had been homeless himself. He was one of The Mission's success stories, having climbed, scratched and fumbled his way out of homelessness and joblessness. Several years prior, he learned lessons in his own Life Skills classes and began working at The Mission, first volunteering for numerous positions, and then eventually applying and securing a job at the front entrance. He was very successful there and moved laterally through the ranks until he landed his current position of programs coordinator. Everyone who worked at The Mission was exceptionally proud of him, but not more than he was of himself. And most of the clients looked up at him with a kind of reverence.

"Zachary, this is David, one of our new clients. He'd like to get set up with the next Life Skills program. Can you help us out?"

"Course, I can," said Zachary, enthusiasm spreading in his voice, in his face, in his whole body as he dragged himself up from his chair and offered his hand to Max. He said confidently, "Nice to meet you, man. Our program can help you more than you know. I'm livin' proof of that. Before I went through it, I had no idea how to negotiate a lease or make friends. Now I even got a paying job here at The Mission."

Only Zachary could say that without an ounce of arrogance, thought Gary.

"So I've heard," replied Max.

"You can leave him with me, Gary," said Zachary. "I know you've got work to do."

"Yeah, thanks. Would you mind reading out loud anything that's written? He has some trouble with reading."

"For sure, for sure," Zachary responded through the grin still spread across his face. "We can even look at some tutoring, if he's up to it."

"I think Life Skills is enough right now," said Max.

"You may be right. Reading skills can come later. And you can easily find someone to help you read any handouts you get in the program."

"Oh," Gary said on his way out the door, "I already told him that I'll take that on." With genuine pride, Gary walked the halls to his office. Not pride in himself but in Max. He was so brave to be taking this on. He was so brave to try to survive.

CHAPTER SEVEN

Gary found it near impossible to concentrate on his paperwork that afternoon and was relieved when Donovan walked into his office. He was an odd man, Donovan was. He bore all the markings of one who had lived on the streets for years, though he retained many character traits he had acquired beforehand. He was very polite. He kept himself as well-groomed as he could given the circumstances. And he still liked to spend Saturday afternoons in Central Park watching the multicoloured passersby. Yet everyone at The Mission knew about his weirdness over that striped shirt he always wore. He was unwilling to take it off, unwilling to clean it, unwilling to replace it. It was these types of dichotomies that fascinated Gary about Donovan.

He had always gotten along well with Donovan, and they seemed to have a good rapport. Donovan would stop by Gary's office every once in a while just to pass the time and exchange pleasantries. "How are you?" "I'm fine, and you?" "I'm well. Keeping busy?" "As much as I can." And those kinds of things. But

Gary felt there was still something between them, a barrier of sorts, like something had always been left unsaid in their conversations. He had no idea what was missing, but he felt it nevertheless. It was this barrier that he always tried to break through in his dealings with Donovan, hoping to delve into deeper conversations that might have more meaning for him if he'd just open up.

The Mission had an open-door policy at all times, except when social workers were with a client who needed privacy to discuss personal matters. It was a regular occurrence to have clients walk in unannounced. Gary didn't mind; in fact, he liked the policy. It created a real sense of camaraderie and warmth, friendliness and friendship in what could have otherwise been a bureaucratic nightmare for all involved. This way, both clients and staff felt like The Mission actually cared about its work, that it urged staff members to work harder to solve the problems that clients presented them with and not become overwhelmed by them.

Donovan was a tall thirty-year-old man, and he was thin as a lemur's ringed tail. His face bore the struggles and exertions of living homeless in New York City. His eyes were ringed with deep, dark bags, and his skin had the unhealthy pallor of a lack of nutrition, which was odd, since he mostly ate at The Mission. Though the meals weren't anything to write home about, they were nevertheless nutritious and satisfactory. His body was unwashed. His clothing was ripped and torn from skirmishes and general wear. His hair was longish, almost down to his shoulders, and was already showing a thin crown of premature balding. It was blond from its roots to its tips—not blond like Max's but an ordinary dirty blond. His fingers were stained from the tips to the knuckles with dirt and nicotine from all the cigarette butts he'd picked up from the sidewalk and smoked down to the filter. He smelled of the street, a dank and disturbing scent that seeped into the air around him. He was unremarkable in all senses of the word and always seemed to creep into the background.

"Hey, Donovan. What's up?" Donovan sat down in the chair opposite him.

"Not much, Gary. You?"

"Same old, same old. Are those the pants you got the other day? How do they fit?"

"Oh, yeah. They fit fine. They've got this elastic in the back, so they stretch when I bend. I like that."

"Great! That's good news. How's the shirt? Still treating you well?" A strange look passed Donovan's eye.

"Uh, fine enough. Why?"

"Oh, just curious is all. Can I ask you something, Donovan? Do you mind?"

"Okay," he said rather reluctantly.

"Why do you love that shirt so much?"

"Do I have to answer?"

"Of course not. But I'd be pleased if you did. It's hard to get to know Donovan the man without knowing about Donovan's shirt. Don't you agree?"

Donovan shifted in his seat. "Can I close the door?"

"Sure, of course," Gary replied, wondering why a conversation about his shirt would require privacy. But then again, who was he to determine what was a private matter for his clients and what wasn't? Donovan got up from his chair to close the door.

"You know, I actually came to tell you something today. But if you'd rather hear about the shirt, so be it."

"Tell me about the shirt first, please. Then you can tell me what you came to say."

Donovan sat with his hands folded in his lap staring at Gary, looking him straight in the eyes for what seemed like forever. It felt like Donovan was sizing him up, trying to decide how trustworthy he was before proceeding. Apparently he passed the test, because he eventually began to speak.

"You know I'm not gay." Now he was searching Gary's face for a reaction to this intimate knowledge he was offering him.

"No, I didn't actually. I don't make assumptions about people one way or the other, because they are most often misleading or flat-out wrong. But what does this have to do with your shirt?"

"I'm getting to that.

"So, about three years ago, I met a man. He was a very kind man, and he used to drop money in my hat every day. I used to beg on the corner of 82nd and Broadway, by the bagel shop there. It was a really good spot because sometimes people would come out of the shop and toss me one, so I'd have something to eat.

"But this guy, George, usually just gave me money—a five-dollar bill, which was a lot. I actually don't think I've ever received that kind of money from anyone else ever . . ."

"Anyway, we got to talking after a while, and I found out that sometimes he left his apartment just to give me money.

"One night, he asked me if I wanted to come over and take a shower. I didn't really want to, but I was really filthy. I told him no because I only had those clothes, so I'd smell just as bad after. I guess he hadn't thought of that. So he offered to wash my clothes in his washer. I agreed." Donovan looked down at his hands in his lap. They were as still and silent as dead things, like birds after having slammed into tall windows and broken their thin, little necks.

"To be honest, it crossed my mind that there might be meds in his bathroom I could nick—just a couple, so he wouldn't know. Enough to get through the night. Because at that time, I was into drugs. Not heroin or smack or any of the really hard drugs. But if there were T4s or morphine pills or pot, I was right into that. And coke, ecstasy and meth. I liked 'em 'cause they would help me sleep or stay awake or just get through the day without thinking about

. . . well, anything. I never poked, though. I didn't think of myself as a drug addict, but how many addicts do?

"So I walked with him to his apartment, but about two or three steps behind him. I was ashamed of my thoughts because here was a guy who genuinely seemed to be trying to help me, and here I was thinking of ways to rob him.

"I was twenty-seven at the time, and George had just turned forty. He would become like a father to me in time. That day, when we got to his apartment at 77 Riverside Drive, he walked me past his doorman. I'm sure the guy had never seen anyone walk in with a filthy, stinking homeless man—the stricken look on his face and his one raised eyebrow said so.

"George had reddish hair and a beard to match. He had a limp that made him walk slower, and he walked with a cane. But even so, he was sprightly and sure of himself.

"Did I mention that he had a musical voice? It went up and down, up and down, and sounded so melodic. He talked with such enthusiasm—nonstop about anything and everything, but mostly about the musicals and plays he'd recently seen or been in. He was a props maker in the theatre, but I got the feeling he wanted to be out there on the stage. And he could have if he didn't have that damned limp. He had such an expressive face that lit up with joy or was crushed by sadness or stricken with anguish at some news he had heard. And despite having to use a cane, he walked as though he were walking on waves of sunshine that shone down upon him and him alone.

"And he was kind, so very kind. I couldn't believe how loving his voice was. His smile and his eyes made you melt. His eyes even made you want to be good, to better yourself. He made me want to rise up above myself. He made me want to be better than I was. I wanted to be closer to him, to have him love me and care about me. It's strange, but I couldn't bear to displease him or be diminished in his eyes, not because it would make me look badly but rather because I couldn't bear to hurt him, couldn't bear to take his love and cheapen it or debase it or infect it."

Donovan looked up at Gary, his eyes glistening. Was he about to cry? It certainly wouldn't be the first time a client had cried in his office. This story was more personal and close to his heart than he had realized. Gary looked away but wasn't sure why.

"I didn't learn all this in one night. It was over time, as I spent more time with him," Donovan said. His lifeless hands were now balled into fists. His knuckles were white, almost as white as his face.

"So anyway, we went into his apartment, and the first thing I saw were the walls. They were loaded with shelves—every wall, stacks and stacks of 'em. They all had a figurine or a greeting card or some memento of some unforgotten past. Oh, there were all kinds of figurines. There were birds and squirrels and dolphins and cute grey mice. And moose with happy faces, and cats with cheshire grins. But mostly there were bears of all shapes and sizes made out of ceramic and painted with incredible care. There were stuffed bears, too. I wondered how many of them were handmade. Quite a few, I thought. I'd never seen anything like it.

"As we walked through the hall to the bathroom beyond, I saw bears of needlepoint and bears behind glass—all kinds of bears. I glanced at George. He even looked like one himself, with his round stomach and red but greying beard.

"'I collect bears, you've probably noticed,' he said to me, gesturing at the walls with a joking smile. I ask him why, and he said his friends always called him Georgie Bear.

"When I went to shower, I found a bottle of T4s in the bathroom cabinet. I swallowed two and pocketed two in the bathrobe he gave me.

"After my shower, I sat with him in the dining room—me on the sofa and him on the piano bench. We talked for hours, long past the dryer's buzzer. Eventually it was late enough that we were both yawning, so we called it a night. He offered me his sofa, but I declined and headed out to the warm subway grate I'd been sleeping on for the past several months. I was clean, smelled clean and had freshly laundered clothes. I felt great.

"I went back to Georgie's often after that. The doorman came to know me by name. Georgie and I would spend hours talking, and I came to realize that despite how exceptionally kind he was, he was also exceptionally lonely. Eventually we got onto the subject of sexuality, and he told me he was gay. At first I was frightened. Was he just courting me with showers and dinners and conversation to get me into bed with him? I really didn't think so, though. He'd never touched me, never opened the bathroom door while I was in there, never done anything that even remotely seemed like a come-on. So though I was a little hesitant after that, I still returned."

Gary was fascinated by Donovan's tale. He was sure taking a long time to get to the point about where his shirt came from, but the details with which he was describing the events leading up to it were rich, telling and curious. He doubted that anyone else had ever sat with him and told him such a tale.

"You see, Georgie wasn't the only lonely one," continued Donovan. "I was lonely, too. I craved companionship. I craved friendship. You don't make many friends when you're living on the street.

"In conversation, I learned that his parents lived in Jersey, in a little town surrounded by trees. They were in their late seventies and couldn't get around much. The same thing that afflicted Georgie's hips and caused him to need a cane was hereditary on his father's side, and his father was close to crippled. His mother was blessed with the same jovial personality that Georgie had—or I should say he got his from her—but her arthritis crippled her almost as much as her husband. So Georgie always traveled to see them, and never vice versa. When he went on these trips, he would ask me to housesit for him, and I always obliged, revelling in the sheer luxury of the place: the softness of the cushions and the freshness of the linens and the comfort of the bed. It was like living as a normal human does, and I looked forward to Georgie's trips to Jersey, despite that I always missed him terribly.

"Georgie told me that money was getting a little tight, with inflation rising but his salary not keeping up. He was thinking about getting a roommate to share the expenses but wanted to offer the spare room to me first. I told him that I just didn't have the money to pay rent at that point. Reluctantly, he agreed that I was right, so he decided to put an advertisement on one of those roommate-finder websites that were cropping up all over the place online.

"'Nevertheless,' he said, looking me straight in the eye, 'you've got to look after your drug addiction.'

"I was shocked. Frozen with fear, actually. It's a disheartening moment when someone finally confronts you with your own addiction. And there was Georgie slamming me in the face with his knowledge of my own. Everything inside of me wanted to run in that moment, to get up and clear the room and get to Central Park as fast as I could, where I knew I could score something to get past those feelings. But instead—and for the life of me, I don't know why—I stayed right where I was sitting.

"At first I denied having one, but he countered by admitting that he'd found the two T4s I'd slipped into his robe on that first night and forgotten to retrieve. He said he always kept a close count of them because he wanted to monitor his own intake, knowing how addictive they were, and that he noticed how many were missing since I'd been coming around.

"I was so ashamed. I couldn't look him in the eye. He produced a pamphlet from a manila folder that was on top of the piano. It was a brochure for a rehab center upstate. He opened it and read it to me, not accusingly, which is what I expected, but lovingly, with the kind of emotion that only Georgie could effect into his voice."

Donovan looked up and over Gary's right shoulder at something Gary could only guess at. He supposed it wasn't the yellow wall behind him but the details of that evening so long ago.

"By the end of the evening, and many tears later on both sides of the table, I agreed to go. Arrangements were made, and Georgie rented a car to drive me upstate for my two-month rehab stint. He told me he was still looking for a suitable roommate via the online source he'd been using.

"I won't bore you with details about rehab. I'm sure you've heard it all before. But as I approached my graduation date, clean as a whistle, Georgie made reservations to pick me up. He showed up that day with a gift for me, wrapped in paper. It was this shirt, the one I'm wearing. And he was so excited because he had someone coming to look at the spare room that night."

Donovan paused, and Gary noticed a tear dripping down his cheek. One single tear.

"So that's why you love the shirt so much—because Georgie gave it to you. That makes sense," said Gary.

"Yes and no. I'm not done."

The room had grown so quiet that Gary wondered whether dinner had begun. He glanced at his watch. It was still about half an hour away.

Donovan continued. "Georgie didn't come by the next day to drop the fiver into my hat. I wasn't bothered by it, since he'd often come late in the evening. Still, it had been so long since I'd had any real time to spend with him that I was excited to leave my post and head down to his apartment.

"I could see the flashing lights from three blocks away, but I didn't think much of it. This is New York, and all kinds of things happen here. But I *was* surprised to see that there were four police cruisers with their lights flashing parked outside of 77 Riverside Drive. I walked past them into the lobby wondering what was up. Some kind of domestic dispute, I figured.

"'You can't go up there tonight, Mr. Donovan,' the doorman told me.

"'Why not?'" I asked, fear rising in my throat.

"'Mr. Georgie's been murdered,' he said.

"I crashed to the floor. I don't remember much except that I was screaming. Screaming and screaming. Tears were soaking my new shirt. And then one of the policemen came through the door.

"'What's going on here?' he asked all authoritative like.

"'He's a good friend of Mr. Georgie's,' the doorman said.

"'He's that homeless tramp from up on Broadway. I see him there all the time. What's he carrying on about?'

"'I told you, he was a close friend of Mr. Georgie's.'

"'Get outta here, you bum,' he told me. 'We've got enough to deal with without you scarin' all these good folks who live here. They're scared plenty already. Get out before I throw you in the drunk tank for the night!'"

The room was dead quiet. Noises drifted into the office from underneath the door. People were lining up for dinner already. The one tear on Donovan's cheek had turned into many raining down his face and onto his shirt. He wiped at his face with the back of his hand and sniffled back the emotion.

"I don't know how I did it, but somehow I got up off the floor and walked back to my subway grate.

"I went back the next day, and the day after that, but the police hadn't finished their investigation yet. When they finally did, they removed the yellow tape from the door to Georgie's apartment. I asked the doorman if I could go up. He said yes but that I wanted to think about what I was doing. 'The blood is still there. His parent's haven't come to clean it up yet. And it's not the building's responsibility. Frankly, because he was gay, none of us wants to clean it up anyway. AIDS, you know. No one wants to catch AIDS from Mr. Georgie's blood.'

"I knew what I had to do: one last favour for Georgie, something only I could do for him. I didn't want his seventy-something-year-old parents to have to go through that, and I knew I could do it—as a gesture of love."

He heaved a heavy sigh and paused. His flowing tears had soaked his shirt by now, and Gary was numb with shock. Surely there were companies that came into houses to do this? But how much did they charge? Certainly Georgie's parents wouldn't have had that kind of money, and neither did Donovan, as he lived on the streets.

"The doorman lent me a bucket and some rags from the back room behind the lobby. I used my own key to enter the apartment. At first I couldn't see any difference in the apartment. I guess my mind just couldn't take in the shock of it all. But then my vision expanded, and I could see everything.

"They had killed him with a claw hammer. They killed him because he was gay. They had trolled the website to find the perfect target, and Georgie was it. Sprays of blood were slashed across the walls where they had walloped him across his head with their hammer, tearing chunks of skull and brains apart. Huge droplets of dry, brown blood were sprayed across all the shelves, dripping from his figurines, dripping from all the ceramic bears. On the floor, bloody handprints crawled from the dining room into the kitchen, where he'd dragged himself up using the sideboard to the hanging wall phone. One single handprint was on the kitchen wall—perfectly formed—where he had tried to steady himself. There was another splash on the sideboard, and one on the wall behind it where it had been pushed out of the way as they pulled his feet out from under him and dragged him back into the other room for more. On the dining room floor was the largest pool of blood, where he laid there dying, where he laid face down, the blood bubbles from his breath dried in circular forms. I'd heard that they'd covered his head with a towel so that he wouldn't look at them as they smoked Colts cigars and used his silver coasters as ashtrays.

"I filled the bucket with warm water, stood there a long time and then finally went to work. I removed boxes filled with books and magazines that he wouldn't have wanted his parents to find: old copies of *Blueboy*, *Honcho*, *Members*—all kinds of gay literature. And when I was done, that home was spick-and-span, fresh linen on the table and all. His parents would never find out he was gay. I felt that if he'd wanted them to know, he would have told them, and I wasn't going to let those bastards who had killed him have the last say.

"Then I returned to my subway grate by the bagel shop. I've been there ever since."

Gary waited a long while as Donovan composed himself. He handed Donovan a box of tissue, which he accepted silently.

"Donovan, what was it that you came in to see me for today, before I asked about your shirt?" he asked.

Through sniffles, Donovan said, "It doesn't matter. I'll come again some other day."

Without another word, he got up, crossed the room and went out.

CHAPTER EIGHT

Max was waiting on the other side of the door to enter Gary's office when Donovan was finished. He sat in the chair beside Gary's desk and looked at him.

"I didn't knock, because I heard voices," he said.

"Thanks. I was busy with someone."

"Everything okay? He looked kind of shook up, that guy who just left."

"That was Donovan," Gary said, hoping Max wouldn't ask for particulars. Part of his job was helping his clients, but another, perhaps larger, part was keeping their secrets. It was the one part of his job that he hated, and he often thought that he should get his own social worker or therapist to tell all these secrets to. Though he'd been trained in school to separate himself from his clients, it was never as easy as his professors made it out to be. It was a huge burden to hold close to his own heart the deep, dark, truly horrific stories they sometimes told him.

Is this what it's going to be like with Max? Holding secrets of trauma at arm's length? he thought. Would he fail Max when he needed him most just because he couldn't separate himself from his brother's problems?

"I know," said Max.

"What? Know what?" Gary said.

"Earth to Gary," he said as he leaned forward slightly and waved his hand in front of Gary's face. "I know that was Donovan. We had dinner with him the other night, and I smoked with him outside the other day."

"In the alleyway, I hope."

"Yes, in the alley. Last thing I need is to get kicked out for breaking the rules."

"We only bar you for three days for smoking on the premises, unless it's in the building. Then it's a month."

"I'm not that stupid."

"It's not about stupidity. You'd be surprised what some clients try to pull, especially when they're staying overnight. Once the lights are off, there's no going in or out of the building. But a lot of them try to smoke in the bathrooms not realizing we check them constantly."

"Ahh, yes. The Bowery Mission," Max said with a grin. They both laughed.

"So is Donovan okay?"

"I'm sorry, but I can't really talk about other clients with you."

"But I'm your brother," Max said a bit churlishly.

"Yes, but while you're here, you're my client. So how did it go with Zachary?"

"Good, I guess. I got signed up, if that's what you wanted to know."

"When does the next program begin?"

"Next week, actually. Three o'clock on Monday afternoon."

"That's great—only half an hour before I usually arrive. It'll be easy to get here early. Do you know where your classroom is?"

"Zachary walked me to it," Max said. "He seems like a nice guy. So does Donovan."

"They both are. Did Zachary tell you his story?"

"Yes, he did. I get the sense he tells a lot of people."

"You are a very astute little puppy."

"Hah. We'll see on Monday." Max began picking at a hangnail.

"Are you worried about your classes?" Gary asked.

Max shrugged his shoulders. "A little. I've never taken a class before."

"Well, time you started."

Gary couldn't help but wonder just how many other differences there were between the life he had so far lived and the life his brother had so far endured. He knew that while he owned an apartment and had an extensive education, Max owned little more than the clothes on his back and did not even know his ABCs. But now he knew of Max's deeper wounds. Max had been abused, even sexually, whereas the only abuse Gary had suffered were the beatings from his mother and foster parents. From what Max had told him, he grew up in an unstable environment, and though Gary did, too, the instability of his was more not knowing how long a foster home would last, and whether he'd made a good enough impression for them to keep him. And Max had spent much of his life finding meals in restaurant dumpsters and taking handouts from those who were generous. Gary never knew that kind of hunger; he had three meals on his plate every day.

Dinner was mostly uneventful. A small skirmish broke out between two men near the cutlery table, but Zachary rose to resolve it in the quickest of moments. Gary chose to help out in the lineup, while Max sat among a group of clients including Samuel, pushing his food around his plate with his fork. Max was waiting for Gary to finish serving so they could eat together. Donovan was noticeably absent. This worried Gary a bit, knowing how heavy this day had been for him, but not for long. He suspected Donovan could take care of himself. Most of his clients could do so in all manner of crises, having learned while living on the grueling, unforgiving streets.

After he and Max had finished their meals, they stayed behind to help clean up. Friday evenings were always slow in the social worker offices. Gary had stuck a note on the door indicating where clients could find him if they needed him, but no one did. After cleanup, Max headed to the alleyway, and Gary sat at his desk to do some paperwork.

By evening's end they were both tired, partly from the day and the incessant heat that just wouldn't break, but mostly from the events of the night before. They were both glad to pass through the Mission doors and head for the subway.

"I used to live down in the subway," said Max as they walked through the train doors. "Worth St. Station. It's an abandoned station from the first subway lines ever built in Manhattan. It's almost directly under the Federal Building on the west side of Foley Square. Apparently, when they were building the Federal Plaza, they had to set the building back far enough from the sidewalk so it wouldn't be on top of the station and collapse into the ground. Cool, huh? I would go down into the Canal St. Station and walk along the subway tracks to get there."

"What was that like for you, Max?" asked Gary, deeply curious. "That must have been exceptionally lonely for you down there."

"I always felt so safe and removed from the world—forgotten almost, like I was buried underneath but could still hear the sounds of the square. It was actually really quiet down there; the only sounds came from passing trains or street kids who came down on a dare to spray graffiti."

The more Max revealed, the heavier it weighed on Gary's soul and the more he found his words escaping him.

They rode most of the way in silence. Gary was still trying to process Donovan's harrowing story, and Max was now concerned about what or whom they might find waiting for them at the apartment. They kept their preoccupations to themselves.

The apartment was dark as usual when they arrived. Gary turned on the lights, and Max headed straight for the shower. Gary decided to set the futon back up as a couch, which they'd neglected to do before leaving earlier in the day. He assumed they'd be up for a few more hours eating ice cream with strawberry-rhubarb glaze and trying to get to know each other more. He was elated that his brother was back in his life but troubled over the enormous scope of the issues Max was presenting as time wore on, and the basketful of anxieties that he seemed to live with. What was Gary to do with his brother? How was he to help him? And what kind of help did he really need?

When he lifted up the futon frame to maneuver it back into position, he noticed something lying on the floor beneath it. Thinking it might have fallen out of Max's pocket, Gary bent to pick it up. It was a brown business card.

Cameron's Flight School
Our Instructors Will Fly You to Heaven
Prices Starting as Low as $4,000 Per Hour
201-942-3728

In the upper right-hand corner was an image of a plane. But it wasn't a plane. If you stared at it long enough, the lines seemed to move and shift into another arrangement, that of a long, thick penis. *What kind of flight school charges four thousand dollars an hour for flight training and has a penis for a logo?*

Gary froze. A grey cloud passed across his eyes, and his tongue dried up in his throat. *No, this can't be. . . . It was all so far-fetched. . . . But then why would Max be carrying it around with him?* He decided to ask Max about it later and set it on the kitchen counter.

After finishing with the couch, he headed to the kitchen, took out the ice cream and jam, and fished out a couple of bowls from the cupboard. Max emerged from the bathroom towel-drying his hair just as Gary was about to dig into the ice cream.

"Man, it feels good to shower again. I don't think I'll ever get clean enough," he said

Gary said, "Get at those nails with that scrub brush I gave you and you'll erase all traces of dumpsters. Don't get me wrong—you look and smell clean enough. It's just your nails. And maybe your feet. How are they doing anyway?"

"They're pretty bad. I have awful callouses, and the soles are cracked and bleeding. It hurts to walk. I just ignore it. I was going to use that scrub brush last night, but I was just so tired. And I told myself I'd do it tonight, but I forgot. I was just loving the feeling of the water on my skin."

Gary looked at the scoop in his hand. The rim of the carton had begun dripping on the counter. "Maybe I'll take a shower now, too. I know I took one this morning, but this heat just sucks the sweat out of me, and I feel sticky all over," he said. He wiped up a couple of drips with his forefinger and licked it clean before putting the pint back in the freezer.

Gary remembered what Max had said about the feel of the water on his skin and wondered whether a shower could ever feel as good to him as the last two had felt to Max. Probably not. As he lathered the shampoo through his hair, the bathroom door suddenly burst open, causing him to jump. Max ripped the shower curtain open.

"Where the fuck did you get this?! Where?!" he screamed.

"What the hell?!" Gary screamed back, holding one hand up and grabbing his crotch with the other. No one had ever invaded his privacy like this. "What's wrong, Max?" he spluttered as he spit shampoo out of his mouth.

"Where the hell did you get this, Gary?" He shook the business card in Gary's face, his eyes wide and bulging.

"Wait a second, Max. I've got shampoo in my hair," he answered, reining in his anger a bit. "And close the damn curtain, or I'll get water all over the floor." Max snatched the curtain shut, the rings screeching loudly. Gary leaned back under the water's spray and rinsed the shampoo out of his hair. He turned off the water and reached his hand out for his towel. Max took it to him. He dried off as best he could and stepped out of the shower with the towel around his waist.

"Do you mind waiting outside while I finish up, please?" he asked. Max stalked out.

As Gary emerged from the bathroom, his anger somewhat abated, Max was standing at the balcony door looking out at the city skyline. The East River and the lights of the 59th Street Bridge were visible from the window. It was a splendid sight at the best of times and a wonderful sight at the worst of times. This, Gary could see from his brother's hunched shoulders and slightly hung head, seemed to be one of the worst times. He didn't hear Gary come from the bathroom, and he swirled around quickly when Gary cleared his throat.

"What is this?" Max asked, a little calmer now. He was holding the business card. "Where did you get this?"

Gary stepped through the living room and into the kitchen. Max watched him like a mouse would a large, fat cat. "I found it on the floor under the futon when I was setting it back up."

Max's face fell somewhat, and he dropped the hand holding the card to his side. "I was afraid you were going to say something like that."

"Where else would you have preferred I found it?"

"I would have preferred you'd not found it at all."

"What does it mean, Max? Why do you have that card? Is this all some kind of sick joke? Is Cameron part of some sick fantasy about your abductors? Is anything you've told me even true?"

Max sat on the futon, practically crumpling into it.

"Is that what you think, Gary? That I'm twisted enough to concoct my whole past? To fabricate some kind of illusion to keep you from the truth?"

"Actually, I wondered if you were ill and have some kind of mental illness like schizophrenia, where your mind creates and distorts voices and images. It's a common ailment for many of our clients."

"And what about last night? What about Quinn breaking into the apartment and abusing me? Did my mind concoct that, too?" asked Max, a little disturbed that Gary didn't even believe him.

"The mind is capable of both wonderful and horrendous things," Gary said as gently as he could. "It can play tricks on us, make us believe in things that aren't real."

"You think I'm sick then," he said, putting his head in his hands.

"Look, Max. All I know about last night is I found you hiding in the closet in the dark and stabbing at things that weren't there."

"But they *were* there, Gary. They were. Quinn was in this room. His hands were on me, and he was massaging my dick. He broke in. I don't know how, but he broke in and was kneeling right beside me."

"Then why didn't he just kill you when he had the chance?"

"Because he still loves me. That's the only explanation. He must have wanted to have me just one last time. I've always been his drug. I can tell—he wants to fuck me one last time before he cuts off my head and takes it back to Cameron."

"Where did you get the card, Max?"

"Quinn must have dropped it on his way out the patio."

Gary placed his hands on the counter a bit more than shoulder width apart, fingers spread wide. He hung his head and tried to process. A long pause ensued until Max finally spoke.

"I'll leave if you want."

Gary looked up at his little brother. He looked so lost. "I don't want you to leave," he said with a lump in his throat. "I just want to know the truth."

"I'm putting you in danger. Last night was bad enough. What happens the next time Quinn breaks in? What will you do when he's standing over your bed with a knife?"

"That won't happen," Gary said, shaking his head.

"How can you say that?"

"I just don't think it will."

"But you don't know Quinn. He's devious. He's determined. And he's deadly."

Suddenly, Gary thought about the building workmen he'd chatted with earlier in the day, two men he trusted and knew to be honest, at least in affairs concerning the building. They told him that someone broke into the apartment next door last night—the apartment that was vacant and still up for sale. There was nothing there to steal, nothing of value, nothing that could be pawned at the nearest pawnshop. Why else would someone break into an empty apartment if not to gain access to another balcony—his balcony? A balcony whose door was ajar when he woke this morning. A door that he always kept shut but seldom locked since he lived seventeen floors up. A door that he seldom locked because no one lived in the apartment next door. A balcony that he always thought was uncomfortably close to the one next door, the one attached to the vacant apartment with the broken lock. The evidence all seemed to point to Max telling the truth, not to mention the look on Max's face when he opened the closet door and found him crouched with a deadly switchblade clutched in his grip. Why was it so hard to believe Max? Was it that the truth was so damn terrifying he didn't dare put stock in it? That he didn't want to believe it?

Max got up and crossed the room to the patio, again looking out at the night. He said, "I've seen this card before, Gary. It's the card that Cameron uses to drum up business. Quinn gives it out to men who will pay big money for young boys. This is his calling card. I saw it one day when I was up on the main floor of the house we were kept in. There was a pile of them on a table. I can't read it, but I'd know that logo anywhere."

And it made sense to Gary then. All of it fit together. In all of Max's stories and the events of the past couple of days, Gary could see one blackened thread: Cameron was a ruthless businessman, and Quinn was his killing machine. Max, he finally knew, was telling him the god-awful truth. Cameron and Quinn lived, and they were the men who stole his brother's childhood.

»

After a night of restless and troubled sleep, Gary awoke to a bright summer's morn. Sunlight streamed in through the window above his bed despite the flimsy curtain that hung there. The air conditioner's hum reminded him how the room was so temperate. He thought about the simple genius of it: Hot air goes in; cold air comes out. He'd never thought about refrigerators or freezers in the same way, but he was grateful for their workings. And right now, he was beyond grateful for the air conditioner in his apartment.

Right now he was thrilled. Gary was, for the first time in days, in a really good mood.

"What's got you so worked up, Gary?" asked Max as Gary emerged from his bedroom humming.

"I've got a date."

»»

Jean was standing on the corner of Hudson and West 12th by the time Gary arrived, several canvas shopping bags in hand. She was wearing another short, black dress, heels and a pearl necklace that clutched her throat and framed her face beautifully. She also carried canvas bags. Gary mused that he'd never had a date with such a beautiful woman. Just what did she see in him?

"Hi, Jean." She twisted in place.

"Hi, Gary."

"You look stunning." Gary leaned in to hug her briefly, but before he could do so, Jean responded.

"Thank you. You don't." Gary pulled back quickly. Noticing his crestfallen face, she hastened to add, "But I don't trust a man who's prettier than me. They're always waiting for the better girl just around the corner. And they turn all the heads in the room, even the guys'. But men should be looking at me. So you look perfect." She nodded for reassurance.

Gary didn't know whether he should be flattered or furious. He settled on flattered.

"Shall we?" he asked, extending his elbow. She wrapped her arm inside it and clasped it with her other hand.

"Let's go."

"I've never asked a girl out to the farmers market before. Always dinner and a movie, even in college. I think college girls feel more grown-up when you take them out for dinner and a movie."

"Like you first suggested to me. Boring. Let me start teaching you—right here, right now. A girl like me needs to be treated special, because she is special and she knows it. A girl like me will see through all your feeble attempts to treat her like anyone else. Take her to The Met or the wave pool or a street fair. She needs to experience new things and live in style. Dinner? I can get that at Zabar's. Movie? I can get that on TV. It's not hard to please me, but if you don't even try, that won't fly."

She smiled up at Gary, and he wondered whether she was reciting something she'd said a hundred times before. He smiled back, pulled her in tighter and walked on.

They took their time meandering through the market—pausing here, stopping there, slowly filling up their bags. They passed numerous stands with an assortment of fresh produce and handmade goods. There were round rutabagas and flowering green broccoli, and potatoes, tomatoes and red, red radishes. Green, leafy lettuces were displayed in all colours and sizes, as well as bunches of dark kale that withstood the heat. They stopped at a table and tasted the smallest dribbles of wine from a vendor, who requested identification from them first. Gary walked away with four new bottles of white wine whose flavour profiles ranged from sweet to dry.

"The man from the vineyard doesn't come often. You have to stock up when you can," Gary remarked as he rearranged the clanking bottles in his bag.

One lady sold honey from the back of her truck, and Gary and Jean spent a considerable amount of time learning about the feeding habits, sleeping habits and mating habits of bees, all of which, according to the bee lady, helped determine the flavour and quality of the honey. They each bought a large jar, Gary choosing a rich, golden clover honey and Jean choosing a dark, mysterious wildflower one. They licked each other's sticky fingers clean after tasting each jar.

True to her word, Jean did know a lot about nutrition. Throughout the morning, she taught Gary that ginger helps reduce muscle pain from exercise by up to 25 percent, that dried fruit has lost massive amounts of nutrient and antioxidant content—up to 80 percent—and that 1 cup of egg whites has as much potassium as a banana. These facts were just the tip of the iceberg of her knowledge.

Somewhere along the array of many tables, they approached a colourful, fragrant and rather crowded table staffed by a short, stocky man with greying blond hair and his portly wife, whose voice was in the range of soprano and had a beautiful sing-song quality.

"We have to stop here. I have to pick up some soap," Gary said. They had to wait for other customers to finish before they could wend their way to the front.

"Hello, Magnus. Hello, Betty," said Gary to the middle-aged couple.

"Hey, Gary!" replied Magnus.

"How are you, dear?" asked Betty.

"Well, it's been a helluva week, that's for sure. And I need more soap."

"Well, you take your pick," replied Magnus, spreading out his hands to show off his merchandise. "If you have questions, let me know."

"I have a question," said Jean. "What goes into your soap?"

"Coconut oil, palm oil and olive oil are my three primary oils," Magnus replied, "but I also include castor oil, shea butter, grapeseed oil, avocado oil and lye."

"Lye?" Jean asked warily.

"Don't let it scare you. Every single bar of soap in this world is made with some form of lye. Lye is the catalyst that combines with the oils to effect a chemical reaction called saponification."

Jean was nodding along, her lips parted slightly and her eyes alert with intrigue. She was drawn up into Magnus's natural charm.

"What about the oils?" Jean asked. "What do they do?"

"Coconut oil is my hard-core cleaner. The other oils are used to complement it."

Gary noticed that Magnus's moustache twitched when he spoke.

"The ingredients are written on the back of the soaps, if you like, miss," added Magnus.

"And so they are," said Jean as she picked one up to look. It was pink and white with lashes of black swirled around each other. She held it to her nose and sniffed.

"That's our Black Raspberry Twist soap," he noted.

She picked up a couple more.

"That's our Grey Panther. We thought it'd be a men's soap, but a lot of women like it, too. It's scented with sandalwood, amber, black pepper and sugarcane."

"Mmmmm. It smells like spicy honeyed candy," Jean remarked, her eyes closed as she took a big inhale of the soap.

Gary chuckled to himself. *Here's another one hooked.* He turned to Betty and said, "What do you suggest to help heal feet that are in real bad shape? My brother's feet have calluses, and they're bleeding between the toes and at the soles."

"Has he tried our Bootylicious Body Butter?" Betty asked. Gary was sure that Max hadn't.

"I don't believe so," he replied as he picked up a jar and flipped open the lid. It smelled like raspberries.

Betty said, "That's our Black Raspberry Twist—same as the soap your lady friend was just looking at. Smell this one. It's our

Satsuma Satisfaction." She held out another jar. Jean smiled, crossing her hands in front of her while Gary smelled the body butter. It was clearly plucked from a heavenly field of oranges. His mouth watered. *How could anyone not love this?* he wondered.

"Hey, Jean. Smell this," he said, passing the jar to her.

"Crack the angel. That smells good!"

"Crack the angel?" he asked, puzzled.

"My own invention."

"But for your brother . . .," Betty gently interrupted. She leaned across the table, her breasts nearly touching the tops of the colourful soaps. "I'd suggest our Plain Jane Body Butter. It works as well as the others, but there's no scent to potentially sting or irritate broken skin."

Gary bought six soaps and three jars of body butter, one Plain Jane for Max, a Black Raspberry Twist for Jean and a Satsuma Satisfaction for himself. Jean purchased four soaps, two each of the Black Raspberry Twist and the Grey Panther. Gary had noticed while walking arm in arm how dry were Jean's hands were. These purchases would be just the ticket.

By the end of the morning, they were both tired from the heat, the walking and the laughter they had shared. They had each bought lots of food. Gary chose things he thought Max might like, as well as stuff for dinner. And Jean bought fresh vegetables and meats for her auntie to use, who was a wonder in the kitchen. She was one of those women who showered her loved ones with food and whose home smelled exclusively of cooking. Onions and garlic were like the air freshener.

As they walked to the edge of the market, Gary was dismayed to see the morning coming to an end. With a frog in his throat that threatened to croak loudly at any moment, he turned to Jean and asked, "Now is it okay to ask you for dinner? It's just that I want to go home and make a great meal with this food, and I'd like to share it with you."

"I could be tempted," she said, glancing up at him out of the corner of her eye and swinging her hips side to side, her bag of groceries swaying with the momentum. It was very coquettish.

"I'm not asking you over for sex," Gary blurted out, stammering over his words.

"A girl can hope."

"Well, I'm not. This is a heartfelt invitation devoid of sexual innuendo . . . though I'm not completely opposed to the idea . . ."

"Tonight? I have things to do this afternoon that just have to get done."

"Drinks and hors d'oeuvres will be at six o'clock. Dinner's at seven. You've got lots of time," he said. *Crack the angel. Don't let me sound like I am begging.* He added, "523 E. 14th Street. I'll buzz you up. Look for Aldertree on the buzzer." Jean pulled a piece of paper from her small, red purse for him to write it all down.

"I'll be there!" she sang. Then she kissed him on the cheek and breezily walked away. Suddenly he realized he'd forgotten to mention that Max would be the second dinner guest.

CHAPTER NINE

Back at the apartment, Gary found Max asleep on the futon. His feet were propped up one on top of the other, and his head rested against the armrest. He was angled in what looked like a very uncomfortable position, but it didn't seem to bother him much. A lightweight cotton sheet lay across him, and his soft snore coursed throughout the room. Gary closed the door quietly behind him, but not quietly enough. Max woke with a start, glanced at his surroundings and then finally registered where he was.

"Hey, sleepyhead. How were your dreams?" asked Gary.

"Not great," Max replied as he pushed himself up to a seated position.

"What were you dreaming about?"

"I was a dog, and my leg was caught in a strong steel trap—a big trap, like a bear trap. Clouds were forming over my head and around me in a dark, dense fog. There were animals everywhere, running past, leaping over me and racing by me. They all looked terrified, like hell was breathing down their necks, and suddenly I knew why. I smelled it at first and then realized that the clouds were actually smoke and the trees were on fire. Sparks rained down all around and were landing on me, burning me." Max held his face in his hands and began to cry softly into them. Gary walked over to him, sat beside him and placed his arm around his little brother's shoulders.

"Max, it's okay. It was just a dream. Just a dream," he said, placing his arm around Max's shoulders.

"Dreams are never just dreams. When I was locked in that basement all those years, I had grim visions that scared the hell out of me, of faceless men coming at me, touching me, fondling me and kissing me, and then . . ."

"Then what, Max?"

"No. I don't want to talk about it," he spat. His dark-blue eyes blazed with fury. He shrugged Gary's hand off his shoulder, stood up and began stalking the length of the room, clenching and unclenching his fists.

"You have to talk about these things," Gary said in as soft and soothing a voice as he could muster. This was his social-worker voice, cultivated all through clinical training at school, that allowed him to register concern while maintaining professional distance.

"But I can't. Not yet. Not today. On a better day."

"There's always going to be a better day. It's like quitting smoking; people never quit because they're waiting for a better day." Gary thought of Jean's comment that morning. 'I don't trust a man who's prettier than me. They're always waiting for the better girl just around the corner.'

"I forgot to mention: Jean's coming for dinner."

Gary stepped around the counter that divided the kitchen from the living room and began pulling groceries out of the bags.

"I figured she might. I can head out. There's lots of stuff I can do. I have some money stashed near the Lexington and 59th subway station. I should go get it soon before someone finds it."

"Please, don't do that tonight. I'd like you here for dinner."

"Won't I cramp your style?"

"Not at all," Gary said, putting the three steaks on the kitchen counter. The meat man, as Gary thought of him, was a regular vendor at the market, and Gary loved the taste of his product. No hormones, no preservatives, oat-fed and not corn-fed. Besides the steaks, Gary had purchased some stewing beef, bacon, salt pork (for the pot of beans he planned on cooking one day soon) and a porketta, all of which he put in the freezer. "Besides, I think I might need a chaperone. Not for me, but for Jean."

"A girl who knows what she wants?" Max said.

"Yes, she's confident and strong like Roseanne Barr."

"Who is Roseanne Barr?"

"Someone quite beyond your years or experience."

"Is she hot?"

"Not at all. Don't even go there. You don't want those images in your mind. You know, Jean is also attractive in a youthful kind of way." Gary took the salt and pepper grinders from the top shelf, where only he was likely to be able to reach, and began seasoning the steaks, which he had assembled on a platter while he and Max were talking.

Max paused. He felt the anger rise through his body. Did Gary actually say what he thought he said? Wouldn't he, of all people, understand the horror underlying his statement?

"Are you telling me that you're attracted to her because she reminds you of a little kid? Don't tell me that, Gary," Max said. He was glaring at Gary, trembling with anger.

Realizing his mistake, Gary hastened to rectify it. "That's not what I meant at all, Max. I just used it as a simile."

"What's a simile? You can't use big words with me, because I can't understand them, especially when you're telling me that you're attracted to children. I'm already worked up." Gary pulled some fresh garlic bulbs from a bag and began peeling a clove. The aromatic scent of garlic filled the room.

"But I'm not saying that, Max. I just said that she has an innocence that makes you want to reach out and hold her and protect her. She's the kind of woman I'm really attracted to."

Max lowered his voice an octave. "Why is that, do you think, Gary?"

"I suppose it's because I'm a social worker and I'm trained to want to save the world."

"Don't give me that. You became a social worker because you *already* wanted to save the world, not the other way around. You *need* to save people. It's the core of your being."

Gary was shocked that Max had read him so well, so clearly, so distinctly. "How do you know so much without having gone to school?" he asked.

"I've learned to read people. You spend enough time living in a locked basement with only other kids as companions and yourself for counsel, you learn to read the signs around you."

"Well, you're pretty good at it. You're a smart cookie," he said as he began peeling onions.

"And what is that supposed to mean?"

"Just be careful," Gary said as he looked over at Max.

»

The phone buzzed at 5:35 p.m.

"Well that's a little early," said Max under his breath, though Gary heard him clearly.

"The subway was probably faster than she expected it to be," Gary retorted as he crossed the room and buzzed Jean in.

"Didn't you tell her six?"

"Yes, Max. Do you have a problem with her showing up twenty-five minutes early? Because I don't."

"Calm down, Gary. I just get anxious when things happen unexpectedly. Like phones ringing and people arriving at unexpected times, or even little things like my delivery food arriving earlier than the person taking my order told me it would. This has nothing to do with Jean; it's my own fear of being unprepared to handle unexpected situations. So, please, just calm down."

Jean was wearing her standard slinky black dress and heels, but tonight she sported a lightweight cream-coloured shawl over her shoulders. Her black hair was up in a bun and held there by a long sharpened pencil. She liked to dress up to look as pretty as possible. It helped to make a good impression. She wasn't good at making friends, so first impressions were important to her . . . and second and third impressions just as much. She smelled of flowers—a perfume that was among her favourites—and the scent drifted about the room around her. It was kind of nauseating to Max; he was used to the smell of base things, like street traffic, homeless people and garbage. It wasn't that he liked these smells but that he distrusted people who didn't smell like themselves, who covered themselves up with perfumes and deodorants.

Gary had the door open in time for them to hear the elevator doors open and close.

"Good evening, Jean," said Gary, giving her a winning smile. She smiled back.

"Hey, Gary. I'm sorry I'm a little early. In my eagerness to get here, I arrived about half an hour ago but got tired of waiting outside alone.

"Now how's that for spouting off my mouth when it isn't warranted?"

The two of them embraced briefly as Gary gave her a peck on the cheek.

"A little hot for this tonight, don't you think?" Gary asked as he removed the shawl from her shoulders. Not wanting to stretch it by hanging it in the hall closet, he decided to place it on his bed. When he returned, Max and Jean were standing in awkward silence on opposite sides of the living room.

"You remember Max, don't you?" he said, gesturing to his brother. Max crossed the room to shake Jean's outstretched hand.

"I thought your name was David?" she asked with a puzzled look on her face. She looked like a squeaky little squirrel.

Max and Gary shared a quick frightened look.

"It is," Max lied. "My middle name is Max, and Gary likes to use it as kind of a nickname."

"Short for Maximilian?" asked Jean.

"Affirmative, ma'am," Max joked as he stood at attention and put his hand to his temple in a crisp military salute. Jean let out her characteristically funny and adorable laugh.

"I like that. I think I'll use it, too," she said. He smiled and nodded in agreement, and as she began to walk toward the kitchen, Gary stole a sly look to Max as if to say, 'My bad.'

"Now what's for dinner? What can I help with?" she asked.

"Oh, he won't let you," Max interjected. "He seems to take great pride in his abilities to create whole dinners without a helping hand. And he claims to be able to have it all ready at the same time, too."

"No, really? Now that's my kind of man!" she exclaimed, winking at Gary.

"Don't worry, you. Whenever I do decide to marry, I'll be expecting the same skills from my wife. I may not even tell her that I can cook."

"That's just downright mean," Jean said.

"You two amuse yourselves," Gary said. "I still have to prepare the steaks. Salad is already in the fridge, and I just popped the scalloped potatoes au gratin in the oven. They'll take about forty-five minutes to cook. Oh, and I almost forgot." He pulled a pan from the cupboard and began filling it with water. "I have to finish the creamed corn."

"I thought this was going to be a farmers market dinner? What's with the can of creamed corn?" Jean teased.

"Do you see any cans anywhere here? How quickly you mistake my veracity for simple smoke and mirrors. It's homemade creamed corn, Jean, with only the freshest of ingredients."

"You're kidding me," said Jean, her eyes widening with curiosity. "I didn't know you could even make your own creamed corn from scratch."

"Kicking and screaming will the masses be dragged into the twenty-first century. Hey, what about some wine? Do you prefer sweet, dry or something in the middle?"

"I like my wines dry, except for my dessert wines, of course."

"And I don't know what I like," joined in Max, shifting slightly in place.

"Then we'll start out with dry and work toward sweet as we finish dinner. And I've got a nice, very sweet dessert wine I've been saving for a while, though I didn't pick it up at the market today; I picked it up there a few weeks ago. We'll finish off with that and a dark chocolate-drizzled peach and blueberry cheesecake."

"Wow!" Max and Jean said in unison. All three of them laughed. Gary was beginning to like Jean's bray. It wasn't getting on his nerves like he thought it would.

"But I do have to confess: I didn't make the cheesecake. I picked it up at Veniero's."

"Who caaaares?" Jean shouted as she tossed her head back for dramatic effect.

"Yeah, it sounds amazing, Gary," Max added.

"Do you both like cheesecake?" Gary asked.

"Who doesn't?" asked Jean.

"Actually, I don't even know if I do. I've never tried it," Max said, looking down. He wondered whether his shame was written on his face.

"How can you never have tried cheesecake before?" asked an incredulous Jean. "This is New York City! Cheesecake is everywhere—the best cheesecake in the world!"

"I haven't eaten in many restaurants, to be honest."

"How do you live without restaurants?"

"Hot dog stands and sausage stands," Max replied. "That hot dog place on 72nd and Broadway—their prices are cheap."

Jean first looked at Max, and then at Gary. The understanding rose to her face. "Max," she said, "you're one of Gary's clients, right?"

Max nodded. "Yes."

"That means you're homeless, like the others?"

"Yes," he admitted softly, his eyes downcast. He wasn't sure he liked where this conversation was going, but he felt strong enough to stand his ground.

"I'm so damn stupid. I'm sorry, Max. So very sorry."

"That I'm homeless? Or that you spoke before you thought?" Max retorted, flashing his eyes at Jean.

"Max," Gary warned, "she didn't understand. She didn't know—"

"Because I was stupid enough to open my mouth before thinking," Jean interjected.

"It's okay. I'm sorry, Jean. I'm just defensive and proud."

"It's because I'm a Sagittarian. We always end up sticking our foot in our mouth. We're so busy looking up at the stars that we don't see the world around us. So we say things as we see them, as truthful as an ox."

"Oxen are truthful?" Gary teased. Jean smirked. He began to shave corn kernels from the first cob.

»»

Candles twinkled on the table, two at each end and one in the middle. Their dirty plates lay in front of them, almost licked clean. Jean took yet another piece of bread to sop up the au jus from the steak. She was making short work of the creamed corn that was stuck to her plate, and Gary wondered whether he'd even have to wash it because it looked so clean. To the side of both Max's and Jean's place settings were their jars of Bootylicious Body Butter, which Gary had wrapped in bright-red paper and placed on their plates when he set the table. The faint sound of his name brought him out of his head and back to the conversation at hand.

"Don't you think, Gary?" Jean asked. She and Max looked at him imploringly.

"Uh, I'd be okay with either," he said noncommittally, hoping the answer would land well enough.

"What?!" Jean shrieked as she sat up in her chair and braced either side of her plate with her hands. "So you believe that black prostitutes and call girls should get harsher sentences so they set a better example for their younger sisters? What kind of racist idea is that? You know, I really thought you—"

"No! Wait! Okay, I admit it! I wasn't paying attention to the conversation. I had no idea what I was agreeing to. No idea at all," he said, breaking into laughter. Jean joined in with her horsey braying, and Max chuckled from behind his hand, trying to keep his food from spraying across the table.

The meal was wonderful, Gary had to admit. The corn turned out scrumptious, as he knew it would. During a lull in the conversation—and there weren't many—Max asked Jean what she did for work.

"She works in that coffee shop, bonehead," Gary said.

Jean added, "Everybody in New York is here to do something, whether they're a doctor who wants to be at the best hospital in the country and cure AIDS, or dancers who want to dance with the Joffrey Ballet School. You must know that by now . . ."

Gary concurred; he was beginning to come to the same conclusion given everyone he'd met in the city. "They're all trying to better their life somehow," he added.

"So. Jean," Max said, "what are your dreams? What are you trying to do? What are you working toward?"

Was it just the wine, or did Gary hear a sarcastic edge in his brother's voice? *What is it? Why does he dislike Jean so much?* he wondered. He'd noticed Max watching her throughout the meal with narrowed eyes and pursed lips, and he had kept mostly to himself. Whether she picked up on it or not, she spoke without reservation, asking them both questions and contributing her thoughts on everything they talked about. She was an open and giving woman—this Gary saw. He wondered why Max was so reserved. Was he jealous of the attention Gary was giving her, afraid that his interest in Jean would take away from his love for him? It was a silly thought, really. Max was an adult; surely he wouldn't be playing these games so readily.

"I'm going to school right now."

"What kind of classes?"

"I'm studying to be a teacher."

"A teacher? That's good." He was holding his wine glass to his lips, nursing the edge of it by licking the rim with the tip of his tongue, pouring a scant amount into his mouth and then licking its rim again.

"It is in my book," she said almost reverentially, meeting his midnight-blue eyes with her deep, dark chocolate ones. "I mean, where would this country be without the educational freedom we have, and the courage to push those freedoms to the core? Well, my parents didn't think it was so noble. They thought that giving me life was enough of a gift, and when I told them I wanted to be a teacher rather than a bank executive or a lawyer or a doctor, they flipped right out on me. They told me I was selfish and stupid, and that I expected more from the world than it was willing to give. I was going to be unmarried my whole life, with no kids of my own." Jean looked down at the table, and Gary noticed tears gathering in her eyes, though not a single one fell.

"That's one of the worst curses you can throw at a Chinese daughter—barrenness," she said, her voice shaking slightly. Clearly, the words landed as heavy now as they did coming from her parents. She sat in silence for what seemed a long time, her hands busy moving around the last of the food on her plate with the remainder of the piece of bread.

Gary glanced at Max to see his reaction to Jean's obvious distress, but Max simply looked away. Jean looked up, sat up straight and firmly stated, "I am a teacher. I was born to teach. It's my passion. It's my be all and end all, and I love teaching, and don't you forget it," she said vehemently as she looked slightly past Gary's shoulder. "Ever."

"We won't. For sure, we won't," Gary said.

"Not you, silly," Jean said, turning to face him. "My parents. They're dead, but I still talk to them. I know they can hear me.

With all the bad things they did, they must be chained to this world as torment upon their wayward souls."

Max glanced at Gary, his eyebrows raised, and then back at Jean. "You believe your parents are here now, in Gary's living room?"

"Yes, of course. Don't you?"

"Well, no."

"You would if I'd told you all they'd done."

Max couldn't argue with that. He, of all people, knew what it was like to be certain of something others might not understand, so he dropped the subject.

"So . . . you teach?" he asked.

"I'm in training now, shadowing another teacher while I work on my graduate thesis," she said as she wiped her eyes with the back of her hand. "You're supposed to be learning how to put theory into practice, but it's really just photocopying and watching the kids at recess. Right now, though, it's summer and the kids are on vacation, so I'm just working on my thesis."

"Do you want a teaching job? After hours, that is," Max asked. "It wouldn't pay much."

"That wouldn't matter. I'd do it because I love it and it might give me some one-on-one training. How big is the class?"

"One single student."

"Is it a special-needs student? Because I'm not especially trained in special ed work."

"No, but the situation is unique," Max replied. Gary sat in awe of the transaction, prouder of Max than he had ever been.

"What do you mean unique? Is this some kind of dangerous thug no one else will go near? But I suppose I could work with that. . . . It's my natural feminine mystique, you know." She brayed, and Gary and Max joined in. As the three new friends laughed together,

Max wondered why he had felt anxious about Jean's presence but decided that it didn't really matter; it was just over.

"But seriously," Jean said, leaning across the table toward them, "my friend Marge started working with a kid who murdered—"
"I'm the student," Max announced clearly and confidently into the room. Jean stared at him in utter shock, as if she'd been through the wringer that morning.

"We could put together a schedule tonight. But here's the catch . . ." Jean leaned in, and Max said, "We have to start with first grade. I don't know my alphabet, so obviously, I don't know how to read. I don't know how to count to a hundred, and I don't know how to add or subtract."

Jean cocked her head to the side. "Wow. You can't recite the alphabet? I . . . I've never met someone in this situation. How did this happen? How did you learn *nothing* in school? Did your parents say they were homeschooling you? I've met so many kids who were homeschooled to the point of ignorance all because their parents were afraid of the established order. They'd rather see Marxism in the classrooms. They'll support quiet revolutions in the workplace and in the common man, but not in their children." She drank a mouthful of wine and poured herself another.

"I didn't really have traditional parents. I was mostly on my own when I was young, except for Quinn," he said, his chin drooping slightly and his eyes sullen.

"Max, I'd like to be your teacher. We'll start with kindergarten and see what you can learn from there. How does Saturday, Sunday, Tuesday and Thursday work for you?"

"Those all sound fine. What time?"

"Evening classes sound okay? I work on my thesis during the day and then go work for my uncle at the coffee shop in the late afternoon and early evening. But I'm free by about seven each night."

"Gary," Max said, excitement obvious in his eyes, "could we use one of the spare classrooms at The Mission?"

"I don't see why not. As long as no one's using them all."

"It's settled then. Jean, you'll be teaching me my ABCs and 123s on Saturday, Sunday, Tuesday and Thursday nights. We can meet at The Mission. You know where that is, right?"

"Great! Yes."

"Could we start this Tuesday?"

"Works for me. I'll need to do some prep work, but I can be ready by Tuesday," she said as she got up and began to clear the table. The two men got up to help, and Gary could hardly contain his excitement over what had just transpired.

CHAPTER TEN

Jean woke with a start, as usual. The night before was a great deal of fun, but she had found herself wondering throughout the evening whether Max liked her even the slightest bit. He did seem pleased that she would be teaching him and increasing his fluency in English and mathematics, hopefully so he could find a job. She had never really thought about the fact that many homeless people must have huge barriers to employment due to a lack of skills and education. Max was obviously smart (Jean could tell from his spoken vocabulary), but if he couldn't read well—read at all, for that matter—or had trouble with math, then his employability factor plummeted down to his ankles. If anything was going to be around his ankles, she'd prefer it were his pants.

She couldn't help it; she found herself attracted to both Gary and Max, despite the fact that they seemed to be close friends. They were a bit of an odd couple, though. Gary had this keen sense of what people needed and just the right words to say. He was astute and likeable and well-read. She liked men who were taller than her, and he must top out at about six feet three inches. Max was shorter, around five feet eight inches, but he had a bad-boy attitude that leaked out of his pores and into everything he said. She was only a smidgen above five feet, which prevented her from meeting either of them eye to eye. Tutoring one friend while dating the other was going to take some getting used to, and more than just a bit of self-control.

Though it was Sunday, the rest day, she still had to work at Uncle Teddy's coffee shop. But she tried not to complain. Uncle Teddy and Auntie Lily had taken her in when her parents kicked her out for having too many American values. Just because she wanted to wear a tight, short-sleeved shirt with a skirt. Admittedly, the skirt was rather short, too, but that wasn't the point. It was that her parents didn't give her the benefit of the doubt. Yes, she was going out with her friends. Yes, she was going out to an all-ages nightclub at the age of fifteen. But she was not going "trolling for sex," as her father had put it.

"You're a tramp! A hussy! A two-bit whore! And your outfit confirms it, Jean. Your outfit confirms it," he'd said, shaking his head ever so slowly. "Now get out of my house. And don't you step foot across the threshold until you can learn to be a good girl." That last statement had stung. Hard. She had always strived to be a good girl, but her standards were obviously different from her father's.

She went dancing with her friends anyway and wound up on Uncle Teddy and Auntie Lily's doorstep. It was either find a family member nearby to stay with or be out on the New York City streets on her own. And if she knew one thing about herself, she knew she wasn't prepared for that.

"Jean!" called Auntie Lily from below. "Bacon and eggs for breakfast. How do you want your eggs?"

"Oh, sunny-side up would be great, Auntie Lily," she called down.

"Too bad. Only scrambled eggs today. So what kind of eggs do you want?"

"Scrambled would be fine," she said, slightly disappointed.

"You're in luck, scrambled is what I've got today!" She went back to humming and whipping her bowl of eggs.

Jean brushed her hair and then grabbed her purse (not before sticking a tube of lipstick in it) and headed down to the kitchen for breakfast.

"Will you be at the coffee shop today, Uncle Teddy?" she asked as she gathered a few other things, tossed them into her purse and hung it on the back of a chair. She'd tried the raspberry-scented body butter on her legs and hands that morning and was delighted with how well it had sunk in, making her skin so soft and supple.

"Not today, Jean dear. Can you handle it on your own?" he replied.

"Yes, Uncle." Of course she could handle it on her own. She had been doing so at an increasingly frequent rate this past year. She didn't like this arrangement much. She was expected to handle so many more responsibilities at the shop, which was taking time away from her studies.

Jean sat at the table and lay her napkin down on her lap. The scrambled eggs went down in a flash. Jean kissed them both on the cheek before grabbing her little red purse and throwing it over her shoulder. She flipped her hair out from underneath so it cascaded down her back as she bounced out of their home to the street below.

She took the subway to the library to catch up on some reading. Today she was immersed in the Understanding Evolution project, a UC Berkeley study that fascinated her in its implications. Its core aim was to teach evolutionary theory with age-appropriate materials. She was mostly interested in how it was possible to lay the foundation of evolutionary thought for students in grades three or four. Though the theories were too advanced for children that age, it was good to teach them anyway, so they would be prepared to learn them at a later date. It was a common problem she was finding in all her studies: How can you teach certain theories if the fundamentals haven't already been laid out?

She wondered about her newest student. He was quite well-spoken, which indicated he was intelligent but said nothing about his educational level. He seemed eager enough. Still, without knowing where he was at in his studies, it was hard to prepare for his first class. So she decided to pick a couple of lower grade level books and a couple of higher grade level books to start him out with, so she could see what he could handle. And with that, she got up and began to scour the children's books for appropriate materials.

She left the library with *The Paper Bag Princess* by Robert Munsch, *Green Eggs and Ham* by Dr. Seuss and *Goodnight Moon* by Margaret Wise Brown. Each book was funny and smart—the kind of book she hoped would hold Max's interest. But who knew how much a twenty-two-year-old would enjoy them? *Now why doesn't Stephen King write for the kindergarten crew?* she wondered. Jean was treading new territory here, but she was determined to make it work. She couldn't bear the thought of someone so interesting and so astute not being able to read. There was a whole universe—no, countless universes—out there waiting for him to open them up to the first page. Pleased with herself and her choices, she almost skipped along the street.

Village Stationary on LaGuardia Place was her next stop. She filled her basket to the brim with school supplies. First were the writing materials: blank recipe cards and a box to hold them, a set of crayons, some black and red pens, pencils and a pencil sharpener. Next, she picked up a couple of scribblers, the kind with large spaces in between the lines and a dotted line running through the middle. For some visual learning, she added some sticker books, one with animals, one with famous buildings of New York and one with food items. The second contained action verbs and illustrations of people running, sitting, boating, driving, eating, reading, etc. The fourth and last was a scratch-and-sniff book of stars of all shapes and sizes and colours and scents.

Illiteracy made you feel poorly about yourself, and Jean was determined to have Max feeling more confident as soon as possible.

After time spent at both the library and the Village Stationary, Jean knew it was time to head back to the Bowery to get to work on time, so she headed back down into the subway. Though it wasn't far, she didn't want to walk anywhere if she could help it.

The Sneaky Bean was blessedly cool. The morning crew was already starting their side work and making room for Jean and her evening cohorts. Everyone knew that when the boss wasn't around, Jean was in charge. There was some dissension in the ranks that mostly stemmed from the familial relationship between Jean and her uncle. Others felt that, despite the fact that they weren't the best workers, they should have been promoted to assistant manager. There were whispers in the back room about how "Of course, Jean got it. She's family." They knew how it was in family-owned establishments: The good jobs go to the pretty daughters and nieces. Since Uncle Teddy (as all of his employees called him) had no pretty daughters of his own, Jean ascended the throne when Margie left. She was quite surprised by the promotion, since she'd only been working for Uncle Teddy for four weeks. But she hunkered down and learned everything she could about orders, suppliers and the pin money that he paid to the beefy thug, Gus, lest he want his store burned down.

Gus offered his "protection" from the seedier side of New York. Uncle never seemed to consider that Gus *was* the seedier side of New York. According to Uncle, they met during the first week of renovations on the store, weeks before they were slated to open their doors. He introduced himself as the "unofficial policing force in the neighbourhood, since there otherwise isn't one." Then he went on to explain that many bad things happened in the neighbourhood, and if one wanted to keep one's investments safe, then one had to purchase insurance.

"You might consider me your insurance broker, Teddy," explained Gus. "You pay me a premium, and I make sure nothing happens to your store." When Uncle hesitated, Gus reminded him that to live without insurance in this day and age was dangerous indeed.

"Do you understand what I am saying here, Teddy? You don't mind me calling you Teddy, do you? I feel that if we're going to be in business together, then we might as well be on a first-name basis." Finally there was something for Uncle to agree with.

Jean had no idea how much her uncle paid, since it was always enclosed in a discrete envelope in the cash drawer. He kept those affairs private. All she knew was orders went out once per week; they touched base with suppliers every two weeks; and pin money was paid every couple of days.

The lineup was stretched halfway to the door when Jean arrived. *No wonder with Myriam working the till*, she thought. She set her small red purse on an free table momentarily and rushed over to tell Myriam to go ahead and finish up her shift, which meant cleaning the display cases so they looked halfway decent and not like some troll had danced zumba on the pastry trays.

In all the hustle and bustle, she couldn't help but notice out of the corner of her eye a huge, imposing man who sat down at the table beside the one on which her purse was perched. He had copper-coloured hair, purple lips and bushy eyebrows that stuck out from underneath long bangs. His forearms were thick and reminded Jean of tree trunks. His veins were like roots twisting this way and that up his arms, disappearing under his short-sleeved T-shirt. He wore tight, tight pants, and Jean could see the outline of a very sizeable bulge between his legs. *Ow, that looks painful,* she thought as she squirmed in place. But she lost track of him due to the numerous clients demanding cappuccinos and espressos and chai tea lattes.

It took about half an hour for things to calm down. Jean was busy wiping up drips of coffee from the counter with a wet rag when she remembered that her purse was still sitting on the table. She walked around the service counter to retrieve it and noticed that the zipper was undone. The copper-haired man was gone, but she didn't think much of it. Customers came and went as frequently as passengers hopping on and off a subway car, so she could hardly be blamed for not noticing when they left. She zipped up the zipper, put it in the back room and then went about her business.

During her break, she decided to look through her Village Stationery purchases. Everything was in order, and she patted herself on the back for being so on top of things. Needing still to copy the amount of the purchase into her little notebook that she carried with her everywhere, she unzipped her purse and was more than a little surprised to find an envelope inside addressed to Maximilian.

She decided not to open it, despite being more than a little curious about the letter's contents. Instead, she held it up to the light to see what she could see. Not much. Frustrated, she dialled Gary's cell phone number and told him what had happened. 'Yes, my purse! While I was at work! I can't believe someone had the gall to go into my purse like that!' She said she would bring it by their apartment around 7:30 that evening after her shift.

»

At 7:05, Jean buzzed the door to gain entrance to the boys' apartment. As she waited for the elevator to lift her up to the seventeenth floor, she held the unopened letter up to the light for the umpteenth time. Still nothing to see. But she kept it in hand so as to hand it off immediately.

Max and Gary were waiting eagerly at the door and answered at first knock. Jean stepped in and handed it to Max. The three of them walked into the living room, and Gary and Jean crowded around Max.

He held it between his thumb and forefinger. He turned it over once or twice to see if there were any clues, but he knew better. There were never any on a letter like this.

"Shouldn't we get it tested for fingerprints first?" Gary asked.

Max shook his head. "Quinn is too smart for that. He would've worn gloves while composing it and slipping it into Jean's purse. I'm just going to open it."

He tore open the envelope and pulled out the note. Jean could see that it was composed out of thick block letters, the kind handwriting experts cannot glean anything from. She waited with bated breath, wondering what Max was mixed up in. Gus used that kind of writing whenever he wrote a note about the pin money to her uncle (which, thankfully, was a rare occurrence).

Anxiousness had blanched Max's face. His fingers pressed into the paper, causing his knuckles to turn white. His eyes were scanning up and down the page.

"You can't read it, can you?" asked Gary.

"That's right."

"Let me read it to you then." He reached out to take the letter.

Max leaned away and pulled the letter close to his body. "But Jean's here."

"Don't let me stop you," Jean said. "Besides, it was delivered via my purse. I should be privy to what it says, too, especially since you both look like you've seen a phantom."

Max looked at Gary. "But we have to keep her out of this," he said.

"She's already a part of it, Max."

"Don't talk like I'm not even here. Go ahead, just read it. I'm not a princess."

"Fine," said Max. "But just for the record, I don't think it's a good idea."

"We take note of your dissent—your minority dissent," Jean said.

"Okay then." Max handed the letter to Gary.

And Gary read:

Max. The other night was beautiful. Touching you again, after all these years. . . . I never thought I would. We could both escape. We could leave all this behind. Leave Cameron behind. I could protect you. You know I can. You know I love you. And I know you still love me. I get hard just thinking about our times together. I'll come to you for your answer. I'm confident you'll choose me over them. But if your answer is no, then your friends will have to go.

Love,

Quinn

They were all quiet for a long, drawn-out moment. The last vestiges of the dying day were screaming oranges and reds into the room, bringing with them a radiant heat that made it hotter than it needed to be. Max could feel the sweat forming beads down the small of his back, tickling the backs of his legs. Jean was simply floored.

"What the hell?" she exclaimed. "What the hell was that? Who writes a letter like that? Who's Quinn?" She'd expected it to be about some unpaid bill, or unrequited love, or something else juicy and sordid. Nothing like this.

"Someone who is very deranged. And very dangerous," Gary said.

Max stood there frozen. Then he said so quietly that they almost couldn't hear, "I have to go. Now. Tonight."

"Where?" asked Jean.

"The streets," he said, dejection in his voice.

"I'll never see you again," said Gary. He didn't dare make it a question—this he knew for certain.

"You'll be safer without me. Look, I survived for nine years on the streets without Quinn catching up to me. And then I find you, and then Quinn surfaces. I can't help but consider that it's not a coincidence. And now Jean's a target. She shouldn't be caught up in all this crap. It's my crap. I'll deal with it on my own."

"There's strength in numbers," Jean said gently.

"There's anonymity in the streets," Max countered.

"Jean, did you see who dropped the letter into your purse?" Gary asked.

"No, but I think it was this big, burly man. He had copper-coloured hair and eyebrows, and bluish lips—almost purple. He had strong arms, too. Really strong arms. And he had a huge . . . how shall I put it? A huge package. That was apparent from his tight jeans."

"You noticed his dick?" asked Gary. "Of all the details to describe someone . . ."

"Well, I wouldn't have, except that it was so obvious. You couldn't help but notice how big it was. It was right there in your face. You'd think he padded it or something."

"That was no padding. She's describing Quinn to a T. And she's right; he has a humongous dick. I remember it well," said Max as he turned away from the others.

Gary's eyes looked wild in a feral sort of way, like a caged animal intent on escape. Who had he invited into his life? What kind of woman went around noticing the size of men's penises for later recall? Maybe she had a thing about them, and he and Max were just given an insight into this strange part of her character. Maybe this Quinn really did have a very large and noticeable penis, one that your eyes couldn't help but be drawn toward. Gary hoped it was the latter.

"What's going on here, Gary?" Jean finally asked as Max crossed the room and sat on the futon. He held his face in his hands. "Who is Quinn? And why does Max know so much about the size of his dick?"

Gary said nothing. The only sounds in the room were the muffled sobs coming from Max. His shoulders were heaving up and down, and he sounded like he was in for some long and tortured dreams that evening.

"Gary and I are brothers," intoned Max. Jean just about choked on her saliva. She coughed and spluttered, and Gary had to pat her on the back hard before she could regain her composure.

"Brothers? Why didn't you tell me? . . . What a strange thing to keep secret."

"Let me finish and you'll understand," Max said. He stood, clasped his hands behind his back and paced the length of the living room a few times. Then he breathed in deeply, and when he exhaled, Jean could hear the shakiness in his breath. He sat back down on the futon. Gary went to sit beside him and motioned for Jean to join them.

Gary leaned over and placed a hand on Max's shoulder, trying to lend him his strength. "Max, you've got this," he said. Max slowly ceased his sobbing and dried his eyes and face with his hands. He gulped down some huge breaths of air and began to speak.

"Gary and I only reconnected less than a week ago for the first time since we were kids. When I was five and Gary was eight, we were playing in a park near our house one day, and I was abducted by a man named Cameron. He took me to Newark and locked me in a basement with other boys, some younger than I, some older. My first night there, Quinn—from the letter—came down and took me into one of the bedrooms. He told me I would sleep there from then on, and that I'd never see my mother or brother again. If I was a good boy and did what he said, then they would be fine. If I was bad and broke the rules, then he would go up to Albany and kill them. I decided then to be good.

"Quinn gave me a bath, dried me off and put me to bed. He was going to give me a massage—to calm me down, he told me. He started with my shoulders and went down my back. Then he turned me over and did my chest. He used this oil that got even greasier the more he rubbed it in. He poured it on my dick and began to massage it. I was too frightened to complain. And I didn't understand why, after giving me a bath and getting me all clean, he was putting this grease all over me. He got up and took off his clothes and asked me to rub some of the oil on his chest. He laid down beside me, and I did what I was told. Then he asked me to rub oil on his dick. That's what he called it, his 'dick.' I'd heard the word before because Gary had teased me that when I got older I'd get hair down there, on my dick. So I rubbed the oil there, too, but I was afraid. And he got hard. He got very hard, and very big, and very thick. He told me to turn on my stomach again, so I did, and he poured some oil into the crack of my ass. And he said, 'It's gonna hurt, but just breathe through it. Don't cry and I'll let your mother live tonight. Don't cry and your brother can live, too. Don't cry, Maximilian. Don't cry. Don't cry,' like he was consoling me. And then he pushed that huge dick into me.

"That was the first night. It wasn't the last. Nameless face after nameless face came through those basement doors. They'd give us enemas so that we wouldn't get shit on the clients. Always an enema, and always a bath before the evening's onslaught of men. I was the most popular boy of them all, with my golden hair and my ability to not shed a tear. And no matter how many boys there were, I was Quinn's favourite. He used me as often as he liked—and he liked to use me a lot. But I just held my breath.

"I escaped at thirteen. When Cameron decided that I was too old to make money for him, he told Quinn to kill me. But instead, Quinn drove me to Queens and let me go, telling me to hide from Cameron so that I wouldn't get caught. Cameron still wants me dead. I'm sure of it. I suppose he's afraid I'll talk and bring the police down on him. But Quinn always loved me, in his own sick way. And I guess he's after me now, but for a different reason."

By this time, Max was sobbing his strong heart out in near-silent breaths. Gary felt his heart tearing at his ribs, clamouring to be freed of its cage. And he wondered whether Max would ever heal from such ardent abuse. Why had he been the one who was blessed with a happier childhood? All those years, all those foster homes, and yet he had somehow believed that Max had gotten the better end of the deal by being whisked away from their mother. Sure, he, too, had been reprieved from her by Child Protective Services, but he had somehow convinced himself that Max was taken to live with a nice family, a good family that wanted him enough to steal him away from his own. All those years of wondering what had happened to Max, and now he knew. What awful knowledge to have. Gary had been whisked away to live in foster home after foster home, and each of them got rid of him because they didn't want to deal with what they called "his problems." But of course he had problems. How was he to deal with the knowledge that his little brother had been stolen from under his nose? The guilt he felt was incredibly damaging; it ate at him like an angry nest of fire ants, chewing at his gut from the inside out. But none of it compared to the sheer hell of Max's earlier life. How could anyone come back from the brink of that hell and still find a piece of heaven for themselves?

Jean was crestfallen, as though the world as she knew it had been ripped out from under her feet. She scooted toward Max on the futon, hoping that her close proximity would help ease his pain.

She was a teacher of seven-year-olds, and she was having an unbearable time attempting to make sense of Max's story while thinking of the seven-year-olds she'd known. They were so small. So precious. How could anyone do something so horrible to a child? She'd heard tales of sexual abuse, but none firsthand and none as big in scope as this. A locked basement of abducted children forced into child prostitution at the tender age of four and five? She cringed at the thought. How could this happen? How could these men not have been caught? How could it have gone on so long without anyone appealing to the police? She had no answers, and it angered her that she didn't. In fact, anger was what she felt most inside, beside the appalling weight of unfairness. And what about Max? Where was he in all this? Caught in a world between then and now, unable to be truly free because of this Quinn, who clung to him like a monkey on his back. She knew nothing in that moment except a burning desire to hurt the men who did this to Max, her new friend, the boy who had vulnerably asked her to be his tutor so that he could better his life. No one she knew had more reason to want to better their life than Max, or more of a right to do so, for that matter. It was a right to better his life but also a right to live. Having endured such a gruesome childhood, Max now deserved to live without fear, without pain, without this Quinn haunting him. Her heart went out to him in that moment, and if she could have wrapped him up in it, she would have. But the unfortunate distance between them, even as Max sat sobbing on the couch and she sat beside him, was too great. Quinn had to be stopped—killed, if that's what it took. And she knew that she could be the one to do it. It would just take a conversation with Uncle to get the necessary props.

She resolved then and there that come hell or high water, she would do anything within her power to free Max. And to help find Max, wherever he may now be beneath all his layers of protection, layers of fear, layers of guilt for what had happened to him down there in that basement.

CHAPTER ELEVEN

Max was throwing clothes into a small duffel bag that Gary had bought him the other day to replace the plastic shopping bags he had been using to carry his stuff. Jean stood back and watched him, fearful that he was really going to go back out on the streets when he had safety here, good food here, friends here to protect him.

"Max, please don't go," Gary pleaded.

"I have to. You're in danger now because of me," he said. He began looking around the living room to see if there was anything he'd forgotten. He stooped to his hands and knees to look beneath the futon and pulled out a pair of dirty socks. "Damn, these are all dirty."

"Stick them in the washing machine, and I'll wash them for you before you leave," Gary said.

"I have to leave now."

"Another hour or two isn't going to make a difference. Let me wash your clothes."

Max paused. "No, I guess not," he relented, handing his bag to Gary. "But hurry, please."

Gary walked to the laundry facilities at the back of the apartment near the bathroom.

Jean implored, "Max, why do you have to go?" Trails of tears glistened down her cheeks.

"Didn't you hear that letter? He knows where I am. And worse, he knows where you and Gary are. The last line was a very real threat. What if he does kill you? I couldn't live with that."

"But I can take care of myself. Don't you see? I'm not a delicate spring flower. I can hold my own with this man. I'm a New Yorker. I've got pepper spray in my purse and heels that will put a hole in him bigger than his asshole. He won't know what hit him."

"Quinn has a gun that'll kill you from thirty feet away. You don't have that."

"My uncle has a gun. He'll let me use it. I know he will. And I'm a great shot; I've been practicing at the shooting range. My uncle started tutoring me when I was fifteen. I'm a much better shot than him. I've even shot a few geese for dinner. Oh, you can't just up and walk away!"

"And why can't I? I've lived most of my life without Gary, and I've only known you for a couple of days."

Jean sat on the futon, and Max joined her. They sat in silence. The faint sound of quickening thumps began to fill Jean's ears. She thought it was Max's heart beating fast but then realized it was her own. His last statement had hurt her. Yes, they'd only known each other for a couple of days. But there was already a camaraderie there, a symbiotic sort of relationship. They were closer than most people who had just met. Jean felt it, and she was sure that Gary felt it, too. Why else would he have let her hear that hateful letter? Max must feel it. He must. Or else why was he so intent on protecting her, on protecting them both? Why the rush to leave and get out on his own? No, she couldn't believe that Max didn't feel it as much as she did.

"We were supposed to begin our tutoring sessions this week. I was so looking forward to it, and I know you were, too," she said.

"But what good is tutoring me if you'd die at my hands?"

"At your hands? The lessons will be challenging, but surely you won't kill me, will you?" She forced out a chuckle, trying to inject some humour into the conversation.

Max was unamused, as she could tell by his blank stare. "If Quinn gets to you, it'll be the same as if I killed you with my own two hands."

"But there's no way to know whether he was telling the truth. And that should be my decision to make. Not yours."

"But it should be my decision whether to walk away, not yours."

"Right now, we're in this together—Gary, you and I. We're a team, and teams are stronger than one. Don't you think that if you leave now, Quinn will abduct you again? That if you walk out that door, he'll be out there somewhere waiting for you to chicken out and leave this all behind? He seems smart enough to bet on that hand, and then you'll really disappear forever. You'll just disappear to the West Coast, or worse, the Midwest, never to escape again. Because it was Quinn who let you go the last time. There won't be a next time. There won't be any bettering of your life, because he's in some kind of insane love fantasy, and he will never let his love object go, and he'll never set you free. Not this time, not again."

Jean could see his gears turning. He slowly bit his lower lip and began picking at a hangnail, his typical nervous habit.

There's some logic there, thought Max. He looked up at her dark coffee eyes and held her gaze. She was right. If Quinn were to capture him now, there'd be no coming back. He'd never live a normal life. He'd never be able to learn and grow. Max wanted that with the deepest of his desires, and Quinn would never allow him that. He'd always be kept as that five-year-old boy Quinn first encountered in that locked Jersey basement, the boy who learned never to cry no matter how much it hurt. *That's who Quinn wants and who he thinks he still has. Not my grown self. Not me as I am now. What happens the day he wakes to realize he's sleeping next to a man and not a five-year-old boy? How long before he finally brings my head to Cameron on a platter to ask for forgiveness and look for another boy?*

He stopped picking at his hangnail, which was bloody and painful now, and in that moment, he realized that he didn't really want to leave. He liked it here, this place with the promise of a new life: a life of learning, good food and better conversations, and getting to know his brother while making a new friend in Jean. He liked his new life. Even if he hadn't had time and had been too exhausted to think it over until now, it was the best life he had had so far.

In the quietness, Max and Jean heard the beep of the washing machine followed by faint footsteps coming toward them.

"Italian, Mexican or Chinese?" asked Gary. "I'm ordering dinner."

»

Under the shower's spray, Gary was frantically soaping down his body. He knew he had to be quick to find some way to head Max from leaving. He'd ordered dinner hoping it would stall him further. After rinsing the shampoo from his hair, he shut off the water and dried himself. How could he convince Max to stay? He had no answer, no reasoned reason for why Max should stay, and he knew he couldn't keep him against his will. But he felt as though this might be the only way to keep him safe—safe from Cameron, safe from Quinn, and most of all, safe from himself. He stepped from the shower and stood in front of the mirror wondering how long the black rings under his eyes had been growing there. Probably all week, but more than likely all his life. After he dressed, he opened the bathroom door, and the steam escaped into the hall in billows around him.

Neither Max nor Jean had heard him. He stood there momentarily, trying to catch snippets of their conversation to no avail. All he heard was mumbling. He cleared his throat and walked into the living room.

"Smells like dinner's arrived," Gary said. "You two could've started without me, you know."

"We were waiting. It's not fair to start without you. Jean paid for dinner, by the way."

Gary fetched his wallet from the counter, fished some money out and handed it to Jean. "Here, is this enough?" he asked.

"Yes, plenty. But I can pay for things, too, you know."

"You're a student, and your source of income is working in a coffee shop. I make a salary."

They each grabbed a couple slices of pizza, sat down at the dining room table and chowed down hungrily.

"Jean, here, is trying her damnedest to get me to stay," said Max, trying not to spit food out of his mouth. "She's doing a good job. What do you have to say about that, Gary?"

"You already know what I think. I think you should stay, if only for your own safety. . . . And for ours. As you said, Quinn will come after us now that he thinks you have told us your story and we are all wrapped up—"

"You are," Max interjected.

". . . and that we'll go to the police. You know what he's like. You know how to thwart him and keep him at bay. You know his methods, his fears and his buttons. We don't. We need your help to keep us safe from this monster. You are our only hope of keeping one step ahead of him. You can't leave now, Max. Don't you see? Without you, we're sitting ducks. Besides! You're just about to start your Life Skills Program and tutoring with Jean—that is, if she still wants the job."

"Of course, I do. I went to the stationary store and the library earlier today and picked up a bunch of supplies to get us going. I'm not about to go back on our agreement just because of some silly old Quinn."

"I'll stay," Max finally said without much certainty. "I'll stay, but only for you two. To protect you, if I can."

A large, radiant smile crept across Gary's face, and Jean let out a small gasp. "How very alike we are, Max," said Gary. "We both want to save the world."

"The difference is that you want to save the whole world, Gary. I only want to save you two."

"Okay," said Jean, clapping her hands together. "Now that's settled. Where am I sleeping tonight?" She grabbed the last slice of pizza.

"At your place, no?" asked Gary.

"I'll just wake my Auntie and Uncle if I traipse in at this time of night. They won't be happy."

"Well, they'd be less happy to learn that you slept in the residence of two men you've only just met. Am I right?" asked Gary.

Jean shrugged. "I'll tell them I was studying late with my friend Anice. She's in my teaching program at school, and I do sometimes stay at her place when we're up late studying."

"Well, the couch is taken, but I've got a queen-sized bed. I only sleep on one side of it. You can have the other half."

"Damn, I was hoping you'd say it was like bunk beds, one on top of the other," she answered with a twinkle in her eye. Both Gary and Max looked distinctly uncomfortable.

"Uh . . . well . . . then it sounds like that's settled, too. Who wants chamomile tea and ice cream? Jean, do you like strawberry-rhubarb jam?"

"My favourite."

"Great. Mine, too. If you want to take a shower, I'll get you a towel."

"A shower sounds like a gift from the gods right now. I'll take you up on it."

With the sound of the shower running, Gary tried not to imagine what a wet, soapy Jean would look like. Pretty damned fine was his conclusion. Except she was so skinny. He thought he might have heard her vomiting before she turned on the shower, but he couldn't be sure. If so, it was probably nerves from all she'd been through that day. She seemed to be taking it in stride, but if she was quietly puking in the bathroom, then maybe she wasn't as strong as she made herself out to be.

Or she might be anorexic or bulimic, he thought. She had the body to prove it: the thin legs, the skinny arms, the figure that seemed lost in whatever dress she wore.

She emerged from the shower looking radiant, her hair dripping down the back of the T-shirt and sweatpants that Gary had lent her. She was damned near swimming in those clothes, but in another way, it was kind of sexy.

Two bowls of glazed ice cream later, Gary said, "Sorry, guys, but I'm out of ice cream. I'll have to pick up some more tomorrow. Or if you want more tonight, there's always the late-night deli on the corner. I could run out and pick some up."

"I don't think anyone should be going out to the deli alone tonight," said Max. "We have no idea where Quinn is stationed and whether he's still watching the apartment or has gone home."

"I agree with Max," said Jean through her second last mouthful of ice cream and jam. She was licking the spoon to get every drop running down its neck. Then she scooped out the last of the melted remnants from her bowl with a dejected look on her face. She'd wanted to stay for the dessert, but she didn't like being a part of this conversation. It was exposing so many of the brothers' secrets and pulling her deeper and deeper into their world.

"Besides, I'm stuffed, Gary," said Max.

"Me, too," added Jean, spitting ice cream at the table. "Oh, my god. I'm so sorry!" She brayed and wiped the table with her napkin.

"Don't worry about it. I have to wipe the table anyway." He and Max both laughed heartily. "You can dress up, but it looks like I can't take you out." He chuckled some more.

"Hate to admit it, you two, but I'm exhausted. Do you mind keeping your voices down while I go to sleep?" asked Max. He crossed to the balcony and checked that the door was locked up tight.

"We'll head to the bedroom," said Jean, and Gary was relieved to hear her say it first.

He got up and gave Max a hug, clapping him on the back as men do. He crossed to the front door to check that it was locked and the chain was in place. He led Jean to the bedroom cautiously and without a word but holding her hand all the while. He opened the bedroom door and closed it behind them. She sat down on the edge of the bed so that her feet could still reach the ground. It seemed as though all his words had left him, and he struggled to find a thread that might lead to a conversation, thereby breaking the thick ice that immobilized his thoughts. But he couldn't do it. It was Jean who finally spoke.

"What an incredible story. It's almost unbelievable at first. Yet all you have to do is watch Max when he tells it to know it's true. He looks completely broken by his childhood.

"What were your lives like before that, before his abduction? I hope they were good, so he at least had that to hold on to." Jean looked up into Gary's downcast face, the face he had half-turned away from her as she spoke her last words. He didn't like to talk about his mother or her predicament.

"Our mother was an alcoholic. She used to beat us senseless on a whim. After a beating, Max would hide in the closet, and I would find him there crying to himself and holding his knees tight to his chest. I used to keep several books in the closet just for those times, and I would read to him. They were stories he liked, sometimes fairy tales, sometimes books that had been kept on the shelves and out of his reach. Christmas and birthdays—that's when we'd receive those books. Our mother never thought to buy them for us. All her money went to booze. Max always liked me to read to him, especially when he was upset. I think it helped him forget what was happening around us, helped him forget the beatings and our mother and our lives. It was like reading to him would help transport him to some other place. He used to tell me that he couldn't wait to be able to read to himself, so that I wouldn't have to. He was always like that, trying to find ways he could look after himself, ways he wouldn't have to rely on me to keep him safe and could transport himself from this world.

"I used to think that Max had had the easier time of it because I thought he was whisked off to a new family who wanted him badly enough to have abducted him. I thought I was the one left with the repulsive life. Clearly that wasn't the case."

"No wonder he wants to learn to read so badly. It must have been awfully difficult for him in that basement without anyone to read to him. That's so sad," Jean said, half to herself, half to Gary. A tear formed at the edge of her eye, but she didn't want to fall apart in this moment. Then she added, "Is your mother sober yet?"

"I doubt it."

"You don't know? Don't you see her much?" she said, interest growing in her eyes as she thought of her own family story.

Her mother was quiet, always subjecting herself to her husband's rants and ravings. She was the perfect housewife, submitting to him in all conversations and growing quiet as some turned ugly around the kitchen table, like when he would talk of Chinese-American social politics, the indecencies of famous celebrities like Jennifer Aniston, Meryl Streep or Glenn Close, or the role of a woman in a well-maintained house in which harmonious relations thrived. Jean had always wondered what he knew about harmonious relations, since he was always the one who broke the peace at home.

Her mother loved her, which was obvious in the way she braided Jean's hair with gentle fingers and tucked her into bed with a softly sung song before turning out the light. But she wasn't strong enough to stand up to her husband the night he kicked Jean out of the house. In Jean's memory, that was one of the worst nights they'd had as a family. Dinner was being prepared when her father came home from the warehouse, where he worked on the assembly line, turning screws into each moulded piece of machinery before the item moved on down the line. He was taciturn and choleric even as he stepped through the doorway.

"Where's dinner, already?" he yelled down the hallway. He took his coat off and tossed it on the floor, despite the closet full of hangers that hung in a neat little row. Dinner was a delicate, precarious and perilous affair that night. Her father asked her to pass the peas, and when the bowl slipped from her hand and landed on the table, he yelled at her—no, bawled at her—about needing to be more mindful about what she was doing. She took it all in, pulled her arms to her sides and hung her head in shame. This was what he wanted. This was the effect he was moving toward. This was the reaction he got from her every night at the kitchen table. But tonight was different for Jean. She didn't know why, but she didn't question the buzz that was flowing through her veins, making her feel bold and out of sorts. She left the table without finishing her dinner, despite her mother's urging her to do so. She softly climbed the stairs to her room and closed her bedroom door without slamming it, which she would normally do. Then she called a few friends and made plans to meet and go out to the club. She dressed in the tightest shirt she could find, a white cotton one with frilly lace on the sleeves, and a short skirt she'd picked up at Winners one day but never had the nerve to wear in front of her parents. Then she painted her face with makeup—not much but enough to know that she had eyeliner, eye shadow and lip gloss. And she walked down those stairs to find her father sitting and watching the late news on the television. She left without saying goodbye.

Gary cleared his throat. "No, I don't. She's in prison."

"In prison! What for? What did she do?"

"Nothing."

"Then how is she being punished in prison if she wasn't charged with something really bad?"

"I didn't say she wasn't charged with something horrible. After Max's abduction, she was convicted of his murder. Life imprisonment, no chance of parole."

Jean suddenly got all happy and jumpy, almost bouncing on the bed. She would have clapped her hands in front of herself if she weren't so aware of how this would make her look like a child. "But now that you've found him, she can be exonerated and released from prison! They do it all the time now, with DNA testing. And this is even better: The dead son she supposedly murdered is actually alive."

"We can't go to the police. If we do, Quinn will definitely murder Max to ensure his safety. And Cameron's."

"But the police will protect him."

"You cannot protect anyone from a shadow, a phantom, a deranged but brilliant killer. And Quinn is all of those."

"But your mother . . . her life is being wasted in prison."

"Her life was a waste outside of it, too. I don't think she knows any better."

"But she should at least have the chance to try. Just like Max."

"I understand what you're saying, but you haven't met the woman. She's cruel. Incredibly cruel."

"But you can't punish her for that. I would understand if she had actually killed your brother, but she didn't. No matter how cruel she was as a mother, that's no justification for keeping her in prison forever."

"I didn't mean that we'll keep up this charade forever—just until Quinn and Cameron are caught. Then there's no way for them to hurt Max when he publicly announces that he's still alive.

"Now, are you going to wear that to sleep? Or do you want something else? Though I'm a little short on slinky negligees at the moment. They're all at the dry cleaners."

Jean laughed.

"I like to sleep in my birthday suit."

Gary tried to hide his grin. "Suits me," he said. "I do, too." He turned away from her, took off his bathrobe and hung it on the hook over the door. Then he backed up a couple of paces and got into the bed, so she couldn't see his front. He wondered why, at the age of twenty-five, he was still so shy in front of a girl. By the time he'd pulled the covers over himself, Jean had gotten into bed beside him. He reached over and turned off the bedside lamp, and the room was plunged into total darkness, except for the glowing night-light that was plugged into the wall.Gary could see the outline of her body under the sheet.

"This is still only our second date," he said, hoping she wouldn't notice the growing bulge between his legs. "I don't usually make love on the second or third date."

"Why is that?" she asked, either curious or concerned—he couldn't tell which. "I hope you're only telling me that to get me to trust you, not because it's true."

"Of course I'm trying to put you at ease. And I'm also being truthful. The two aren't mutually exclusive." The bulge between his legs had begun to stiffen more. He knew what was coming next if he didn't concentrate on going to sleep: a trip to the bathroom, where he could be found sitting on the toilet and beating his meat until he blew a geyser. He really didn't want to do that, not with Jean in the next room and possibly listening.

"Can we hold hands while we go to sleep, then?" she asked somewhat cautiously. She didn't know why she was so nervous about asking for something so small, but she almost felt like a little kid asking for a cookie from the cookie jar just before dinner.

"That'd be nice," he answered, wrapping his fingers in hers.

They lay quietly like that for a moment or two. Then, Gary felt her fingers disentangle from his and begin stroking his hand, petting it. He was immobilized. He couldn't move even if he wanted to. He was caught, trapped by her five little fingers that circled around and around. They had the softest touch, and they knew exactly what they were doing—teasing him, traipsing up and down the skin of his hand. One finger trailed up his arm to his shoulder and then back down. It did this a few more times. His bulge was rock-solid, and his mouth was as dry as a brown, dead ravine in the heat of an Indian summer. He shivered and hoped she didn't notice. But she did. She was getting the reaction she wanted: him lying there helplessly under her fingers. She used a nail now, lightly scratching his arm and then soothing it with the pad of her finger.

She wasn't usually so bold with men. Truthfully, she had little experience at all. Actually, she had no experience at all. She had experiences with boys, those fumbling things who scraped and clawed at her with too many hands to try to get what they wanted no matter what the price, the ones who she told no but never listened. She gave up with some of them and let them have their way. But she always felt lost and contained terrible remorse inside her as she walked home to her Auntie and Uncle's those nights. Though she hadn't had much experience with men, her character was one to know what she wanted. And right now, she wanted Gary. Every inch of Gary. Gary beside her, atop her, inside her. Her back arched suddenly, and she felt the stirrings of desire flow through her. She'd never spent the night with a man like him, a man who knew what he wanted and wasn't afraid to go for it. She continued to trail her fingers up and down his arm.

"Is this okay?" she asked in a small voice.

"Yes," he breathed. "Don't stop."

Her fingers traced the curves of his body down his chest to his nipple. She raised one finger to her mouth, stuck it in, pulled it out and put it back on his nipple, circling it until her saliva had dried.

"Is this okay?"

"Yes, don't stop."

And so, she traced her finger down, down to his long, narrow cock, dragging it along the length of it to the tip, where precum had gathered. She wiped it up with her finger, brought her finger to her mouth again and sucked it clean. Then she grabbed his cock in a strong grip and pulled up, causing the foreskin to close around the head. She squeezed once. She squeezed twice.

"Is this okay?" she asked breathlessly.

"Agh. . . . Yes, but stop."

"Why do you want me to stop?" she asked, hurt registering in her voice as she pulled her hand away. Gary grasped her hand and held it tight to the mattress. He was breathing hard. He turned his face to look at hers beside him.

"Because I'm too close already." She laughed. "I'm going to get you back for putting me in this situation!"

He pushed her from her side onto her back and kissed her hard. She kissed him hard back. He moved to her neck, laying soft and gentle kisses there that were of fire and rain and ice all at the same time. She was so beautiful. But as his hands moved down her sides, he could feel her ribs protruding. Yes, protruding, frighteningly so. She was unhealthily skinny, so much so that you could almost see her skeleton in the dark of night. He wondered whether something was wrong with her, whether she had some disease that wastes its victims away to nothing. Her butt was almost nonexistent. It was jarring. But he banished the thought, especially since his hands had arrived at her perky little breasts. He moved down to suck on her nipples, one of his favourite things to do with a woman in bed. She had stunning breasts, just itty-bitty bumps on her chest that could fit right into his mouth.

Then Gary was moving again, moving on down until he arrived at the beautiful patch of hair between her thighs and her delicious pink cake, a treat he had learned to appreciate with previous lovers. His tongue got to work, and soon she was bucking and grinding and mashing herself into his face. This was what he loved. This was what she needed. He saw just how close he could bring her to orgasm and then pulled back, forcing her to calm down before going back at it again. His tongue was diving deeply and licking her clitoris slowly, ever so gently. Her breathing had become so heavy up to that moment, that place only he had brought her. And then he backed off again, teasing her mercilessly with his tongue, his chin, his whole face.

"Oh, God, Gary." Jean was thrashing in the bed, twisting this way and that, her back arching, her fists pounding the mattress.

Gary wondered briefly whether Max was listening, and then he didn't care. This was his moment, his moment alone with Jean.

He sat up, picked up her legs, bent her knees and leaned over her, his long cock touching her lips. He paused in stillness. He could feel her wetness against him, teasing him, taunting him, testing him. He was up to the test, and he knew it. He was loving the moment, and knew that every inch inside was going to be pure heaven, pure ecstasy. He loved Jean in that moment and knew that it could only get better.

"Is this okay?" he teased.

"Yes. Yes! Don't stop."

He didn't.

CHAPTER TWELVE

In the morning, Gary woke first. It took a moment before he realized Jean was in bed beside him. But it didn't take long to remember what had transpired after they'd come to bed the night before.

She was uncovered now, having kicked off the light cotton weave in the night. And she was naked, of course. She looked . . . how could he put it? Skinny. Very, very thin. Emaciated, even. Her ribs showed, and the skin actually sunk in between them. Her hips were nonexistent. All that remained was her pelvis bone. And for the first time, he noticed her face. She was obviously adept at using makeup to fatten her cheeks and give the illusion that the sunken areas beneath her eyes were just normal bags that anyone gets. But on her face, they were sunken suitcases. She looked almost grotesque. Yet in another way, she was beautiful, so beautiful—a fragile thing, a broken gift that he might have found or that might have been given to him.

He wondered what was wrong with her. Anorexia, for sure. And bulimia? Hadn't he heard her puking in the bathroom after dinner? This city had a way of attracting the beautiful and the damaged, and the beautifully damaged, too. Gary felt that Jean was one of those beautifully damaged, filled with inner beauty but cursed with a body that worked against itself, fought itself, and a mind that made it all the more worse. Anorexics had an incredibly sad self-image, one of fatness and worthlessness to the point of sheer ugliness. They believed themselves incapable of being lovable or finding love without being always thinner. They were tortured by the mirror and the bathroom scale, both of which only served to reinforce their badgering thoughts and accusing eyes that raked over their bodies, always so critical. His clinical eye should have picked up on it, but try as he might, he couldn't imagine this vibrant young woman having those problems.

"Mmmmph," Jean moaned. She was slowly waking. Though he didn't want to, he pulled the thin blanket over her in case she was uncomfortable with her exposed condition.

"Mmmmmm, nice. You're a nice kind of toy," she said, slowly opening her eyes. Sunlight was pouring onto her face from the window above the bed, making her irises the colour of dark, rich coffee grounds. Though it was Monday morning and he knew that they both had things to do, he didn't want to say goodbye to her, didn't want to let her go, didn't want to exchange numbers and speak about how one would call the other. But he was sure that those exchanges would be more than just words and they were sure to be seeing each other again.

"Good morning, sleepyhead," Gary said.

"Is it still morning? That's a good thing."

"What are your plans for the day?"

"I have to go to the library and study. Then work, and then home, unless I have a better offer." She pulled the blanket up to her neck and smiled mischievously up at him.

"I could do with another date, if you still desire my presence," he said, putting emphasis on "desire."

"Oh, I do. I do."

She pulled him down and kissed him, long and slow. His hands moved to cup her face. He held her gently, like a delicate crystal vase that threatened to shatter under his touch. He thought of the word "love" and then banished it quickly from his mind. It was too early for that. But he'd never felt this way about a woman before. This attraction, this desire, this need to hold her. This *need*—that summed it up. He needed her like he'd needed nothing before, needed her to soften his rough edges, to mirror his strength, to watch football games with him and go to the market with him and accompany him on the thousand other things he did.

Max was preparing to make oatmeal when Jean and Gary arrived in the kitchen dressed and ready for the day ahead. He seemed to be having trouble with the directions on the side of the box.

"Hey, do you add the oatmeal to the salted water right away, or am I supposed to do something first?" he asked.

"You have to bring the water to a boil before adding the oatmeal," said Gary. He stepped closer and reached for the box. "Here, why don't you let me do that?"

"I can't read the directions on the box," he said sheepishly.

"That's nothing to be ashamed of, Max," said Jean. She reached up and put a hand on his shoulder. "You'll be reading soon. I have some great plans for how we are going to do this—together. As a team, you and I. We'll have you reading books in no time. Not *War and Peace*, mind you, but grade-appropriate books nonetheless. It's still reading. And every book opens a universe of possibilities for the mind. You'll just love it. I know you will."

Max was visibly shaken, unsure why he deserved such kindness.

"So, Gary and I have been discussing our plans for the day. What are yours?" she asked.

"I'm going to head up to 59th and Lexington. I've got some stuff stashed there behind a dumpster that I'd like to pick up."

"And I'm going to go into work early," added Gary. "I've got some paperwork to catch up on. Make sure, Max, that you get there by three o'clock for your first Life Skills class."

"I'm heading up to The Mission as soon as I'm finished getting my stuff. I'll see you then," Max said.

"And I'll meet you both there after I'm done at the coffee shop," Jean said. "I finish before you do, Gary. For safety, we should travel together as much as we can."

"Agreed. But where do you even live, Jean?" Gary asked.

"Uptown. But that's neither here nor there. I'm spending the night here again." And with that, she turned toward the bathroom to put her makeup on.

»

They parted ways at the subway station, Max and Jean heading toward an uptown train and Gary heading toward the Bowery. When Max exited the train at 59th and Lexington, he climbed the stairs with more than a little trepidation. Boy, didn't this feel familiar? How many times had he used this station when sleeping in the alleyway nearby? *Too many to count*, he thought. As he walked out onto the street, he couldn't help but wonder whether any of the neighborhood tenants could recognize him. He looked so different now with his golden hair clean, his body clean and his clothes new. Not to mention how clean he smelled. That soap Gary bought was wonderful. And the body butter seemed to be working. Though it was hard to tell, it appeared that some of the cracks on his soles had healed already, and his socks weren't as bloody at the end of each day. He usually had to peel them from his mangled soles, as the rivulets of blood soaked them and lacquered them to his feet.

Ahead of him, standing in front of the jewelry shop was Ivan, the shop's owner. He wore a double-breasted suit even in the heat. "David? Wow, you're cleaned up," he said as Max walked past.

"Hi, Ivan. How are you today?"

"Not bad. Not bad, my boy. Did you find a place to stay? Are you off the street now?"

"Yep. Staying with a friend down in Stuyvesant Town."

"Good for you, boy. Good for you. You deserve it. Hey, there was some guy around here earlier asking about you. Did you know?"

"No, I had no idea. What did he look like?"

"He was a big, beefy kind of guy with blondish-red hair and really big arms, like he works out constantly."

Max cringed inwardly at the thought of Quinn knowing one of his secret hiding places, the sleeping spot he had felt was most secure from his prying eyes.

"Did he give you his name?"

"He did, as a matter of fact—some weird kind of name, like Gunn or Kane or some such thing."

"Was it Quinn?"

"That sounds right."

"Okay, thanks for letting me know, Ivan. Did he say what he was after?"

"No, he just asked a lot of questions. He seemed really interested in finding out what time of day you usually show up here, like he was trying to get ahold of you or something."

"Okay, Ivan. Thanks so much for telling me." He waved goodbye and walked down the street to the stinking alleyway. He turned the corner and walked about halfway down. There was trash

stashed there, like in every alleyway in the city, and the smell of the
dog shit during summertime was nauseating. Why people didn't
clean up after their dogs was a question he'd like the answer to.
He'd seen many of them walking their schnauzers or Westies or pit
bulls and leaving their dumps on the road. There were laws about
that kind of thing, but who had the time to prosecute some old lady
because her tiny, little Tinkerbell had crapped in the alleyway
where he lived? No one cared. That was the thing about New York:
If it wasn't big news or big politics or big entertainment, then
nobody gave a damn. Certainly not about the stinking, dirty
homeless man who slept in the alleyway next to Tinkerbell's crap.
But he cared. Because he was that homeless man who lived in the
alleyway, and truthfully, no one cared about him either.

The nicest thing about the new life he had stumbled into was
that there were people who cared. First Gary, and now Jean. They
both seemed to care almost to the point of loving him. They both
seemed to think that his future was something precious, worth
saving, worth working toward. Gary invited him into his home and
into his life. Jean wanted to teach him. He'd never had anyone care
about him before, except Quinn, and that could hardly be called
caring. Quinn had an agenda that Max fit neatly into, one based
upon his own sick desires. He wanted Max for one thing and one
thing only. He cared not about Max's future, his dreams or his
desires. He didn't care that Max wanted to learn to read with a
passion that was hard to explain. He didn't care that Max wanted to
find love, because for Quinn, love was his disturbed fascination
with the memory of a five-year-old boy he'd once known and
abused mercilessly in the confines of the basement. No, Quinn
didn't love him.

He looked around the alleyway and saw bags of garbage, a
rotting pool of what had once been water but was now just city
juice lying stagnant on the asphalt, and a dead bird lying close to a

brick building. There was his bed, a crumpled green garbage bag stuffed with newspapers that lay against the building. Another lay beside it, the newspapers inside crunched up and flattened. He used to lie on the one and use the other as a pillow. *Comfortable enough—for a homeless guy*, he thought. He knew he'd have a hard time returning to this life. And there was the dumpster. He used to crawl through that restaurant dumpster at the end of each day to scavenge for scraps of food. He usually found lots to eat in there— fatty pieces from some diner's pork chops; quarters of baked potatoes wrapped in tinfoil, sometimes even with sour cream and chives; bacon slices and orange slices and lime slices, too; and the odd half a coffee in a takeout cup. The coffee was always cold, but beggars couldn't be choosers now, could they?

He wedged himself behind the dumpster. He had placed the plastic shopping bag far enough behind the dumpster so it was impossible for anyone else to reach, but even he had trouble reaching it. Hooking the handle with one finger, he pulled it free and opened it up. Both items were there: the rolled up stack of money held together with an elastic band, a total of $953, and his wallet, which carried nothing of value except some photo identification in the name of David Commely.

He heard a rustling, like the crunch of a paper bag being stepped on, and his head snapped up in surprise.

"Hello, Maximilian."

"Hello, Quinn."

»»

Jean had lied. She had no intention of going to the library. She went home instead.

The scent of warm pancakes hit her nostrils the moment she opened the door. So much for arriving before anyone woke up and pretending she'd spent the night in her own bed. Oh well.

"Hi, Auntie! Hi, Uncle!" she called from the boot room with extra enthusiasm. Neither one of them said anything back. *Oh, shit.* She walked into the kitchen and gave Auntie a kiss on the cheek.

Auntie packed a powerful emotional punch that could wither the strongest of men with just one look. It was almost a look of disgust, but not quite. It was almost anger, but not really. Almost a deep sadness, but not wholly. Disgust, anger, sadness: It was all of these things and more, some indescribable quality of her displeasure that couldn't quite be pinned down. She flashed her niece this look as she pulled away from her kiss.

Jean noticed the strands of grey that had gathered on her head over the years. Auntie was a short woman, reaching only about five foot zero, so she was evenly matched to Jean. Despite this, Auntie seemed so much taller. It was certainly in the way she held herself but also in her demeanour. She *felt* so much taller than her short stature allowed, especially when she wanted to, like when she was cooking up a storm. She was in her element then, mixing batter, cutting veggies, slicing fat off of meats. She was an excellent cook, and she used food to bring people together, to calm tempers and bring forth her love. Auntie was always cooking, it seemed to Jean, and Jean wondered where all the food went. She knew that she herself ate a large portion of it, as Auntie was always placing plates of Chinese cookies and dumplings and sesame noodles in front of her to accompany the steaming bowls of wonton, egg drop and sweet-and-sour soups that were her idea of healthy snacks. Never did they have leftovers. Those were fed to the garbage pail in the corner of the room, and though it never complained about these feedings, it always seemed to be bursting with fullness.

"Don't you 'Hi, Auntie' me. Where were you last night?" Auntie asked.

She was mixing more scallion pancakes to join the pile that was already cascading over the side of the plate. Uncle Teddy sat in his chair, his eyes fixed on a point straight ahead.

"I stayed the night with a friend."

"And you couldn't call?"

"It was too late to call."

"It's never too late to call."

"I would've woken you both."

"No, you wouldn't have. We were both awake."

"It really was very late. I'm sure you were sleeping."

"Neither one of us slept all night. We sat up worried. No phone call. No Jean. No word of where you were. I was up all night because I was calling the police and the hospitals. Your uncle was up, well, because he's your uncle—he worries. And because he loves you. We both do. And it was too late to call?" She slammed the mixing spoon down in the bowl and put her hands on her hips.

"Do we know this friend?"

"No, you don't," admitted Jean.

Auntie Lily's voice was decidedly frosty when she spoke again. "Will you be seeing this *friend* again?"

Jean thought about her options. She could lie to her auntie, try to convince her that she stayed with a girlfriend. Or she could tell the truth and let the chips fall where they may. Finally, she said, "Yes, Auntie. Yes, I will."

"You tell this friend—you tell him that the next time he decides to keep you overnight, he'd better call me. Not you. Him. He should have had the decency to call, even if you didn't. What kind of man leaves Auntie to worry? What kind of man leaves Auntie to stay up all night calling emergency rooms? You could have died, for all we know. You could have died, and I'd be none the wiser." She picked up her spoon and began to stir the batter furiously again. "Better yet, bring him by to meet me before you spend another night with him. I deserve at least that."

"I will," said Jean, in a voice no louder than a baby racoon. "Uncle," she said as she turned to him, her voice stronger now, "I need a favour from you." He didn't respond. He didn't even turn his head. "It's a big favour. I need to, um, borrow your gun."

Jean looked at Uncle and tried to meet him eye to eye. There had always been a fierce kindness deep inside his eyes. She tried to will him to understand the importance of what she was requesting from him.

"Borrow his gun!" screamed Auntie. "What do you need his gun for?"

"It's just for, um, target practice. I want to go and practice."

"Don't you lie to me, young lady. What kind of trouble have you gotten yourself into?" she asked, sounding remarkably like a hissing mongoose. "Why do you need a gun?"

"I haven't gotten myself into any trouble. I just need it."

"Well, no, you can't have the gun. It's for target practice, not to be carried around with you when you're with your boyfriend."

"She can take it."

"Did you say something, Uncle?" asked Auntie, her husband's words not fully registering.

"The gun is not for target practice. Target practice is for the gun," he said.

"I said, did you say something, Uncle?" asked Auntie as she slammed a plate down in front of him.

He took a scallion pancake from it and dipped it in the thin, gingery sauce. Then he said, "I taught her to use it so she could use it against Gus if she ever had to. But I've never needed it. As long as I've had the money on time, there's never been any problem with him. Jean's a smart girl. She knows the gun is only for emergencies, and if she has some kind of emergency, then I'll give it to her. I trust her to know the difference between a whim and a place inside oneself that instinctively knows right from wrong."

With that, he finally turned to her, and with a look of desperate love in his eyes, he fished a key out of his shirt pocket.

"Thank you, Uncle. Thank you so much." She took it and turned to run upstairs to where Uncle kept the gun under lock and key.

»»»

The subway took Gary to the Spring Street Station, where he ascended the stairs and began the short walk to work. What an incredible night he'd had. And he hadn't expected it either. This morning, he had felt a closeness to Jean that he hadn't felt before, as though they were somehow connected, somehow lost in each other. Though he'd just left her less than half an hour before, he missed her already. He couldn't get enough of her, couldn't relinquish the feel of her hands on his body, her fingers trailing up and down his arm, his chest, his dick. And the feeling of entering her—he'd never known such pleasure. He'd never felt such desire as when he shot his load deep inside her. And here he was, almost at work, feeling like a teenage boy at the front of the class as he tried to hide a raging hard-on. But he lost it quickly enough when he saw the crowd at the end of the alleyway. This couldn't be good. It could only mean a fight between clients. He hurried his pace and pushed his way to the front of the crowd.

There was Zachary, arms outstretched to block the impossibly wide alleyway.

"Oh, Gary. Thank god. The police haven't shown up yet, and I'm havin' the damnedest time tryin' to keep everyone away," he said.

"But what happened?" Gary asked.

"Look for yourself," he said. Gary looked around and didn't see anything of interest at first. Then he noticed the pile of red and white rags laying against some garbage bags at the end of the smoking section. He walked toward them.

The pile of rags wasn't a pile of rags. It was Donovan. A dead Donovan. His face was slashed, as though cut with the razor-sharp edge of a knife, and a trail of blood ran down his cheeks. His arms had puncture wounds all over, and blood coursed down each one of them to his fingertips, where it drip, drip, dripped to the ground below. He'd been stabbed repeatedly in the chest. There was clearly no need for the ambulance to hurry. But the strangest, most troubling thing Gary noticed was that he was naked—buck naked. Gone were the pants he'd received from The Mission the other day, and gone was his favourite shirt. His red sneakers were tossed to the side. There was something sticking out from his tightly clenched hand. Gary stooped down and took it from the dead man's grasp. It was a green-striped cotton square, the pocket of his beloved shirt. He had ripped it from its stitching to keep for himself while whomever had done this had so cruelly disrobed him and left him there in the stinking street to die.

»»»»

"What are you doing here?" asked Max.

Quinn smiled. "I came here for your answer to my letter," he said, not even remotely thinking that things wouldn't go his way today.

Max quickly glanced down the alleyway with a subtle turn of his head. If he tried to run for it, with this distance between them, Quinn would surely have time to catch him by the arm, or worse, tackle him into the stinking bags of garbage. He would have to keep

Quinn talking and wait his chance. *Show no fear,* he told himself. *If he knows you're scared as hell, he'll have the upper hand.*

But Max was frozen with fear. This was the closest to Quinn he had been in years besides the break-in the other night, and he wasn't the more comfortable for it. He distinctly disliked being so close to this man, this man who had abused him, this man who had hurt him, his abductor, his keeper, his jailer. When he said goodbye to him at thirteen, he hoped it would be the last time he would ever set eyes on him again. This day came none too soon.

"You want me to come away with you," Max stated.

"Of course, I do. I love you. I always have. And I know you love me, too."

"But I don't love you, Quinn. I never have."

"You know, as a child you were sexier than any of the other children."

"Quinn, children aren't sexy. They aren't supposed to be sexy. They're supposed to be children and be protected."

"I did protect you. You have no idea how many times I protected you from Cameron's rage. You know how he'd get. He'd get frighteningly angry and then go downstairs and fuck one of the boys. He'd hit him and bang him up good, use huge dildos on him, and sometimes even the handle of the toilet plunger. I'd hear those kids crying out, and I prevented him from doing that to you. I'd talk him out of it, convince him to use another boy."

As he spoke, Max slowly edged toward him to close the distance between them. He thought that if only he could bridge enough of the gap, then he might be able to run clean past him and out of his reach.

"But not always, Quinn. He did those things to me, too."

"Only when you deserved it. And those times I couldn't interfere, because to interfere would have been wrong. Sometimes you needed to learn a lesson."

"It was wrong to do it. Period. And it was wrong to let him. You had the power to stop it. And what about the other boys? Didn't they matter at all?"

"They weren't my concern. I didn't love them like I loved you."

"But you could've protected all of us. You could have killed Cameron, taken *his* head down to the nearest precinct and told them where to find us. But you never did."

"How could I? I needed what he had to offer. It's hard to find this kind of gig, Max. You must believe me. I protected you as best as I was able. I kept the worst of Cameron's wrath from touching you. Please believe me. I couldn't live with you not believing me.

"I don't know any of the other providers who'd take me on this late in their game. I got on with Cameron early, when we were both young. We've grown together. We've groomed a lot of boys, and they're the best product out there. And you. You were the greatest one of all. You never even cried when the men were with you. You were strong and stalwart. You were more than we could have asked for. And Cameron knew that. That's why you survived down in that basement until you were thirteen. Most of the boys were dispatched by age eleven. You know that."

"I felt *soo* protected," Max said sarcastically.

"You were. And you still are. Didn't I let you go when Cameron called for your head? I tried to talk him out of it, but it was no use. 'No dangling threads,' he always said, and you were no exception no matter how much I pleaded. So I brought you here to New York and set you free at great personal risk. And for years, I've been watching you and making sure you were okay. Cameron still thinks I'm looking for you and I'll bring him your head. But I won't. I can't. I love you too much."

Quinn looked proud of himself, as though he'd just caught a fat, juicy rat.

"I'm still not coming with you," Max said. "And I think it's time for you to go."

"But why?"

Max thought for a moment. "Because I don't love you."

"But you do! You must, after all I did for you."

"You did those things for yourself, Quinn. You kept me alive so you would have continual access to me. You couldn't bear to see me marked up or banged up or killed, because you wanted me clean and unharmed to complete your fantasy of our mutual love. But that love only exists in your imagination."

They were even closer now, about fifteen feet from each other, as Quinn was moving down the alleyway toward him.

"I don't know who's been feeding you these thoughts, Maximilian. Is it your brother, Gary? I'll kill that man if I get my hands on him—and his little Chink girlfriend, too. I don't know why you're so angry. Has Gary been planting awful thoughts about me in your brain while you've been cozying up to him, and soaking him for money and a place to stay? Or is that girlfriend of his using her sex to plant dirty thoughts in your mind? I'll kill her, too. Don't think I won't. I'll take them both away from you until you have nothing left, no one to turn to but me. Or how about that friend of yours at The Mission? That Donovan guy. Had he been soaking you for money and cigarettes in exchange for blow jobs? Our love puts them to shame. The things—"

Max broke into a run for his life. He ran quicker than he'd ever run before, and as he angled past Quinn, he felt Quinn's hand grasp his shirt before it was ripped from it, useless. As he turned the corner, he pushed past angry people and ran down streets and side streets and avenues toward The Mission, the only safe place he knew of. He ran until his breath was a painful stitch in his side, until his feet were throbbing and and the cracks had opened up again and were slippery with blood. He ran until he was finally able and ready to look over his shoulder behind him.

No one was there. No one except strangers milling around and heading to work, eyes pointed to the ground. Had any of them even seen him being chased? He didn't care. If they hadn't, they wouldn't be able to confirm a sighting of him for Quinn.

He slowly got his bearings and saw that he'd run to Astor Place, the perfect area to effectively lose someone. There were hundreds of people here, many of them just doing their thing unaware of the golden-haired man with bleeding feet who was running for his life, running for his future, running toward the only people who cared. He was exhausted, so he descended into the subway and passed under the fluorescent bulbs that hung there showering the tunnels with grainy, dim light. It was supposed to show off the tile work, the other passengers and the arriving trains but, after years of accumulated grime on the bulbs, was unable to do so properly.

He hopped on the train that would take him the rest of the way to the Bowery. Upon arrival, he ascended to the street and headed toward The Mission. About halfway there, when he could barely see the red door down the way, he turned away from his destination. He wasn't sure he was ready for all the people with concern in their eyes to ask questions. There were sirens in the street coming toward him, but that was par for the course in this city. He wound up walking the few short blocks to the Sneaky Bean, hoping that Jean would be working.

When he entered, he noticed Jean right away, serving customers at the till. He crept up alongside the line and caught her eye with a bit of a wave. She took one look at him, at the pink colour that had risen in his face from the exertion, and then motioned to someone from the back room to come up front and take over her station. She came out from behind the counter and took Max by the arm.

"Max, what's wrong with you?" she whispered in his ear.

"Quinn cornered me in the alleyway when I went to get my stuff. He was going to kidnap me again, and he threatened to kill you and Gary. I feel all shaky inside, like I'm going to puke."

"Come to the back with me, and I'll fix you an iced green tea. It'll help cool you and calm you."

Behind the counter they walked, Jean's arm in his the whole time, holding him tightly to her. She sat him at a table that was mercifully out of view of the customers and employees out front.

Max placed his strong hands over his face and clenched them. The muscles in his forearms flexed and straightened. He began rocking back and forth, just subtly at first and then gaining momentum the longer he did it. Jean sat in a chair opposite him. Another employee brought the tea to the table, and she placed it in front of him.

"Thank you, Carmen. I appreciate that."

Carmen nodded and walked away gingerly.

"Tell me what happened, Max."

He spoke from behind his hands. "I went to 59th and Lex to get my stuff—a bag with my wallet and some money. I heard something behind me, and when I looked up, Quinn was standing there. I looked for a way to escape, but he was blocking the passageway too well. So I tried to keep him talking until I could disarm him, until he began to relax. And he told me some things that he was going to do, and they scared the hell out of me."

He looked as though he were trying to hold the moment in, even as he was trying to tell her about it. Jean was having a very difficult time reading him, something she usually prided herself in being able to do easily with her friends. She noticed that tears were leaking from between his fingers and under his palms onto the table. It was a heartrending sight, this strong, grown man dripping all over himself and his torn T-shirt. His rocking increased dramatically, and a wail escaped from between his lips—a long, desperate whimper punctuated with little screeches here and there. She had never heard anything like it. He seemed lost in another world, another place, another time.

"Max, what's happening? Max, where are you?"

He just kept sobbing, the sound muffled through his hands.

"Max? Where are you, Max?" She reached toward him and placed a hand on his shoulder. "Can you feel my hand rubbing your shoulder? Can you feel my touch?"

Max nodded his head with effort. He was trying hard to listen to Jean's voice, but the images in his mind were powerful and difficult to dispel.

"Max, listen to me," she said calmly. "Feel your feet planted on the ground. Feel the concrete under them. Can you do that for me? Can you feel your legs attached to your feet? Feel my hand on your leg now. Feel my hand rubbing your knee."

Max concentrated on her words, and some of his body slowly came back to him. He'd felt her warm hand rubbing on his shoulder, back and forth, the friction with the fabric of his shirt creating a warmth that radiated out. Then his arm came into his consciousness, and then his elbow and his hand that was held tight to his face.

"Where are you now, Max? Tell me what you see."

"I'm in the basement," voiced Max, "and Quinn is walking down the stairs. I can recognize his walk. It's large and lumbering; his feet pound on each stair. He's coming for me. I know he's coming for me again. Then he's in the doorway, one hand resting on the doorframe. The smell of his sweat crawls into the room, and I know what's in store for me tonight. It's going to hurt so *much*, Jean. And there's nothing I can do to stop it. I can't play sick, because that never works. I can't play tired, because he doesn't care.

He just wants one thing. And then he's there, standing over me, taking off his clothes, rubbing himself with one hand, and . . ."

Max hesitated, and his rocking increased. Jean grabbed his arm. Her touch was strong and forceful. She was careful not to hurt him, but she needed to bring him back to the room.

She held the iced tea in front of his face and placed the straw at his mouth. "Here, Max. Take a sip of your iced tea. It's good for you and will help steady your fear."

He did, and the straw came away with a string of saliva. Slowly, his eyes glazed over again, and he was back in the basement. But his rocking slowed somewhat, and he seemed more in control.

He continued. "After it's over, when I just want to be alone and cry myself to sleep, he wants to talk, to tell me his troubles and the stress in his life. And I'm lying there hating him, wanting to kill him.

"This is what he wants for me again—those same conditions. And today he almost got me. And it terrified me, Jean. It terrified me that I came so close to having him in control of my life again, when I've worked so hard to hide from him all these years."

He was sobbing now, deep, tortured bawls, and he couldn't catch his breath. Jean put one arm around his shoulders, gripped his forearm with the other hand and just held him until it felt like the right time to speak.

"Max, look at me. Look at me, Max." She cupped his face in her hands and turned it toward her. From this vantage point, she had a front-row seat to his anguish, fear and anxiety. His pain was palpable and seemed to emanate from his very muscles that trembled visibly. "Max, you're safe now. You got away. He didn't get you."

"You don't get it, Jean. I'm never safe. He's there in my dreams. He's there when I wake. He's there outside the shower curtain when I'm trying to soap up my body. He's there behind me when

I'm walking, there beside me when I'm sitting, there inside me when I'm thinking. He's there when I smell man sweat on someone nearby. He's there when I hear a dog's warning bark. I'll never be safe because I'll never be free. I'll never be alone. He's with me forever. He's with me as far as the day is long."

His eyes glazed over again, and he looked out and over Jean's shoulder. She wondered where his mind had taken him now. She was about to snap her fingers in front of his face to get his attention back to the moment, but he came back to her on his own. His eyes slowly lost their unfocused look, and he looked straight at her.

Jean said, "You've got friends now, Max. We'll find a way to beat him. I picked up my uncle's gun today. It's in my purse, and if he comes anywhere near you when I'm around, I'll kill him. I swear I'll kill him. I won't let him touch you. I won't let him take our Max, because he has no right to you. He *never* had any right to you. He's sick, this Quinn, but that sickness is no match for my aim. I'll shoot him dead, Max. I promise you that. I'll kill him for you so you'll always be free. I've never wanted to hurt anyone so badly as I want to hurt Quinn for what he's done to you. I swear on my mother's grave that I'll kill him. I will kill him to protect Gary and myself, but especially to protect you. You have so much ahead of you, a life filled with learning and loving. Yes, a life of *loving*, because I'm sure you will find someone, a strong woman such as you, who will love you more than the sun. You have so much to offer a woman, so much of yourself to give. You feel like you've been damaged and cruelly destroyed, but you haven't. You've remained intact. God knows how, but you have all these years. You will find love in this world, Max. I assure you of that. And that love will dry your tears. You have nothing to fear anymore today. Quinn is gone. You lost him. He won't come here, or to The Mission, because there are just too many damned people. He won't try anything more today, Max. He won't get you."

»»»»»

It was only upon arriving at The Mission that Max and Jean realized where all those sirens were headed. There was an ambulance out front, and Jean was worried that someone had been hurt. Though Max didn't talk much and subsequently didn't make many friends, he knew enough about people to know when something exciting was going on. Jean pushed her way to the back of the crowd and jumped up and down to try and see what lay beyond. But it was no use, since the police were cordoning it off to keep out the curious. Max thought he could see an empty body bag being lifted from the trunk of one of the police cars. He thought it might be a good time to turn away.

"What do you think is happening?" he asked Jean.

"I'm not really sure. Do you see anything?" she said.

"They're bringing out a body bag. Let's go in. You don't want to see this."

"No, I do, but I *can't*. I'm just too damned short."

"Let's go in. Gary's already here, I'm sure."

"I thought he'd be out here, what with a body bag in plain view. The clients are probably causing a ruckus . . ." She trailed off, hoping to glean some further knowledge from Max about how Gary reacted in a crisis.

"Let's go check how he's doing, then. It must be difficult. Maybe he was close with whoever they're stuffing into that bag."

Jean noticed that Max was biting his nails. "Maybe," she said.

She turned and walked slowly toward the front door. Max caught up and put his arm through hers, hooking them together so they could hold on to each other. Feeling her protruding bones, he understood why Gary had said she was fragile. They walked through the door and presented themselves at the front window,

Max as a client of Gary's and Jean as Gary's girlfriend. They were buzzed in.

They noticed several cops who were congregated down the hall in front of Gary's office. Saundra stood in the doorway answering questions. Two more were walking down the hall toward the cafeteria, talking in loud voices about something other than the murder victim being stuffed into the black body bag. Max and Jean glanced at each other but did not deign to comment. They'd save it for when they were with Gary. So they went off to see whether they could track him down.

After a bit of searching and a conversation with Zachary, who told Jean his rags-to-almost-riches story and kept wanting to steer the conversation back to the Life Skills Program that Max was supposed to begin later that day, they finally found Gary sitting at a large desk at the end of one of the otherwise empty classrooms. He was a shadow at first, with his back to the sunlight shining through the window behind him, and only his profile spoke of his features. *Even without his face he's recognizable*, Max thought. When he cleared his throat to announce their arrival, Gary jumped. Jean laughed.

"I don't suppose you know why this place is crawling with cops, do you, Gary?" asked Max.

"In fact, I do. There was a murder late last night in the alleyway. The victim was our client, and he was found early this morning—completely naked except for his sneakers."

"That's horrible," said Jean, her eyes wet and glossy. "Do they know who did it?"

Gary shook his head. "They have no idea. He was shy. Kept mostly to himself. A really nice sort, but very shy. Everyone liked him, though. And there wasn't much to take, but they took everything he had."

"What do you mean everything he had?" asked Max.

"I mean his clothes. They stole his clothes. Even the shirt he loved so much."

"Are you talking about Donovan?" asked Max.

"Yes. Donovan," Gary answered. "But everyone liked him, so who would do such a thing?"

Max was shaken, his eyes wide and his lips pursed in a tight line. After the emotional outburst he had just had at the coffee shop, this was almost too much to bear. He let out a shallow exhale and said, "Quinn. Quinn would do this."

"Why? Who is Donovan to Quinn but another one of our clients?"

"Quinn thought he was my friend. And it's partly true. He's the only other client I've spent time with. And the other day, he told me something . . ." He stared up at the wall high above.

"What did he tell you, Max?" asked Jean, softly touching his arm for reassurance.

"He told me he'd overheard other clients out back talking about a big dude with copper hair who was asking them all about me—where I stayed, who I was friendly with, how I got my money. They thought he might be a cop, so they mostly clammed up with his questions. Donovan didn't believe the rumours at first, until Quinn had cornered him moments before dinnertime when the alleyway was almost empty."

"He should have told me," said Gary angrily. His hands were clenched into fists, and his arms were rigid by his sides. "I need to know these kinds of things. If someone is stirring up trouble, I need to know."

"Gary," Jean said softly, "right now? This isn't about you."

He knew she was right.

"He tried to tell you, Gary. The other day while I was with Zachary, he came to tell you, but for some reason he didn't," Max said. Gary thought back to when Donovan had visited his office and confided in him that harrowing murder story. He'd felt like there was something left unsaid, but they'd agreed to discuss it during his next visit. Now there wouldn't be a next visit.

"So, Max, you think Quinn did this? Why would you jump to that conclusion?" Gary asked.

"Because Quinn told me so this morning. At 59th and Lexington. He cornered me in an alleyway and listed off all my friends. He mentioned Donovan, but I didn't know that he was dead. Now it makes sense. He saw us smoking together and thought that we were bosom buddies or something. This was his revenge for us scaring him away the other night when he broke into the apartment."

He thought for a moment, chewing on one of the hangnails he'd missed during other sessions with his fingers.

Finally, he added, "This is his way of reminding me who is in control."

CHAPTER THIRTEEN

Max walked with trepidation toward the classroom door. As he rounded the corner, he saw a small crowd of about six or eight milling just outside. When he approached, he was told by one of them that it was locked.

Was he imagining it? Or had their conversation ceased as he approached? Yes, they had been talking about him. He hugged the manila folder that Gary had given him close to his chest. He would use it to keep handouts and other papers from the class together in one place, so that either Gary or Jean could read them aloud to him at a later point in time.

Five classes in five days . . . it sounded like a lot, especially considering he'd never before sat in a classroom. In his right breast pocket he had a tiny digital voice recorder so that he could record the class and play back the lesson later. Both Jean and Gary had offered to take notes from these recordings for him. Max knew he was fortunate in having the chance to take this program, and he didn't want to screw it up.

"Good afternoon, everyone," called a cheery voice from down the hall. When Max looked up, he caught sight of Zachary, who was sporting a light-blue dress shirt that was decidedly too small for his humongous frame.

"I see we're all here," he said as he unlocked the door. They filed into the classroom and each took a seat. "Actually, we're still missin' Samuel. But we're a little early, and I'm sure he'll be comin' soon enough."

Everyone but Max turned to someone else and began to speak in hushed tones. Finally, one of them called out, "Hey, Zach. So what's the story with Donovan? What happened out there last night?"

"You know I don't like the name Zach," Zachary said.

"Yes, I do," said the speaker. He folded his arms and leaned his chair back onto its hind legs. Max wondered whether they were going to break under the pressure. "That's why I call you that." He snickered.

"Then call me Zachary, and maybe I'll answer you." He looked down at his desk and rummaged pointlessly with some papers. When the speaker addressed him again, he almost jumped.

"Zachary, then," he said with a sneer, putting extra emphasis on the name. "What happened last night?"

Zachary walked around and sat on the front edge of his desk. He said, "Donovan was murdered last night, here in our alley."

"How was he killed?"

"He was stabbed to death."

"He was a faggot anyway. Good riddance to bad rubbish."

Zachary jumped up and took a firm stance. He was fuming.

"You *will not* speak that way about other clients of The Mission!" he shouted. "How are you somehow privileged with this information, huh? Did Donovan ever confide in you about his sexuality? Or did you two ever sleep together?"

"Ah, fuck that. I'd never sleep with no goddamn queer. I wouldn't even invite him into my house."

"You don't have a house."

"If I did . . ."

"Maynard, why don't you just shut your trap for once?" said another classmate. She looked to be in her forties and had grey hair that had once been dyed red but was a faded scarlet now.

"You can go to hell, Eloise. Nobody cares what you think," Maynard retorted.

"I care," said Zachary. "I'm sure most of us would rather hear from Eloise on this matter than you, Maynard."

Maynard was visibly dumbfounded. It wasn't often that people didn't like to hear him. With his bald head and his fat gut held together by a frame that might have once been muscular, Maynard certainly wasn't attractive. But he was a favourite to listen to if you wanted a dose of shock jock. With as many sour opinions as Howard Stern and Dr. Laura combined, he was an imposing figure out in the alleyway, where he could spout his mouth off without being challenged by staff. Inside, however, he kept mostly to a small group of comrades who looked up to him because he handed out smokes. They could always be counted on to lie for him when he stepped over the line and either pushed or tripped another client who opposed him.

"Zachary?" queried Eloise in her small, frail voice. "What did happen? There's so much talk, and none of it makes sense, and no one has told us anything."

"I can't really give you much information, Eloise, but I know that Gary and Saundra are workin' on it. They're coordinating a town hall meeting for later today. There are signs up in the halls already. And they'll be doin' another tomorrow morning for those who miss today's. You can ask questions then. They'll be more prepared to answer them than I am right now."

Zachary looked around the room. "Does that satisfy your curiosity, at least until then?"

Some of the students nodded, while others only grumbled, Maynard included.

"Okay, then let's get started without Samuel."

»

In their office, Gary and Saundra were working against time to prepare for the town hall meeting. This was supposed to be their time to gather information and coordinate their stories. It was hard work, since the police had learned precious little by the time they'd left. And the things they did tell them Gary could have surmised from a quick scan of the murder scene.

Donovan was dead, murdered at the hand of a deranged killer—deranged or furious. With the haphazard stab wounds all over his body, it was as though the killer had slashed him over and over to ensure that he was bled thoroughly dry. He had been left naked, and neither the police nor the staff had been able to find his clothes. It was enough to give them all nightmares. Were there fingerprints or boot prints or hairs left on Donovan's body? Forensics would have to answer these questions at a later date. Was he attacked because he was homeless? Or because he was in the wrong place at the wrong time? Nobody knew. Did it happen because he was gay? He'd asserted to Gary that he wasn't, but who knew for sure? They did know this: Donovan's murder would not go unsolved for very long. The police would put every effort into finding his killer and bringing him to justice.

Yeah, right.

Gary was sure the police weren't inclined to put much effort, if any at all, into finding the killer of a thirty-something gay homeless man. That was something else that he and Saundra agreed on. But they couldn't say that to the rest of their colleagues and clients. He had hoped that a police spokesman would come and talk to the crowd for them, but at his suggestion, they had simply said the police didn't have the staff. It seemed no one cared what the homeless clients of The Mission had to deal with when one of their own was murdered in cold blood. Not knowing much about the murder—the who, the when, the why—would only instill greater fear into an already frightened community. But the police didn't seem to see The Mission as a community; they saw it as a place where the degenerates gathered for a free dinner and a place to sleep. Gary knew that apart from a possible visit from officers to ask a few questions to a few people, this was going to be the last they heard of Donovan or saw of the police. His murder would go unsolved.

But this wouldn't be the last of his killer for Gary and Max and Jean. Not if Max was right, and Gary and Jean had every reason to believe his theory.

The story of Quinn cornering Max in the alleyway was disheartening, but in some ways it wasn't as disheartening as Donovan's murder. Quinn was obviously capable of anything and willing to go to any lengths to get what he wanted. And right now, he wanted Gary's little brother. But Gary wasn't going to let him have him. He wasn't going to stand aside when his brother needed him. Max had been ripped out of his life as easily as Donovan had ripped off the pocket of his treasured shirt. He would not let it happen again.

And to top it all off, it was August 24, the anniversary of Max's abduction, though he doubted that Max knew this. He was so young when he was taken, so fragile and frail. A child that young would have no idea what date it was on any given day, except Christmas and his birthday. And he himself wouldn't have known the date either, except that every year afterward someone seemed to remind him. "Honey, how do you feel today?" they would ask. "Are you missing your brother? You know, this is the day he was taken." August 24. Always reminded of August 24. He doubted that Max's captors had given him this incessant reminder. They had other ways of torturing him.

Jean had left for work about an hour before, and Max was still in his Life Skills class. It was lonely without the two of them and just Saundra to talk to—or rather, Saundra to talk at him. He kept mostly quiet, while she talked almost incessantly. One of her primary subjects was her displeasure at having to stay late for the town hall meeting because she'd had to make alternate arrangements on the fly for someone to pick up her daughter from her after-school program. But Gary knew better. She'd had to stay late with him on other occasions, and she always maintained a backup plan for her daughter, where her sister would pick the child up. Nevertheless, she complained a lot about the inconvenience of it all. Gary was lucky. Since he worked the evening shift, he rarely had to stay late, except when one of the nighttime monitors didn't make it and he had to fill in and watch over the sleeping clients through the night.

Saundra had only had to stay late on a few occasions. There was the time one of the cooks broke her ankle climbing the stairs to the pantry where the potatoes, onions, carrots and such were housed. Saundra was asked to remain and help cook until dinner was over. And there was that enormous snowstorm, when the roads were impassable and the subways had shut down because mountains of snow hadn't been cleared from the exposed tracks. She had to stay overnight then. Come to think of it, those were the only times he could remember her having had to stay late.

He stopped working for a moment and thought about Jean, about the anorexia that could be killing her. How could he reach her? How could he help her? Anorexia was a very difficult disease to treat. She might need to go away to a treatment facility that specializes in eating disorders, or be hospitalized so she could be given medical treatment. Group sessions and therapy could help her shift her skewed views about her body, rectify her self-image, re-establish her destructive thinking patterns that were destroying her from the inside out. He didn't have that kind of power or that kind of training. In school, he'd specialized in poverty and child-abuse issues. He'd always thought that eating disorders were best treated by women, for sharing a gender identification with their clients would allow them to be more easily trusted. He'd also thought that mostly women were plagued by eating disorders, though he'd learned later that men were almost as easily afflicted by these diseases, especially with the advent of more and more magazines sporting scantily clad men who were just as thin as their female model counterparts.

"Hey. Earth to Gary. Wake up, kiddo," Saundra said.

"I'm awake."

"But only barely. You've been staring at that police statement for about fifteen minutes already."

"Sorry. I guess I'm not going to be much help this evening."

"Neither of us are. There's no real information to tell them."

"But the real reason we're doing this is to open a conversation about Donovan's murder, to give the clients a point of contact to take their feelings to. That we can do. At least it's something."

"I wonder how scared they are."

"I think many of them will take it in stride. They've seen a lot already on the streets. What's a murder when you've lived the kind of life most of them lead?"

"Just another event, I suppose."

"Just another event."

Knock, knock, knock.

"Come in," they said in unison. They laughed as Max opened the door and entered the room. Since both of the chairs were taken, he stood in the doorway.

"Hi, David," said Saundra. "How was your class?"

"Great. Found a new person to hate, though, which is always nice."

"Who is that?" she asked, not looking up from the paper she was scanning.

"A dude named Maynard. Really prejudiced. Really angry. Really not my type."

She looked up, surprised. "Oh, are you gay?"

"No. I meant he's not my type of person to have as a friend, not a lover."

"Sorry. Jumping to conclusions, I guess. I don't usually do that, but I'm not really myself today."

"None of us are at our best today, Saundra," said Gary. He looked up at Max, and a knowing look passed between them. Both of the men knew that the other was still shaken by Donovan's murder, probably more so than anyone else in The Mission. But they had more reason to be shaken up, since they both knew that Quinn had been at the blunt end of the knife that killed Max's "friend." They both knew the act was for them—it was personal.

"I'm going to step outside for a smoke, but I wanted to ask where we're supposed to do that now that the alleyway has been closed off," Max said.

"We've asked everyone to smoke at the end of the street, at least until the police have finished their investigation. You can crush your butts on the ground and put them in a city garbage can," said Saundra.

"Until they've removed the yellow tape," Gary added. "Things should be back to normal pretty soon, I suspect."

"We'll have to figure out how to clean up the blood, Gary."

"Won't the police do it?" Max asked.

Saundra explained, "No, they don't do that. It's up to the property owners to clean up after a murder. Or if it's in a home, then it's up to the family to clean up. Sometimes it's left up to the building management, and in this case, that's us.

"I don't want any of our clients cleaning it up, because it'll only scar them worse than the murder itself. And I'm not sure I want to do it either. I go home each night with enough memories to wound an elephant. I just don't need any more."

"If no one offers, then I guess I'll do it," Gary said.

"I'll help," added Max. He was clearly concerned about his older brother, though he couldn't show it to Saundra. He didn't want to blow his cover.

"Gary, feel like taking a break with me while I head out for a smoke?" he asked.

"Sorry, but no can do. I've still got to finish preparing for the meeting."

"Your loss."

»»

"Well, if it isn't the man of the hour," said Maynard as Max approached the small group of smokers that had collected at the end of the street. Max looked at him questioningly, a little shocked to see that he was addressing him.

He added, "The golden boy. The popular dude. The one that everyone wants to know about." He let out an abrasive, mean laugh. "I suppose you're special and that's why everyone's looking for you. Or maybe you're just another miserable fuck that's messed up in something bad." His eyes narrowed, and his lips pursed.

"I don't suppose you'd like to stop fucking around and just tell me what's up your ass, Maynard," said Max, his ire rising despite his conscious attempts to control it. Losing it right now, with everything that had already happened today, was not advisable. He didn't need to get barred from The Mission for any reason, especially one as stupid as fighting Maynard in the street.

"There's someone looking for you, man. And he doesn't look nice."

"And why does that bother you so much?"

"Because if you're in trouble and you're bringing it here, it'll cause trouble for the rest of us. Just ask Donovan. Oh, wait. You can't, because he's already dead."

"I'm sure you bring enough trouble here on your own. Or is it just that you're afraid of losing your position as head fuck-up?"

Someone laughed; it sounded like Eloise.

"It's got nothing to do with me. But I've been wondering about you. You show up this last week with your golden-boy looks, and you're showered with clean clothes on, and you never stay the night. You've obviously got some other gig going on. It's like you're not even homeless, like you got a nice, cushy pad to crash in, but still you're here every day except the weekend.

"And then there's this big, burly bodyguard type who's asking questions about you, needling the rest of us for answers and giving out smokes in exchange for information. And he's interested in you—not me, not Eloise, not anybody else. He was talking with Donovan the other day. I heard them. And no matter how much he tried, he couldn't get a clear answer from him. And he looked mad when he left—real mad. Now what's that supposed to make me think, huh? I'll tell you what I think. I think you're here to hide, to cover yourself up with The Mission. I'll tell you what I think." He pointed a long, crooked finger right at Max. "I think he's looking for you but he found Donovan instead. It should have been you in that alley this morning. It should have been you all cut up and left for dead. It should have been you that was stripped of your clothes, with all your faggoty lies and half-truths. That's what I think, David. That's just what I think. You can fool some people some of the time. But you can't fool me."

»»»

"Can I help you?" Jean said to the customer standing before her.

"A cappuccino, please."

"You want cinnamon or chocolate on that?"

"Mmmm. Chocolate, please."

Jean looked around as she was frothing the milk. Her favourite drink was a chai tea latte, and she was itching for a break in the lineup to make one.

The shop had been busy since her arrival. Customer after customer had come through the doors wanting to be served quickly so they could hurry on their way. That was one thing she didn't understand about New Yorkers: Why did they need to hurry all the time and go about their business without reflecting on the passing day? She liked to cruise through life, to stop and smell the roses, as it were.

The line finally thinned out and then broke about twenty minutes later. She made her chai and tasted it silently, letting the hot liquid sit on her tongue before swallowing. She stood at the cash register and waited for more customers to walk in. She was almost alone today, and her uncle was due to show up at five o'clock. There were two others on the clock, but one of them was on a break and the other was in the back doing dishes. If the time was correct, Uncle was running a bit late. He didn't usually run late. It was his custom to always show up on time and to leave her alone with the store only if he needed to.

She quietly surveyed the room. It was quite full of customers drinking their coffees, their cappuccinos, their lattes, their teas. She felt a sense of pride in that moment, knowing that she had accomplished some little bit just by serving them. It wasn't the best job in the world. She knew that. But she also knew she was helping Uncle out big time by being his second in command. She didn't talk back to the customers. She kept the place reasonably clean. She didn't steal from the till. And she wasn't going to up and quit just because she'd found a job at another coffee shop closer to home. Uncle knew that he could trust her to stay, that she was loyal to him and his enterprise, if only because she was family. She looked up at the clock just in time to see Gus come through the door.

Gus was a very tall man, about Gary's height, with a crop of thick red hair. His eyes were narrowly set on his face. The combination of it all gave him the look of your stereotypical Irish mobster. But that was where the resemblance ended. He was attractive despite his age, for he had a dynamic, alluring quality about him. He seemed almost magnetic, an energy that began with his full lips but continued into something that was hard to describe. It was in his nature itself, betrayed in his way of carrying himself, his way of cocking his head when he was listening. It was in his way of looking at you with those deep-set eyes that held yours steady and firm in their gaze. It was in his way of listening to you, seeming so interested in whatever it was you were saying. It was in his way of standing, how he leaned into your conversation and favoured you with his attitude. Yes, he was an attractive man, but he was a dangerous one, too, and Jean always kept that in mind.

He was robbing Uncle blind, taking pin money each week as a kind of blackmail. He had told Uncle enough times that if the pin money wasn't waiting, something could happen to the coffee shop, like a fire or some other kind of "incident." Jean wasn't quite sure what he meant by this threat, but she was astute enough to always make sure that the money was ready when he came. Today was no different, so she pulled the envelope from the cash drawer and waited for Gus to come.

Gus never spoke much. He usually just waited in line until he was at the till, reached out to take the envelope and left. But today, Uncle entered on his heels.

He looked the worse for wear. He was disheveled, unkempt and frightened. Jean froze and watched him limp toward the front of the store. Gus hadn't noticed him at first, but he did as Uncle came around behind the counter.

Besides the limp, he had scratches on the side of his face, and his jacket and pants were torn as though he'd been dragged along the pavement. The blood on his face was still wet. He took a napkin and tried to wipe it off. His hand had seen better days, and Jean wondered whether his pinky was broken due to the angle at which it was bent. And his hair, his always combed and always gelled black hair that usually shined in the sunlight, was messy and dusty.

"Did you arrange this?" he asked Gus.

"Arrange what?"

"For someone to beat me up. They didn't even take my wallet. They just wanted to hurt me. And they would have hurt me more if I wasn't so short and such a fast runner."

"I had nothing to do with this, Teddy."

"Are you sure? Because I don't deserve this."

"Not from me you don't. You always pay on time, and you always have the correct amount."

"That's why it's wrong that this was done."

"It wasn't me, Teddy. I have no idea who did this to you."

"On your honour?"

"On my mother's grave."

"Then do you have any idea who did this?"

"I haven't heard of anyone with a cause to hurt you. Or your premises. You're pretty well off the radar."

"Gus, can you do me a favour?" asked Uncle. He looked almost sheepish, not knowing where to start, and then said, "I know I have no right to ask you for anything. But I've been a good client. You even just said that I always pay on time. Surely that counts for something."

"It does. But I'll wait until I know the favour. Some things cannot be given."

"Will you keep your ear to the ground and let me know if you hear anything, anything at all that might indicate who did this?"

Gus thought for a moment, his eyes wandering up and left toward the ceiling. Finally, he looked back at Uncle and said, "I can do that for you, Teddy. I can listen to the ground for any news of you, your coffee shop or your family. And I won't charge you extra for listening either. I can do that for you."

Jean held out the envelope, and he took it without looking at her. As he turned to walk away, Uncle slipped into the back room. Jean skipped toward the door to catch up with Gus.

"Gus, can I speak with you outside of here?" she asked.

He turned back around and looked at her square in the eyes for the first time since entering the shop. He raised his eyebrows, thought momentarily and then said, "Yes."

»»»»

Max was furious. He finished his smoke as quickly as he could, crushed the butt and headed back to The Mission.

Why had Maynard decided to single him out? Was he was just picking on the new guy? Or was he holding his cards close, having figured out more than he was letting on at the moment, and waiting to play them at just the right time? Max didn't like poker games. He didn't like poker faces either, and Maynard was playing his for all its worth.

He climbed the front steps, pulled the red door open and waited at the window to be let in. He was thankful for these doors, this window, the locking mechanisms that kept Quinn out. But how long would it last? How long before Quinn was actually admitted to the place while pretending to be homeless or in need of a meal?

"Hey, are you David, the new guy?" the gatekeeper asked.

"Huh? Oh, yeah. Affirmative," answered Max, almost forgetting his cover and the name he used in the outside world.

"I've got something for you. Looks like a card of some kind. I can't tell, because it's in a sealed envelope." He was clearly disgruntled by not being able to read the correspondence. "Come on in, and I'll hand it to you."

Max walked through the door as it buzzed him in. He stopped at the gatekeeper's door, and the guy handed him the envelope. It was rather large, larger than a letter and not quite the shape of one either. "David Commely" was written on it. He walked to Gary's office without opening it.

"Hi, David," said Gary as Max knocked on the open door.

"Hi, Gary. Could I talk to you for a few minutes? Alone?"

Saundra looked up and then placed the papers that were on her lap onto the desk. "Sounds like my cue to exit," she said. "Do either of you want a coffee? My treat."

"Not for me," said Gary. "I've already had too many today. I want to be calm during this meeting and not get flustered when I'm speaking."

"I'll take one. Black with cream and six sugars, please," Max said.

"I'll be back in fifteen. Is that enough time for you, David?"

"Should be. Thanks, Saundra."

After she left, Max handed the envelope to Gary. He turned it over and over trying to decipher the contents.

"Should I open it?" he asked, looking at Max for approval.

"Yes, please. I can't read it."

Gary tore open the top and pulled out a greeting card. He froze, and Max could see the anger rising in his face. He was turning red in the cheeks and neck. He gripped the card tightly, pressing his fingers into it, and then looked up at Max.

"Do you know what today is, Max?"

"It's Monday."

"No. Do you know what the date is? It's the twenty-fourth of August."

Max shrugged. "And?"

"That's the date you were abducted."

"And what's that got to do with this card?"

Gary held out the card. "It's an anniversary card. Quinn's wishing you a happy anniversary."

»»»»»

Gus was a man of few whims and many desires. He had no whim for a fancy apartment on the Upper East Side, but he had a strong desire to live his life fully and to the best of his ability. He had no whim for a relationship with a loving and caring woman, but he had a strong desire to fulfill his sexual needs on regular occasions. He had no whim for camping adventures in the wilderness, but he had a strong desire to hike the four-day trail to Machu Picchu. Though to many people whims and desires were almost synonymous, for Gus, they were easily distinguishable as things he didn't want and things he desperately longed for.

As a younger man, these things were more fluid. He hadn't yet categorized life into what he sought after and what he was willing to leave behind or untouched. But that was before he'd become a hired gun, a common thug, a man who extracted what he wanted from the weaker ones around him—a time before Mornie had been murdered. He could still hear her screams when he closed his eyes at night.

He'd grown up rather poor. Money never came easily to the O'Connor family. Now that was a name he'd left behind a long time ago, too. He first used a pseudonym but eventually changed his name legally so he could finally leave his father's legacy where it belonged: on his gravestone. Kiran O'Connor was a petty thug. He took contracts to rough men up in back alleys and on the piers of the Manhattan waterfront. Kiran O'Connor was a mobster. But he never amounted to much. He never rose through the ranks. Good positions were reserved for family, extended family and friends of family, none of which he could call himself. Rather, he was a dirt-poor wretch born of an unwed mother who had come to America on a boat from Ireland. Gus didn't know much about his grandmother. She'd died of the drink long before he was born. His father had grown up in poverty, an economic vice he never rose above or escaped. He had gravitated toward lowly mob work as a young man, searching for his way in the world but never able to find it. He resolved to doing the dirty work of those who were quick to hire his weathered fists and strong, stocky frame. Like a mail messenger in a fancy corporation who dreams of one day being discovered within its halls, he lived his life waiting, dreaming, hoping for the day that he would get that one job, that one contract, where his usefulness would be noticed. But it never came. Until his last day on Earth, he was slated for crappy jobs, like beating some guy who hadn't paid a bill or sticking a knife into someone who had crossed the wrong boss.

Gus had grown up with his father's eternal presence overshadowing him. Kiran O'Connor had big hopes for his son and never tired of trying to convince Gus that he was meant to go places, be somebody, leave their world and their family behind. 'Stand up straight, boy! You'll never get anywhere if you slouch through life,' he would say. 'Work hard, so you won't end up like me. Keep your chin up, and don't look so cross—smile more. Strive hard. And get your ass to school!'

Gus's mother cut a strong figure. Brita O'Connor was quick with an insult. They were most often directed at her husband, though she never held back on her children. She kept a clean home—no, a spotless home, overwhelmingly clean. She scrubbed her wood floors like she was trying to exorcise demons from their slats. But despite her efforts to make improvements, the apartment always looked dingy, drab and dreary. The sun never shined through the windows, for despite their spotlessness, the apartment was on the ground floor of a four-story walk-up, and each window was fitted with black wrought-iron bars. Three families lived above them, all equally poor and equally ashamed of themselves and the lives they lived. Brita was fighting a never-ending battle in her tries to better their lives through water and soap. Nothing she did seemed to lift them up. Nothing she did seemed to work.

Gus's twin sister was the shining star of the family. She was pretty and kind, gentle and warm. She walked lightly, as though held aloft by the breath of angels. Her body twisted like spun glass, fragile and temporary as though she were not meant for the life she was born to live. Her name was Morna, but Gus called her Mornie, a pet name that was used by no one else in the family. He loved her more than life itself, and nothing could prevent him from catering to her every whimsical notion. She was a simple girl. Some called her slow behind her back, but Gus didn't care. Though he knew that she had a moon-shaped face similar to the boy down the street who never went to school, he loved her dearly. But that was a long time ago. Gus tried not to think of Mornie anymore.

At seventeen years old, Gus was introduced to Abela. She was the daughter of a friend of his father's, and though she was only fourteen years old, they quickly started up a friendship, a friendship that turned into passionate fumblings in the dark. They kept their relationship a secret. It wasn't good form for them to be doing what they were doing. Even they knew that. But where the heart goes, the body will follow, and Gus's body followed Abela's into her bed as easily as he could count to three. Before her fifteenth birthday, Abela had missed three periods, and Gus didn't know what to do. On a whim, he decided to leave it all behind. His father. His mother. Abela. Even Mornie. He wanted out. He needed out. He envisioned himself trapped forever in poverty and anger, trapped eternally in that place where his father was trapped.

The night Abela told her father that she was pregnant with Gus's child, Gus left for good. He packed a satchel with a few clothes, a comb and $253 cash he had stolen from his father's bedside stand. In his haste, he forgot his toothbrush.

Three days later, Abela's father enacted his retribution. Gus could see the flames from four blocks away, where he was trying to hustle some guy for his wallet on a street corner. He hadn't gotten far since abandoning Abela and her fate, a seven-block radius to be exact. He was just too frightened to leave completely, too sad to leave Mornie behind. He had hopes of seeing her walking around the block one day, as she liked to do. When he caught sight of the flames, he dropped the wallet and ran toward home. What he saw would be indelibly etched in his mind.

Flames were pouring out of all those spotless windows, through the black wrought-iron bars and up into the dark sky. He looked at Mornie's bedroom window and saw his sister trapped inside, screaming and beating against the bars and trying to break them down. She wasn't screaming for help. She wasn't screaming for mercy. She was just screaming, a sound that tore the darkened night apart. Gus just watched her, unable to get near the heat of the flames and help her. Soon, Mornie was engulfed in them. Her long red hair was curled up in cinders by this time, and the skin on her hands and face began to bubble. Eventually, she dropped out of sight, and Gus knew it was over. His family was dead. Mornie was dead. And it was his fault.

»»»»»»

"Gus, it's me."

"Sorry?" he asked. They were standing on the sidewalk next to an old, abandoned brick building about a block from the coffee shop.

"It's not Uncle they're after. They attacked him to get to me, to scare me off."

"Why do you think that is?"

"It's hard to explain, but there are two men, Cameron and Quinn. One of them wants my friend dead, and one of them wants to abduct him. Neither of them like me helping my friend out."

Gus pulled a pack of Camels out of his shirt pocket and lit one. When he blew out the smoke, it went straight into Jean's face.

"Do you mind?" she said as she waved her hand through the cloud.

"And why did you decide to help someone with a price on his head?" Gus asked. He took another drag of his cigarette and this time blew it away from Jean.

"He's my boyfriend's brother. And my friend."

"You're a good girl, Jean. But you've gotten in over your head. Your friend is already dead. He might walk and talk, but he's really just biding time and waiting for his sentence to be carried out. And if they're using you and your family to get at this friend, then they'll do anything to get him. Your uncle could have died today, and there's nothing you could have done to help him. Take my advice: Stop helping your friend. Stop hiding him. And stop trying to save him. You can't save someone who's already dead."

"But you could help him. You could save him. You have connections that I don't have. You know what's going on on this side of town. I know you can help."

"But what if I don't want to help? What if I don't want to get mixed up in this?"

"Then I guess I'm wasting my time."

"Maybe. Maybe not. How willing are you to help your friend?"

"What do you mean? I'd do anything to help him."

"Anything is a lot to offer, especially to a man like me."

"Please help me, Gus. Please say you'll help."

"I'll help. But I want payment."

"I have no money," she admitted. "I'm a student."

He wrote an address down on the back of an old business card that he pulled from his wallet. Then he said, "Come to this hotel room at eight o'clock tonight, and wear your little black dress. I'll help you, Jean. But you're going to pay." He handed it to her and walked away.

She tucked the card in her purse and then looked up to see that Gus had already disappeared around a corner. *What have I done?*

CHAPTER FOURTEEN

Gary was worried. Max was sitting there with his eyes at the floor. His back was slumped, and his shoulders were heaving. He was taking in short, drastic breaths, and he seemed lost in his own visions. Tears were coursing down his cheeks. He was chewing on a hangnail, and a bit of blood had gathered at the corner of his mouth. This had been his state since Gary had read the inscription in the card.

My dearest Maximilian,
I hope you remembered this day. I certainly did.
This is the anniversary of our first date, when you came to me and we consummated our love for each other.
Love always,
Quinn

Gary was shook up from those words. What must they have done to Max?

Max was thinking about that night, the night Quinn first raped him. Hadn't Quinn told him he'd kill his mother and Gary if he were to cry and complain? He wanted to save them. So he didn't. He laid there stiff as a board, with his thin legs opened wide by Quinn's hands. And he remained that way, the way Quinn wanted him. It was always for Quinn. Everything for Quinn. But that was then, and this was now. Max knew he'd never give in to Quinn again. Not willingly. Not without a fight. He'd never let that man inside him again.

But Quinn was inside him. He was in his mind and his thoughts and his memories. What would it take to excise Quinn? What would it take to erase Quinn? What would it take to kill Quinn? He knew he had the guts to do it in the real world, but he wasn't sure how to kill the part of Quinn in his soul. They were twins in a way, stuck together in a parasitic relationship, a horrendous coupling. Quinn had control now—enough to make him cringe and cry with something as simple as a greeting card. Max hated him for this, possibly above all else. He was taking control of Max's life in a way that derailed him, denounced him and destroyed him.

Finally, Max spoke through his tears.

"That first night was so awful. All those days and nights were awful. But I guess that first night with Quinn was just so frightening. I had no idea what he was going to do to me. All I knew was that I was in a strange basement with strange people and other kids were crying through the walls. All I wanted was to come home to you and Mom. I even missed Mom's beatings then because they reminded me that all was normal and all was okay. But there, in that basement, nothing was safe. Quinn's hands were on me and rubbing me in that oil, and the worst part of it was that some part of me, some childlike part of me, liked it. It felt good to have someone caress me. It made me feel like everything was going to be okay, like it was just a blip in time and an error had been made and they'd grabbed the wrong kid. I thought they'd take me back the next day and give their apologies for having picked up the wrong kid.

"But then he was on me with his huge, hairy chest, and his dick was pressing up at me, pushing against me, forcing me open and pushing into me. I can't tell you what it did to me when he finally entered me, when he finally pushed that huge dick into me. It hurt *so bad*, Gary, like nothing I'd ever felt before. And that first time hurt like no other time afterward, like there was a hot poker searing my insides and tearing me apart and ripping me open. I tried to push him out by contracting my muscles, but I couldn't. I just couldn't. And a part of me blamed myself for not being able to push him out. Can you believe it? I blamed myself for having this man inside me, like I'd allowed it somehow by liking his hands on my body and feeling calm from him rubbing the grease. But I couldn't push him out, Gary. I couldn't push him out no matter how hard I tried. So I laid there and held back my tears because I was afraid to cry. I was afraid it could get worse. As if anything could have been worse than what was happening right then, in that room with the lights on.

"He liked the lights on, you see. He liked to watch himself in the wall mirror by the bed. I think he liked to see me just lying there still while he plugged me. Most of the men were about the size of my hand as it is now, but Quinn was larger, so much larger. And it hurt, Gary. I can't tell you how much it hurt to just lie there and take it. 'Take it like a man,' he said to me that night. 'Take it like the man I know you are.' And I did, Gary. I took it like a man. I didn't cry. No matter how much it hurt that night, I took it like a man. And there's a sick part of me, Gary. There's a sick part of me that's still proud of how I took it without tears, without crying, without whining."

His tears had stopped, as though he were recounting an event that had happened to someone else, some awful secret he'd been entrusted with, a secret that he'd held close to his heart and hadn't confided to anyone else but Gary. Gary knew this to be true, that his little brother was speaking words he'd never spoken before, words he'd never shared with anyone. And a part of Gary felt honoured that Max was finally confiding in him, finally sharing the deepest, darkest pain he'd known. But he wondered how he'd ever walk straight again after being burdened with this knowledge. And yet, another part of him, a healthier part that had roots in that day Max was abducted, had developed a rage he'd never known before that was eating at him like fire eats at kindling on a darkened winter's night. It was a good thing, this rage. He had heard somewhere that in order to heal from one's past, one must embrace the demons that live there. He was afraid, though, not for himself, for he felt he really had nothing to fear, but for Max. How could his little brother ever heal from his past?

"You want to know something?" Max asked.

Nodding was all Gary could manage. He was afraid that if he spoke, this fire inside him would consume them both.

"I don't even know if I'm gay or straight. I've never had the chance to be with a woman. I've been on the streets since I was thirteen. Homeless men don't have many chances to make love to women. And I . . . I've never even kissed a woman. I've never held one. I've never made love to one."

"Would it be so bad if you were gay, Max? I mean, would it be such a devastating sin?"

"No, of course not. I don't think there's anything wrong with being gay. But I want to know. I want to try making love to a woman at least one time in my life. But how do I know I'm not like him? Like Quinn? How do I know that after what's been done to me, I won't want little boys instead of a grown woman?"

Gary had no idea what to say, or how to comfort him. With all his training, he had no idea how to counsel him as a brother would help a brother.

"I don't want to be like that, Gary. I don't want to hurt little kids."

"There's no reason you have to, Max. There's nothing that indicates you want to, unless you think of little boys when you masturbate." Gary looked straight at his brother. So lost. So forlorn. So damaged. "Do you do that, Max? Do you think of children when you masturbate?"

"No. No, not at all."

"Then I don't think you have anything to worry about."

Knock knock knock.

"Please, we're busy at the moment," Gary called out.

"Gary," said Saundra, "it's time for the town hall."

"Shit," he murmured under his breath. "Okay, come in."

»

Jean left work early without giving any excuse. She grabbed her purse from the back room and looked at herself in the mirror that hung on one of the crew lockers. *God, I am getting so thin,* she thought. Though she knew she had to go to the doctor—and soon—Auntie and Uncle didn't have a lot of cash to spring for it right now. And lord knows she didn't have the money herself. What was the cost of a doctor nowadays, anyway? She had no idea. But she also suspected that it wouldn't be just one doctor visit. No one lost this amount of weight in such a short span of time without something being desperately wrong. And that's what really kept her from going: the fear that something awful and irreversible was wrong with her and it would take test after mysterious, expensive test to get to the truth. *Cancer. It's probably cancer—of the cervix, most likely.*

It had started one morning after breakfast. She was sitting at the table digesting the oatmeal that Auntie had made her when, without warning, she felt the urge to vomit. She scurried up the stairs trying not to alarm Auntie, who had just sat to eat her own breakfast. She almost made it to the bathroom in time, but not quite; there was a mess to clean up off the floor. She puked until it felt like her insides were ripping out, like the threads that tied her stomach to her intestines had suddenly been shredded and were coming up her throat, into her mouth and down the toilet.

That day was just the beginning.

Before long, she was feeling a dull pain in her sides that crescendoed into intensely sharp stabs.

"You have to eat more, girl," Auntie had said to her one morning after she'd pushed her breakfast away. "You're thin as a rake."

And she was. Though she hadn't noticed it until then, Auntie was right. She was wasting away before the mirror, sinking into herself, disappearing into the gloom that was slowly becoming her life. What was happening to her?

Then, one day, Auntie asked her whether she was vomiting on purpose. "What are you doing to yourself?" she asked as one hand caressed the side of Jean's face and then turned it this way and that. "I'm not doing anything, Auntie. It's just because it's spring. I always lose some weight in the spring," she lied. She kissed Auntie on the top of her head and breezed out the door.

"We're going to have to get you to a doctor," Auntie called out after her. But Jean knew it was an impossibility because of the money. Doctors cost a lot of it. Too much of Uncle's money went to Gus, Jean suspected, for how else could the shop be so busy and they still live like paupers?

Jean stood at the entrance of The Mission waiting to be admitted.

"We're in the middle of a town hall meeting, miss," said the gatekeeper. "But you're welcome to sit in on it and wait for Gary there." He buzzed her in and directed her to the cafeteria.

She opened the door quietly just as Gary looked up to see her coming into the room. The cafeteria was a long, narrow room with tables and chairs standing along the length of the space. All the chairs were occupied by clients and staff, and coffee cups and small plates with the ends of desserts on them were scattered about. The clinking of coffee cups on the table sounded a bit like wind chimes. Jean gently closed the door behind her. She waved a little wave at Gary and crept along the side wall until she stood beside a woman dressed in jeans and a light-coloured shirt, whom Gary and Max knew as Eloise.

"But can you tell us more about why anyone would want to kill Donovan?" she asked Gary.

"Because he was a faggot," Maynard catcalled from the middle of the room.

"There's no need for that kind of language, Maynard," scolded Gary. "The police have no reason to believe that Donovan was murdered because of his sexuality, whatever it may have been."

"Maybe he tried to touch the wrong person, someone who wasn't afraid to fight back," Maynard called out.

"And maybe your homosexual panic button is too obvious for any of us to take you seriously," said Zachary.

"Thanks for adding that bit of reality, Zachary," added Eloise.

"Ah, shut up, Eloise. No one wants to hear from you," said Maynard.

Gary had fire in his eyes. "Okay, Maynard. That's it. One more word out of you and—"

"And what?"

"You'll be kicked out on your ass," added Zachary.

"I see that this is going nowhere fast," whispered a voice in Jean's ear. She jumped and turned to see Max at her side.

"Oh, it's you, Max," she said.

Max winced. "You have to call me David in here. No one knows I'm Gary's brother. They all think I'm just another homeless client."

"Right. Sorry, uh, David."

"I didn't know you were coming."

"I wasn't. I mean, I didn't know about the meeting. I was just coming to pass the time with you and Gary for a while. I'm still creeped out over the body in the alleyway. Plus, I can't ride home with you two tonight. I'll have to meet you at the apartment later."

"Why is that?"

"I have to pick up some stuff at the library for school."

"We'll come with you."

"There's no need for that. I'll be fine. I'll meet you there. Besides, the library will be closed by the time Gary gets off work."

"Why do you have to do so much for school when it's summer? Don't you ever take a break?"

"I'm in graduate school, and I'm working on my thesis. There's never any rest with a thesis breathing down your neck."

"Want to see the card I got today? It's very thoughtful. It's from Quinn." He handed it over and watched her face turn from tense to horrified as she read it.

"My god, Max—er, David. Why would he play such a game?"

"Today is the anniversary of the day they abducted me. He believes wholeheartedly in what he's writing. I told you, he loves me and he thinks I love him, too."

"But to send this . . . it's just cruel."

"Not in his eyes. In his eyes it's a love note to his beloved."

"Jesus, David. How are you handling this?"

"I've had better days. First Donovan. Now this card. It's hard to understand why all this is happening. It feels like Donovan's murder is all my fault."

"But it isn't. And you can't blame yourself for it. All you did was try to make a friend. It's Quinn who did this, Quinn who sent you this card. It's his fault, not—"

"Could you two in the back please take your conversation outside the room?" ordered Saundra. "We haven't finished the meeting, in case you were too busy to notice."

Jean's face went red with embarrassment over the chastisement. She wasn't used to being singled out in a group, and being singled out to be called to order was a deep shame for her. She hung her head for a moment and then lifted it to Max's.

"Look, I've got to run," she said, careful to keep her voice to a whisper. "Please tell Gary that I'll be at the apartment as soon as I'm done at the library."

"Sure thing." He hugged her quickly, and as she walked away, he thought about how that hug sent a shiver down his spine.

»»

When she arrived at home, the lights were off. She was thankful that both Auntie and Uncle were out. Uncle must've still been at the coffee shop, and it was Auntie's card night. She and her friends played cards at each other's homes on a rotating basis, and obviously it wasn't her turn to host the other ladies. She unlocked the door, removed her shoes and climbed the staircase to her room.

It was just as she'd left it. Her bed was unmade. Numerous pieces of clothing, mostly dresses, were slung across the bed, the nightstand and the chair beside her pink vanity. She picked up a black dress, removed what she had on and wriggled into it. It hung off of her like a drape hanging off a window and looked ridiculous.

Oh well. I can't do any better than this, she thought. She gathered some more makeup and stuffed it into the case in her little red purse.

She sat down at her little pink vanity table. Uncle had bought it for her about six years prior, when she first landed on their doorstep, as a kind of welcome gift. He and Auntie worked so hard back then to make her feel at home in their three-bedroom house. Uncle purchased her gifts he thought a girl should have, while Auntie combined her sewing room and her cold cellar (which wasn't really a cold cellar but a bedroom at the back of the first floor) to free up a bedroom. They had no children of their own, and they treated her as though she were their own blood, their own child, their own gift from heaven.

Jean rounded out her cheeks by downplaying her cheekbones and applied lightener to the bags under her eyes. At last, she searched for the bag from Village Stationary. Despite the fact that she was angered by what she was about to do with Gus, she was excited to begin lessons with Max the following night.

She knew deep inside that Gary could be hurt by her actions tonight—severely hurt. But she had no choice, right? She had to do whatever was in her power to save Max, to save them all, and this was something she could do. What was one indiscretion when it could help so much? But it was no small indiscretion. It was huge. She was going to betray his trust, the fragile trust that was growing between them. Sexing Gus could destroy Gary, for all she knew. And it definitely threatened to destroy her. She pushed all the emotion away and banished the fear of what was about to happen into the nether reaches of her mind. But the guilt she felt was overwhelming, frightening and impassable.

Before leaving the house, Jean wrote a note to Auntie.

Auntie,

I brought my friend Gary by to meet you tonight, but I forgot it was your card night. I'll bring him by again soon.

Love,

Jean

She left it on the kitchen table, where Auntie was sure to find it.

»»»

When the meeting was over, Max walked to the front of the room and waited for the crowd that had formed around Gary and Saundra to thin.

Finally, Gary turned to him and said, "That didn't go so well, did it?"

"Not really. There's a lot of fear flying around this place. I hope you can manage it."

"That's why I went to school for six years. And Saundra and I, we have each other in this. It's what we do. There's always a crisis to handle."

"Hey, where's Jean? I thought I saw her here."

"She had to run off to the library to pick up some stuff. She'll meet us at the apartment later."

"I'm not sure I like her being off by herself."

"I tried to talk her out of it, but it was a no-go."

"I guess we'll have to live with it. I'm beginning to think Jean does what she wants when she wants. But her walking out there alone with Quinn having just killed someone . . . I don't like it much."

"I don't either."

When Gary had finished his shift and The Mission was beginning to bed down for the night, he and Max headed for home.

The subway ride was uneventful, but neither of them could dispel the fear for Jean that was slowly twisting a knot in their guts.

She'll be all right, Gary assured himself. *She's a strong, smart woman who knows her way around the city. She'll be all right. She has to be.*

»»»»»

When Jean arrived at Gus's location, she hesitated. It wasn't the best part of town: a darkened street in Brooklyn that housed some five-story flats, a bodega or two, and a motel. The address was that of the motel, which had seen better days. She walked the length of the building until she came to room number thirty-four.

This was the last moment she still could walk away from Gus, his nasty intentions and the desire he obviously felt for her. How long had he harboured these ideas? How long had he wanted to have sex with her, to let himself loose upon her and inside her like a feral cat?

She didn't want it. She didn't want any bit of it—not his urge, not his desire, not any part of him, especially his penis. That was something she definitely didn't want any part of. But she had to do it, for Max, for Gary and for herself. She had to protect them in the ways that she could.

Finally, she knocked on the door just to get it over with. He answered wearing a pair of loose Adidas shorts and an undershirt—nothing else. He placed one hand on the doorframe above and leaned forward. Dull yellow light spilled onto the step.

"Hi, Gus," she said, looking up at him straight in the eye.

"Hello, Jean. You came. I wasn't sure you would."

"I always keep my word."

"Even when it means betraying your boyfriend."

"Especially when it means *saving* my boyfriend."

"So that's what this is about: Florence Nightingale ministering to her mate, attempting to keep him alive with whatever means she possesses." He laughed, not unkindly.

"That's right. Now, will you invite me in, or are we going to do it out here on the lawn?"

Gus looked over her shoulder at the street beyond.

"I could be tempted," he said with an uncharacteristic smirk.

"I couldn't," she retorted as she slipped under his arm and entered the room.

The place was a pigsty. At one end of the room was a single-sized bed that was obviously hastily made. Newspapers were strewn about, each opened to a different section—some to the business page, some to entertainment, most to sports. Styrofoam cups were perched on the small table in the corner of the room, the dresser and the bedside table. Takeout containers still containing vestiges of food were scattered around. Beyond the room was a small kitchenette with an apartment-sized refrigerator, an electric coffee pot that looked like it could make two cups at a time and even a small microwave. Dirty dishes were piled sky-high in the sink. The dim yellow light was cast about the room by a single lamp that stood on the bedside table. Jean had guessed correctly that this motel catered to long-term residents rather than overnight passersby gliding through town.

Jean turned to face him and said, "Do you live here, Gus?"

"I do."

"Nice pad." This is what you always say when you walk into someone's place.

"It's home."

"I've never done this before," Jean admitted.

"You're a virgin?" asked Gus, delight registering on his face.

"I didn't mean that. I meant that I've never paid for anything with sex."

"There's always a first time. And sometimes more than that. It's like marriage: A woman pays her husband with sex for upkeep and protection. It's just sex. Nothing to worry about, nothing to write home about—unless it's great sex. But it usually isn't when it's done like this."

"Then why do you want it if it's not so hot?"

"I didn't say it couldn't be hot."

"Well, if it's not great, then why do men go to prostitutes for it?" she asked, genuinely curious for his answer.

"It is what it is. And it fills a hole."

Jean raised an eyebrow. "Nicely put."

"That's not what I meant. I meant that it fulfills a need that is always there, always eating at me.

"So let's get it over with, then."

"How romantic."

"I'm not looking for romance—just sex."

He pulled off his undershirt, exposing thick, red hair that travelled from his manly nipples down to his navel and disappeared into his Adidas.

Jean began to slowly pull her dress up and over her head. She stood there in her bra and panties wondering what she should do next. She didn't like standing there like that, exposed and desperate, but there was no other way to feel. Gus was obviously not a romantic man, but at the moment, Jean wasn't sure whether romance would have made the moment easier. Probably not.

Gus pulled down his shorts and kicked them off with his feet. His penis was short and thick, but she knew from her limited experience that those things could grow much larger than their initial appearance. His eyes focused in on her body, and his face dropped, his mouth hanging open.

"Christ! What's wrong with you? Do you have AIDS or something?"

"I don't!" she cried as she grabbed her dress from the floor and held it up against her ugly ribs and wasted hips.

"Are you anorexic? I had a girlfriend once who was, but she never looked as bad as you."

"You're so charming. Every girl likes to hear that she's hideous."

"I'm not trying to hurt you. I'm just shocked. What *is* wrong with you, Jean?"

Tears of frustration and anger and fear welled up inside her, and she couldn't hold them back, not in front of this almost-complete stranger, this man who stole her uncle's money and wanted her sex in payment for his protection. She dropped the dress, put her hands up to her face and cried into them. Her shoulders bounced up and down with each intake of breath, and snot ran out of her nose.

"Here," said Gus, surprisingly kindly. "Take these." He handed her a few tissues from a box on the table. She wiped her eyes and blew her nose. Suddenly she stopped crying almost at once. It was as though someone had turned off the taps behind her eyes.

"I'm sorry, Gus." She didn't know why she was apologizing, but it felt like the right thing to do. "I don't know what's wrong with me, and I can't go to the doctor."

"Why can't you go to the doctor?"

"We have no insurance, and Uncle can't afford to send me because he pays you so much money."

Gus looked anguished—horrified, really. And guilty. Surely she saw guilt in his eyes. He looked down and to the side of her to evade her gaze resting upon his eyes. Still, he handed her more tissues as if they could solve her problems, at least in the moment.

"I can't have sex with you now," he said.

"Because I'm so ugly?" she spat out.

"No, because I'm so sad."

"You? Sad?" In all her thoughts of Gus over the years, she'd never imagined him getting sad.

"Do you want to try this another night?" asked Jean. She was intent on getting her payment over and done with as soon as possible.

"No."

"Why not?" she asked almost petulantly.

Gus had been here before, in this "place of no return," as he sometimes thought of it. Once he got close to a woman, there was no turning back; he would forever retain that closeness with her, which was a frightening thing for him. He didn't like getting close to women, especially not as quickly as he had with Jean. Then again, it wasn't quick with Jean either. How long had he known her? Several years now. He had slowly come to know her over that time. And now there was no return from it.

"Because I've seen your heart—here, tonight," answered Gus. "I can't have sex with a woman once I've seen her heart." He looked down at the green carpeted floor.

"You can't have sex with a woman who has touched you with her heart?"

"No."

"That's so sad, Gus. You must be filled with sadness." She pulled her dress on over her head. When her head emerged, she noticed his gaze was still fixed at the same spot, so she went to him.

She reached up, placed her hand on his heart and said, "I hope you heal this, Gus. I truly hope you find a way to heal."

"I do, too."

She reapplied her makeup and then left Gus alone, a damaged heart in an empty room thinking about his future.

»»»»»

It was early evening, and Maynard was walking one of his favourite streets, Avenue B along Tompkins Square Park, toward the alleyway where he liked to sleep. The park was one of those green Manhattan oases, a patch of nature in a jungle of concrete. He decided to take a few moments' respite from the unbearable heat and sit in the park.

He entered the park through one of its many pathways, found a bench and sat his bulky butt down. *Whew. This heat is going to kill me before long*, he thought. Soon his mind wandered—as he was prone to let it—over the day's happenings. First there was finding the dead faggot's body in the alleyway. Yes, it was he who'd found Donovan. Thrilled with the news of a drama in the making, he'd rushed in to tell the only person he could find: that damned nigger Zachary. Then Zachary took over, as he always did, for he loved to be the one in control of a situation. But he wasn't much in control, was he? Maynard chuckled to himself. There he'd stood at the front of the swelling group holding his arms out and telling everyone there was nothing to see, when clearly there was. And the crowd didn't listen at all. He kept everyone back for a few moments. But as soon as there were enough of them, they swarmed past him to get a good, solid look at the cut up body that lay there. Maynard chuckled again, this time louder. He really got a good kick out of it. Then there were those endless conversations about the whole thing in the halls and in the classrooms, and there was that fiasco of a town hall meeting. Who did they think they were trying to fool? The police knew a lot more than they were letting on. They always did.

He heard a rustling in the wind. It sounded like newspaper. And then the wind did it again. But there was no wind. Strange . . .

Maynard turned to look behind him but saw nothing of interest. Then came the sound again, a little bit closer and to the left this time. He twisted his body around and looked the other way.

"Who the fuck is it?" he called out with as much rancour as he could muster. No one answered. The rustling sounded again.

"Who's there?" he called out, his voice slightly shaky.

Maynard wasn't a man prone to fear, though. He took life as it came and spat it back out. Care be taken by anyone in his way. Even as a boy, he had been one to be reckoned with. His foul mouth and racist charm made him enemies as quick as they made him friends. He attracted more than a few who wanted the protection of his forceful ways and his vicious tongue. Even at The Mission he had his followers.

"You've been spouting your mouth off, Maynard," a voice called out from a stand of bushes. "You've been a very bad boy."

He spun around and gripped the back of the bench tight. "Who are you, you sick fuck?"

"I'm the one who's going to teach you a lesson."

Maynard felt a cold shiver down to his toes. Every fibre of his being went numb in fear, a feeling he wasn't used to and didn't quite recognize at first. His mind began to race. What to do? He knew he wasn't a fast runner. He had a big gut and never exercised, except if you were to count walking from the subway to his destination as quickly as possible. What reason did he have to exercise anyway? The streets would kill him long before a heart attack ever would. Then he thought of Donovan. Maybe the streets would get their revenge tonight. But he didn't want to go now. Not like Donovan. Not like that faggot out back in the alleyway.

A thought struck him: Maybe if he'd been nicer, this wouldn't be happening tonight. . . . But he didn't believe in fate. He didn't believe in karma. He did believe in retribution, and if this were that sicko with copper hair who offed Donovan, then he didn't stand a chance. So he stood up and turned to face the voice.

"Okay then. Show yourself."

Then the man with the copper-coloured hair tore himself away from the shadows. In his hand he held a long, sharp knife.

»»»»»»

Gary buzzed Jean into the building and met her at the apartment door. She heard him unlocking it and sliding back the chain, and then he was there, silhouetted against the glare of the lights inside. She flung herself at him, wrapping her arms around his chest and burying her head into his blue shirt. She began to cry out the frustration, the anger, the hurt, the embarrassment that had transpired in Gus's rundown motel room. But her illness had saved her from having to give her recompense for his protection.

"Hey, what's wrong?" he asked. He tilted her head up to his face with his hand. "Has something happened? Did you meet Quinn?"

"No, it's nothing," she blurted out.

"Then why so many tears?"

"I'm just relieved to see you. Both of you." She looked around and past him at Max. "You're safe and sound."

"Everyone's fine here. At least step inside." He closed the door behind her and locked it. "Have you had dinner? I just ordered pizza."

"I'm starved. Why didn't you eat at The Mission?"

"Too worked up, I guess. I had no appetite after the meeting."

After dinner arrived and all the pizza was eaten, Gary and Jean bade Max good night and slipped away into Gary's room. Once the door was shut, he took her in his arms and made love to her slowly, gently, but with an urgency at the end that surprised him. In the midst of the passion, he was nudged by intruding thoughts of his earlier conversation with Max. *He's never made love. He's never had the chance. He's missed all this. The only thing he's experienced is rape and abuse.* He tried to banish the thoughts, but they kept creeping up on him, testing him, demanding him to listen. When he was finished, he rolled off of Jean and lay down beside her.

"Gary?" she said.

"Yes?" he answered, though his mind was still on Max's inexperience.

"I'm not really done."

"You didn't cum?"

"Not enough. My thoughts kept bothering me."

"Mine, too."

And then a thought struck him, and he knew it to be true.

"Jean?" he asked.

"Yes?"

"How much do you trust me?"

"With all my heart."

"Is there anything I could ask of you that would make you hate me?"

"No. I don't think so. I could always say no, but I wouldn't hate you for asking."

"Would you go to Max? Please?"

"What? You can't be serious."

"Please. While you're still excited and wanting more. Would you let him finish you off?"

For a moment, Jean was shocked and angry. How could Gary ask such a thing? Was he wanting to parcel her out like a pimp? Then, a small thought intruded upon the affront: This was something she wanted. She couldn't deny it. She was attracted to Max's blond curls and bad-boy attitude more than she cared to admit.

"That's a strange thing to ask of your girlfriend," she said.

"He's never made love to a woman. He's never had the chance living on the streets. The only thing he knows is being raped by

Quinn and a whole cadre of other men. I want you to do this. For me. And for him."

Jean lay there thinking of the events of the night. She'd been so willing to have sex with Gus to protect Max just a few hours before. Was this any different? *It's different because I want to do this*, she thought. And so, she kissed Gary on the lips long and soft and then got up quietly and walked out the bedroom door.

»»»»»»»

Max was almost asleep when Jean sat on the edge of the futon.

He popped his eyes open and let them focus. "Jean?"

"Shhh," she said, pressing her finger to his lips.

She placed her hand on his chest. His blond hair grew in thickets there, and she ran her fingers through it. Shivers ran down his spine, just like earlier when he hugged her at The Mission. Her hand was so warm. She reached her other hand up to cup his cheek and then leaned down and kissed him. Max reached up and tangled his hand in her hair to pull her closer. She kissed him with a desperate passion, her tongue slinking in and out of his mouth. He followed suit, and soon their mouths were filled with each other, saliva passing back and forth. He felt her hand reaching down and into his pants, and she squeezed his hardness. It was like nothing he'd ever felt before, and he was afraid that he'd never feel it again.

She lay down beside him and pressed her body against his. He felt her breasts touching his chest, her nipples hard and taut. He moved his hand from her hair and cupped one breast, massaging it, kneading it, pinching her nipple softly between his fingers. He twisted onto his side, pressed his body against hers and pulled her tightly toward him. His kisses began moving down her neck and tentatively toward her breasts. He took each one into his mouth, one after the other. He was so damned nervous, but he continued anyway. She moaned softly, and he heard her breath began to quicken. He propped himself up on one elbow and slid down and across her abdomen to the dark patch between her thighs. It was damp, probably from Gary making love to her moments before. His tongue caressed her soft lips. Then he licked her deeply, tasting the sweet, salty, wet crevice. He licked at her clitoris. She grabbed his head and thrust her hips up and against his face. Evidently that was the right spot. So he continued and continued, and she came in little orgasms.

"Enough. That's enough. Now, Max. Now," she pleaded.

He straightened up until he was on his hands leaning over her, his whole body trembling. He tried several times to enter her but kept missing. Finally, she reached down and guided him in. He began rocking in and out, in and out. In truth, it was only a few moments stolen from his life before he came deep inside her. Without removing himself, he reached down and caressed her clitoris with his thumb. His hands fumbled a bit with excitement, but he kept with the motion until she came again, this time hard— really hard. She bit into his chest to prevent herself from screaming, so hard that she drew blood, though Max didn't feel a thing. Finally, he withdrew from her, dripping with her cum and his own, and lay on the bed beside her. After they caught their breath, he spoke.

"Did Gary send you out here?"

"Does it matter?"

"Yes. I don't want him to know if he doesn't already."

"He does, Max. He sent me out."

She kissed him hard and went back to Gary's bedroom, leaving him to the dark, noisy night.

CHAPTER FIFTEEN

In the morning, Gary woke first and crawled out of bed. He watched Jean lying in his bed, resplendent in her beauty. She didn't have a shower before bed, so she still had her makeup on, which hid the hollows of her cheeks and the bags under her eyes. But there was no hiding her rib cage or her pelvis or her thin legs. His eyes travelled up her body, drinking in every inch of it. She was more than beautiful; she was his.

But was she anymore? His mind went to the night before. It was his choice to ask her to go out to his little brother, his inexperienced little brother who had cried in his office and divulged his fears surrounding his sexuality. But from what Gary had heard in the other room, he wasn't inexperienced anymore. Though Gary had felt like he was giving Max a gift, he now wondered whether it was such a good idea. It seemed like one at the time, but he couldn't shake this niggling feeling that gnawed at his heart this morning. Of course she was his. She came back to *his* bed after having sex with Max. Or did they make love? There's a huge difference between having sex and making love. And did he really want them to make love? Or did he want her to have sex with him? He wasn't sure anymore.

"Why are you just standing there? You look worried," Jean said as she drifted up from sleep and opened her eyes.

"Just thinking about Quinn and everything going on, that's all."

He couldn't tell her the truth. Not now. He remembered suddenly that there had been no real hesitation in her getting up and walking through that door to Max. She did it on her own free will, because he asked, and she accepted. She wouldn't have done it without his request. Or would she? Was her making love to Max, or having sex or whatever it was, inevitable? Gary wanted to show Max how loving and intimate sex can really be. He'd asked Jean with a straight face and love in his heart, though he had to admit that he'd opened the door a crack and listened to them and it tore a tiny, little hole in his chest. But of course it would tear a little hole, no matter how unselfish the sacrifice.

That's what it was, he realized now: a sacrifice, however small. He'd sacrificed a small amount of himself to give this gift to Max. How much of a sacrifice had it been for Jean? What if it hadn't been a sacrifice at all? What then? He didn't want to think about that possibility.

Was this jealousy he was feeling?

"Come back to bed, my love," Jean said.

"Oh, '*my love*'?" he said. A twinkle in his eye replaced the tension in his face.

"Yes, *my love*. Because that's what you are. That's what you are to me." She lifted the covers, and he crawled back into bed.

"Tell me something," he said.

"Yes?"

"Did you enjoy yourself? Last night, with Max?" Though he was afraid of her answer, he needed to know. He wasn't sure why, but he needed her answer. She hesitated, as though thinking about how to word her response. She trailed her fingers across his chest and played with the hair that grew there.

"Yes," she said finally. "Yes, I did."

"You had to tell me that, didn't you?" His body stiffened as he thought about her answer.

"Well, you asked."

"But I wanted to hear that it was a chore, something you only did because you had to. Not that you enjoyed it."

"Max is attractive. I won't deny that. And though he was nervous as hell, he is a gentle lover. Every girl would enjoy that."

"And am I a gentle lover?"

"Gary, you're different than Max. You can't compare yourself to him. I don't compare the two of you, and you shouldn't either. Not now; not with everything going on. You and Max are brothers. Even if you weren't, you couldn't expect me to compare the two of you. I won't play this game of jealousy. If I'd known that you'd react like this, I never would have agreed. I would have stayed with you, because it's you I love."

"You love me?" he asked incredulously. He hadn't thought about his feelings for her up until this point, but if he had to pin them down, he'd admit that he felt something for her he'd never felt before. But wasn't that what he was thinking just this morning as he walked to work? Maybe he thought about it more than he realized. Was that love? Maybe it was. He didn't know, since he'd never been in love before.

"Yes, I think I do," she answered.

"How long have you known?"

"A few days at least. It happened fast. The night before last, when we made love the first time, was the first time I admitted it to myself."

"Do you always fall in love so fast?"

"You say it like I've felt this before. I haven't. In fact, I've had remarkably little sex. You're the first man I've ever fallen in love with."

His body finally relaxed. "I like that. I like that a lot," he murmured as his lips found hers. And then, before he knew it, they were making love again.

When it was over, they crawled into the shower together, Gary having set the water temperature before letting her climb in. They took turns soaping each other up with a facecloth and the soap he'd bought at the market.

"Jean?"

"Hmmm?"

"What is this about?" he asked, running his hand down her ribs, across her pelvis and back up again. "Are you anorexic?"

"Why does everyone think that?"

"Because something is clearly wrong. Something is off. You don't have the personality traits of an anorexic, but I can't think of what else it could be."

She slapped him with the wet cloth—hard—and it stung.

"Why does everyone think I'm doing that to myself? Huh? Why do you think I hate myself so much that I'd starve myself to death?"

"I don't know of any other explanations. What else would decimate your body like this?"

"I don't know."

"You don't know? How can you not know? You must have been to a doctor by now."

"I haven't," she said as she turned away from him. "Now quit asking questions and wash my back, please."

"But you're wasting away! It could be anything. It could be cancer even," he said, voicing her greatest fear. He wrung out the facecloth, soaped it up again and then leaned over slightly to wash her back.

"It's not cancer, silly."

"How can you know if you haven't been to the doctor?"

"I just know. It can't be. Besides, I don't have insurance."

"What?"

"I have no medical insurance. My uncle can't afford it."

"You haven't been to a doctor, because you don't have insurance?!" he almost screamed at her. "Can't you just pay the doctor?"

Now she was angry. "With what money?" she spat. "I'm a student, Gary. I work in a coffee shop. How much money do you think I have?"

"I guess I wasn't thinking."

"I guess you weren't."

"I'm sorry, Jean."

He was sorry about more than what he'd said. He was sorry about her situation. She was like his clients at work: None of them had insurance, so none of them could go to the doctor. That's why they had doctors who volunteered their time at The Mission to treat the homeless, to diagnose their ailments and give them medical assistance, to call on their doctor friends for favours with tests and procedures and other things Gary didn't know. Even his clients had access to as much medical treatment as The Mission could provide. But Jean? She didn't even have that. She was caught in that netherworld of medical care, that place in America where so many people were caught: without insurance, without answers, without care, without hope.

Neither of them said much as they dried off. Gary thought about Jean being caught between the poverty-stricken and the middle class, caught in the working poor. They had escaped the dangers and the pitfalls of the most desperate in society, but they struggled daily to maintain their position, to ensure they didn't fall through the cracks and descend again into their greatest fears:

having no food, no home, no life. And they had all of the trappings of the middle class: too many worries, not enough vacation pay and not enough health insurance.

Gary was one of the lucky ones. He'd been slated to be one of the working poor, but he'd escaped through chance, education and sheer determination. He hadn't been saddled with kids by age eighteen. He hadn't been plagued with a debilitating illness he couldn't control. No, he had crawled up with his teeth and his nails to a first-rate education. He now had health care through his work, but he knew how precarious his situation was. If he were to lose his job, then he'd lose his health care, and he wouldn't be able to afford it with his meagre savings.

As for Jean, Gary now had an idea. However brave he needed to be, it was an idea that could work.

»

Max woke to the sound of voices, harsh voices, coming from Gary's room. *Oh, God. They're fighting. Probably over me and last night,* he thought. He pulled the blanket up over his head, but the voices travelled through it.

What a night he'd had. Jean. Beautiful Jean. She'd come to him and taken him to a place he'd never been before. What did it mean, her coming to him in the darkened night? That she loved him? No, that Gary loved him. It was Gary who sent her to him. Gary loved him, not Jean. And in the light of day, it didn't matter who loved him last night. What mattered was that someone did. Gary loved him enough to send her to him. And Max had enough love for Gary and Jean. That's what mattered. He had enough love to share with both of them. He had enough love, and that was a miracle. Enough love. Enough of himself to share, to give and to explore.

He wasn't gay. He'd proved that to himself last night. Would it be so bad if he were? No, it wouldn't. Donovan was probably gay, and it didn't matter to Max. He knew enough about the world to know that the men who'd used him and abused him when he was young weren't gay. They were child molesters, and that was a violence, not a sexuality. None of them were interested in maintaining a healthy, loving relationship with an adult male. No. They were interested in abusing boys, and possibly girls.

If he were interested in adult males, wouldn't he have tried to get something going with Donovan? Wouldn't he have tried to court that man? Donovan was attractive enough. Max could discern that. He wasn't that much older. And he seemed to have been slowly on his way up and out of homelessness, like Zachary. But Max never even wanted to begin anything with Donovan.

Then along came Jean. This little spitfire, this powerhouse of energy and veracity and integrity had come to him in the night. It didn't matter that Gary had lent her to him for his pleasure. He knew that Gary meant well, that Gary meant to help him. Still, with the sound of their argument reaching his ears this morning, how was he ever going to face them? He didn't have to wonder for long, because they entered the living room momentarily.

"Up and at 'em, sunshine!" called Gary, announcing their arrival.

Max sat up.

From their wet hair dripping down the sides of their necks, Max surmised they had already showered. Gary was glowing. Max had heard about that look before. People in love wore that look. He had his arm around Jean's shoulders, and she was absolutely radiant. Whatever they had argued about, they had worked out their differences and now seemed completely, totally in love. A sadness crept into Max's heart, displacing the joy he'd felt moments before. He was happy for them, sure, but a part of him still wanted

Jean, still wanted to hold her close, to keep her for his own. But from the looks on their faces and their body language, it looked like that would never happen. They were in love—that was apparent. He should be happy for his brother. And he was, but he wasn't.

"What are the plans for the day?" asked Max. He expected Gary to answer, but Jean was the first to speak.

"I have to go into the shop for an errand for my uncle," she lied with that smile still plastered on her face.

"I thought we'd stick together today, given everything that's happening," countered Gary as he looked down at her.

"I can't get out of this, Gary. I'm sorry. I still have to take care of my responsibilities."

"Then we'll come with you."

"No, you won't. The last thing I need is my uncle questioning me about the two of you. Now, let's get ourselves fed and get on with our day. I'll meet you at The Mission as soon as I'm done. It's only two blocks away; nothing's going to happen."

"Do I have any say in this?" asked Max.

"No, you don't," they said unanimously. All three of them laughed. Max got up from the futon. He kept his back to them while he dressed, pulling a clean shirt over his head and pushing his legs through a pair of jeans. Gary's living room doubled well as a bedroom for Max, but it didn't afford him much privacy. He then opened the patio doors wide to let in the moist morning air.

With a deafening thud, the apartment door burst open, and Quinn was standing in the doorway.

»»

The first thing Gus did when he woke that morning was masturbate. He thought about Jean—a different Jean, one without indentations and crooked angles where flesh should be, one with a little meat on her bones. When he was finished, he got up, showered and poured himself a bowl of Shreddies.

While eating his breakfast, he wondered what he was getting into. The girl had explained the whole story about the boy who'd found and was now being chased by a madman, and his brother, whom she'd fallen in love with. She didn't use the word "love," but he saw it in her eyes, heard it from her lips, watched it in the way she held her arms close to her as she spoke. Yes, she was in love with this boy, and a part of him was angry that he hadn't been able to interrupt that, to break that by taking her roughly in his arms and then roughly in his bed. On the other hand, a more nobler part of him believed that he was put in her life to help her, not to fuck her. He usually pushed that noble part of himself to the side when it reared. He wasn't a noble man—never had been, never would be.

But he had a job to do, and it was to kill Quinn.

This wasn't the sort of job he usually took. For starters, he usually got paid. A lot. And he usually worked for husbands who had something going on the sly and wanted to off their wives because they saw no way out of a marriage that condemned them to a life of misery. It wasn't his place to ask questions, though he sometimes did. When that noble side came to the fore, he tried to talk them out of it, mostly to no avail. Days, or even weeks, later, he'd read in the paper about a murder in Queens or Brooklyn or Long Island and recognize the bereaved husband as someone he thought he'd talked some sense into. They always found another hand to hire when they were intent on changing their lives— branching out, as it were. And then he'd be sorry, not for the dead wife lying on her kitchen floor—he never felt sorry for people he'd never met—but for himself and the money he'd missed out on. That was why he usually pushed his conscience aside and simply took the job, no questions asked. It was a foregone conclusion anyway. And he liked the money.

He was saving his money in seven different bank accounts. He knew he had a lot at the moment: over four million dollars. That kind of money would go a long way in other countries. He'd earned it the hard way, the very hard way. And it was earning interest even as he sat and ate his Shreddies. It was money he'd saved by living cheaply, in dirty motels in the worst parts of town. He was saving it so that one day, one day soon, he could get away. Like some of his clients with their insurance money they'd won through their hard decisions, he wanted to leave this stinking hellhole of a city that he hated. It had been good to him, there was no denying it, but he wanted to leave nevertheless. Jamaica. Mexico. The Dominican Republic. Peru—especially Peru. He'd always wanted to climb the trail up the steeply rising mountainside to the ancient Inca city of Machu Picchu that was so beautifully preserved. He'd seen pictures so long ago and fallen in love with the idea of that bright, golden city in the early-morning light. And at the age of forty-four, having never smoked a single cigarette in his life, he knew he could master the Machu Picchu trail. If all those pretty boys at the gym could master the StairMaster, then he could conquer that trail.

He dressed slowly, taking his time. There was no reason to hurry. He grabbed his black leather gloves from the chair on which he'd placed them the week before after a job. Then he opened his nightstand drawer, pulled out his Glock 19, stuffed it into his waistband and covered it with his untucked T-shirt.

He had some grocery shopping to do early this morning. Then he would be ready to meet Jean.

»»»

The first thought that burst through Max's mind was that his knife was under his pillow, where he could reach it quickly during the night but not now. This is where he'd always kept it while living on the street, no matter what he was using as a pillow. The second thought, the one that caught his breath in his chest and wouldn't let it go, was that Quinn had his own blade, a sharp blade similar in length to his, and it was dangling by his side in his hand. Max looked up to see that the doorframe was splintered, and the lock was twisted. *God, his strength.* All this he thought in an instant, before anyone else had had a chance to move.

Gary reacted quickly, lunging forward to try and slam the door in Quinn's face, but Quinn raised one hand and pushed hard against the door, his strong forearms straining. With one great shove, he threw it open and stepped over the threshold.

"The famous Gary," he spat. "So you're the one who's tied up my Maximilian." Pure hatred radiated from his eyes.

Max was incredibly relieved that Gary wasn't alone in the apartment. Surely, Quinn would have killed him. *Might still kill him if he gets a chance—if we don't all die here this morning,* he thought.

Quinn stalked into the room and stopped to face them. Gary was unwilling to move until he could take better stalk of the situation. Jean was at the end of the hallway. Max was still standing by the balcony, feeling the morning breeze on his neck. Quinn lifted up his knife and caressed the sharp blade with one finger.

"So, who's going to be first?" he said. "The protective big brother who's lucky he wasn't picked up himself that day in the park? Or the little fucking Chink whore who uses the smell of her stinking pussy to lure my Maximilian in and confuse him with thoughts of sex with women?

"C'mon, which of you wants to die first?"

"He goes by the name Max now, you sick, twisted fuck," snarled Jean. She was looking around desperately for something to use as a weapon. But her eyes found nothing. All the knives were in the kitchen drawers, and Uncle's gun was still in her purse in the bedroom.

"Don't you speak to me, you little whore. I've met your kind before. You're nothing but trash."

"Don't you speak to her like that, Quinn," said Gary as he slowly inched away from the door and toward him noticed.

"Let's go, Maximilian. We're leaving. Together," Quinn said.

"I'm not going anywhere with you, Quinn. It's over. Your sick fantasies have brought you this far, but that's it. It goes no further. Not now. Not ever. I'll never leave with you."

"Well, if you're not willing, then I'll take you unwilling. And believe me, I'll *take* you. I'm sure you remember what's that's like— when I'm pissed off at you. It'll hurt. I'm sure you remember what it's like to hurt, Maximilian."

"I remember, Quinn. You'd take me however you wanted to, whenever you wanted to, no matter what I wanted."

Suddenly Gary rushed Quinn, taking him by surprise. He almost toppled him, but not quite. He had a mind worth reckoning with but a body that was useless in a fight. Quinn easily deflected him and knocked him to the ground. He lunged at him with the knife not once, not twice but three times. Gary twisted on the ground, and the blade just missed him.

Then Jean was on him. She ripped his hair out in handfuls and used her perfect nails to scratch at his eyes, but she didn't make contact. He was thrashing too quickly and trying to climb on top of Gary. With one hand he backhanded Jean, and she went flying back. Her head connected hard with the futon frame. A sickening thud carried through the room. Max gasped and held his breath. He was relieved when she sat up seconds later and rubbed her head. Gary had almost wriggled free, but Quinn had a hold on his legs. He thrust the knife down again, this time connecting with Gary's calf. Blood spurted out and down his leg.

"Quinn, stop!" screamed Max. He ran straight through the balcony screen door. "Stop, Quinn, or I'll jump! I swear I will!"

Quinn froze and looked up. So did Gary and Jean.

Max had climbed up the safety railing. One leg was over the edge, while the other remained on the cement floor.

"I swear it, Quinn. I'll jump. I'll die. And you'll have nothing left. Nothing to chase. No prize to take home."

"Max! Don't do this. Don't jump, Max. Please," Quinn cried.

"I swear I will, Quinn, if you hurt them again."

Quinn released Gary, who lay there with his leg bleeding on the carpet. Quinn got up from the floor and slowly walked toward the balcony. Max climbed a little higher.

"Put that knife down. Put that knife down, and come out here to talk," he said.

Quinn placed it on the coffee table and walked toward the balcony slowly, so as not to startle his Maximilian. His one Maximilian. The Maximilian who had come to him so many years before, who was just a child with golden ringlets that curled down his forehead. His dear Maximilian. His only desire.

He slid the screen door open, stepped onto the balcony and said, "Come down, Maximilian. You said we'd talk. Come down from there. Don't hurt yourself over these pieces of trash," he said, gesturing to Jean and Gary.

"You're wearing Donovan's clothes," Max observed. Quinn was sporting the brown khakis and Donovan's favourite green shirt, now with the pocket missing.

"They make me feel closer to you. That's why I took them. Come down, and let's talk, like father and son."

Max climbed down. Gary noticed that he was angling himself between Quinn and the door.

"I'm not your son, Quinn. I never was. I was always just a boy who Cameron stole and you fell in sick love with. I've only ever been a fantasy for you."

"You've always been more—more to me than you'll ever know. I love you, Maximilian. I love you with all my heart." He put his face in his hands and began to wail. His great body shook with the force of his sobs. It was almost obscene to see this great hulk of a man doubled over in emotional pain. It almost would have broken your heart if it weren't so sick.

Here was Max's opportunity. He struck Quinn with one solid punch to the face. Like a grenade bursting on an unsuspecting bus, he lunged out and *Crack!* Quinn crumpled from his knees and fell to the ground. Max jumped inside, slammed the door shut and locked it tight. Quinn was stunned to see the object of his desire now on the other side of the plate glass. He hurled himself at it and was pounding on it, raging against it, fuming over the hand that Max had just played. He screamed incoherently through the glass from a mouth that was sideways, crooked and wrong.

"Get your things. Quickly! We have to get out of here!" said Max.

Jean ran for her purse, and Gary tried to get up but was unable because of the bleeding gash in his calf. She knelt down beside him and looked at his wound.

"Oh, Gary. I'm going to have to get you to safety. We can't go to a hospital. They'll ask too many questions. I'm not sure what we'll do, but we'll figure something out."

Quinn was still pounding on the door, the sound of which made their pulses race.

"We have to stop his bleeding, Max—before we leave. He can't stand," said Jean.

Max grabbed an old T-shirt from his pile of clean clothes. He ripped a long piece off and carefully bound it around the wound. He ripped another piece to use as a tourniquet, and it slowed the flow of blood from a geyser to a trickle. Then he got on the side of Gary's bad leg and lifted him with one arm nestled under his shoulder. They hurried out of the apartment and closed the door behind them.

Jean attempted to hail a taxi while Max tried to keep Gary upright. Thankfully the bleeding had mostly stopped. He had no idea what he'd do if it were to start to bleed through. They had to get him someplace safe, and fast. They couldn't go to the hospital; the staff would call the police, who would ask questions they'd have a hard time answering. No, the hospital was out. They'd have to find another safe space and hope for the best. When Jean finally succeeded in hailing a taxi, they all climbed in, she in the front and they in the back. Because of Gary's height, Max had trouble getting him into it comfortably, but he did it.

"The hospital, I suppose?" asked the driver.

"No. Canal Street subway," answered Max.

"That guy looks like he needs a doctor."

"Nevermind what he needs. We need the Canal Street subway. Fast," he said as he turned to look at Gary's building behind them. He thought he could see Quinn emerging from it.

The ride seemed to take forever. Was it because there was more traffic than usual? Or because they all felt that no matter how fast they moved, no matter how far they ran, Quinn would be right behind them and and deliver a sentence only he could devise?

When they arrived at the station, Max pulled his roll of cash from his pocket and paid the driver. Jean wondered where he got that thick roll of twenties, but she didn't ask. Now certainly wasn't the right time. They piled out of the taxi, and the driver turned back to look at the seat.

"I hope he didn't bleed all over my cab," he said before taking off in search of another fare. Jean gave him the finger as he sped away, a feeble gesture that made her feel a little bit better but a whole lot smaller.

In the subway station, Max paid for them to enter the platform. He directed Jean to the end of it, near the gated entrance into the tunnel where the subway personnel often went on mysterious errands with flashlights in hand.

"Damn. We don't have flashlights," Max said. "Jean, go back up please. There's an army surplus store across the street. They'll have some. Get three, and don't forget batteries. Get twice as many as the flashlights take, because we may need extras. I'll stay here with Gary." He flipped off a couple of twenties from his wad, and she ran as fast as her short legs could carry her down the platform, up the stairs and out the exit.

Max sat Gary down on a bench and straightened out his leg.

"That was a great shot, Max. You really nailed him good. How's your hand?" Gary asked.

"Don't worry about my hand. Nothing's broken. It's your leg we have to worry about."

"Where are you taking us?" he asked weakly.

"Save your breath. And your strength. You'll see in a bit."

"Is it safe?"

"As safe as anywhere could be."

A train sped into the station and slowed to a stop as it neared them at the end of the platform.

Max watched it crawl its last feet and said, "No one ever jumps from this end of the platform. They always jump at the entrance. The trains move too slowly here to kill them. If you want to do it right, you do it at the beginning of the platform where the trains enter."

Neither of them spoke after that. They waited for Jean. When she returned, she was carrying a black plastic bag that was hanging low from heavy weight.

"Jean, please put the batteries in the flashlights. I'm trying to stand Gary up," Max said.

Jean did as asked, and soon they were back at the end of the platform.

"Okay, let's go," said Max. He pushed the gate open and helped Gary hobble through and down the steps to the pathway that was there, provided to take workers from station to station to clean the tracks or clean graffiti off walls. Jean followed.

She soon understood why they needed the flashlights. The tunnel was dark, so dark compared to the morning light outside that the flashlights were barely able to cut through the gloom.

"I tried to get good flashlights. I'm sorry, Max."

"You did good, Jean. It's just too dark down here."

The tunnel stank. It had a cloying feeling, like the walls were closing in on you, trying to smother you with their stink. It got in their throats and made them want to spit it back out. Try as she might, Jean could not get rid of their flavour that curled up in her mouth and died there. It was like cold, wet rust and sewage and used diapers, and she would remember it until her last days. It made you imagine things, the worst of things, like gooey monsters oozing around corners, or enormous alligators lurking in the shadows, or Quinn stepping out from behind a pillar with his blade in hand, iridescent in their flashlight beams.

It was cool down here, probably because of all the condensation dripping down the walls and onto the tracks, where it then sat with no place to go and morphed into city juice. Rats scurried from the light, but not always before being caught in their flashlight beams, and Jean saw their red eyes reflecting back the lights.

They walked on and on in the stinking dark. It clutched at their imaginations, turned their thoughts to imaginings of camouflaged sentries, concealed enemies and undesired unmentionables. Max had trouble trying to hold Gary upright with his arm around his back because he was so much shorter. Jean could see the darkness changing just ahead of them. It seemed to take up greater space and consume more light. The tunnel opened up into another station, a station that looked as if it hadn't been used in years.

"Where are we?" asked Jean, her eyes wide as they took in the graffitied walls, the unearthly quiet, the high ceiling.

"Now we're in the Worth St. Station. It's been abandoned for many years. Trains don't stop here anymore. The only people who come down here are street kids on dares, usually to add to the graffiti on the walls. But they're rare, and they won't bother us. The only thing is that a couple of the trains still pass through, so we could be seen by the driver or the passengers. But there's a recess in the wall about fifty feet down, where it's just too dark for them to view us. We'll stay there right now, until we can figure out what to do."

He turned to Jean, touched her face with his hand and turned it up to his. "We'll be safe here. I promise. Now, we have to find a way to make ourselves comfortable. I have no idea how long we'll be here."

True to Max's word, they came to a recess in the wall. It was about ten feet wide by fifteen feet deep. Most of it was hidden from view by a wall that reached up about seven feet. They could easily rest comfortably without any passersby being the wiser. They could probably even stand. Max lowered Gary to the ground, laid him down and straightened out his damaged leg. Jean began to cry, and Max put his arm around her.

"Don't cry, Jean," he whispered. "We need to be strong right now. Strong for each other. Strong for him." He turned his face to Gary, who seemed to have fallen asleep.

He continued, "You know, I used to come down here when I was living on the streets, when I was afraid that Quinn was getting closer to finding me. I'd hear other homeless people talk about him questioning them about me, and then I'd retreat down here. And even though I was lonely without anyone to talk to and I had to go up top to get food and money and supplies, I always felt safe here. This is the one place where Quinn never found me. Had I stayed here, I would have disappeared completely. This was a safe place then, and it's a safe place now. There's nothing to be afraid of here, Jean. Nothing at all."

He let her go and went to Gary, his brother who loved him enough to have sent him love last night . . . a time that felt so long ago. He felt Gary's forehead.

"Gary. Gary, can you hear me?" His eyelids fluttered, but they didn't open. "He needs to sleep. He's gone through a lot, and he lost a lot of blood back there. We need to stay the night here."

He got up and searched the station for anything Gary could use as a pillow. There weren't even any newspapers to ball up. The space was devoid of anything useful, and Max now remembered why he'd abandoned it so many months ago. No matter how safe it was, it just wasn't practical.

"Jean, I'm going to go up top and buy some bedding for us. There'll be blankets at the army surplus store we can use, and I'll get some water, too. And maybe a few disposable cups and some instant coffee for the morning. You stay here with Gary and try to comfort him. Maybe let him use your legs as a pillow until I get back. Will you do that for me?"

"Of course. I'd do anything for either of you. Will he be okay, Max? Do you think he'll be okay? He was only stabbed in the leg. I mean, how bad could it be?"

"I won't lie, Jean. I don't know. I really don't know."

He cupped her face in his hands and kissed her forehead before setting off down the tunnel, flashlight in hand.

Jean sat down beside Gary. She scooched her bum and legs over, lifted his head and wriggled over a bit more so she could place it on her legs. Then she leaned back against the wall and promptly fell asleep.

She dreamt that they were in a high-rise building with glass windows all around. The sound of *drip-drip-dripping* water was coming from somewhere, and it made her teeth chatter. Quinn's face was at every window. His hulking copper-topped face was searching for her, searching for them. They were well-hidden behind a counter in the middle of the room, but they couldn't move, lest they be noticed in this glass graveyard that was so silent except for the dripping water. She wanted to get up and shoot Quinn with Uncle's gun, but she couldn't find her purse anywhere. And besides, there were too many of him; she'd shoot one and there would be a thousand more Quinns to take his place.

And then Auntie was there on the outside of the building, feeding Quinn dumplings with chopsticks she held deftly between her fingers. She fed the first Quinn lovingly and then moved on to the next, feeding them all, bringing them all under her spell. How was Auntie appeasing him when Jean was trying to hide his utmost desire from his sights? Then the scene went dark, and Jean was lost in an empty, dreamless state.

>>>>>

When she woke, Max was just returning. He carried a large camouflage duffel bag on his back and several plastic shopping bags in each hand. He set them on the floor near her feet and slung the duffel bag around his body and off his shoulders. Jean began to rummage through the shopping bags and found several jugs of water, oatmeal bars and packages of easily cooked food, like instant oatmeal (several kinds and lots of it), instant rice and Kraft macaroni and cheese. From the duffel bag, Max pulled several wool blankets and pairs of socks, comfortable-looking track pants for Gary, sugar, dried milk and instant coffee, as well as a tabletop cookstove and three small tanks of propane.

"You did good," said Jean. She was still wiping the sleep from her eyes. She hadn't had enough of it.

"How's he doing?" Max asked.

"I'm sorry, I have no idea. I fell asleep."

"He seems okay," said Max as he felt his brother's forehead. "No fever yet, at least."

"What time is it, Max?"

He checked Gary's watch. "About one o'clock. It's earlier than I thought."

"I have to go. Now. I have somewhere to be at two."

"You've got to be kidding. You have an appointment? Today? And you're still going to keep it?"

"It's very important. You've no idea how important it is."

"Okay. . . . You'd better hurry. Will you be long?"

"I don't think so. I have to go to my uncle's coffee shop. There's someone I have to meet. School stuff." She was hellbent on leaving, and that was that.

"Please hurry. I'll worry the whole time you're gone." He'd think the worst: that Jean was abducted by Quinn and used as bait to lure Max out, or that he'd outright killed her as she exited the tunnel with a blow to the head.

"I'll stop by The Mission and tell them that Gary won't be in for a few days. I'll make some excuse."

She picked up a flashlight and rushed along the tracks through the tunnel that would take her out to the real world.

CHAPTER SIXTEEN

Gus was already waiting for her at the coffee shop when she arrived. Uncle wasn't there, and the staff members working complained to her the moment she walked in the door about the lack of help that day. She didn't have patience for this, so she turned her back on the girls and told them that they'd just have to deal with being short-staffed for a few days while she was busy with school. She made a cappuccino for herself, and one for Gus as well, and then went to meet him at a table in the far corner of the room.

"Problems, I see," said Gus.

"Just the usual when you run a small business. The staff is always complaining about how hard-pressed they are to perform the jobs normally expected of them."

"So what's new? With you and your boyfriend and his brother?"

It all came out of her mouth in hushed tones but in a torrent.

Once she finished and took a breath, Gus said, "I know that station. I've seen it from the train many times. You're staying there?"

"It's the safest place for us right now . . . well, the only place for us . . . until this is all over."

"Gary needs to go to a doctor. He needs to be tended to by nurses, not his homeless brother and a girl with no medical training."

"It's all we can do right now, Gus. Please, you know where we are. Can you keep us safe?"

"I can try my best. I'll be there within an hour."

After leaving Gus in the coffee shop with his cappuccino and his thoughts, Jean headed to The Mission. She told Saundra that Gary was sick, too sick with who knows what to call her himself. Saundra complained all through Jean's recounting of Gary's imaginary symptoms. Finally, she relented and assured her that she'd manage without him for a few days.

As she rode the subway back to the Canal Street Station, she reflected on her feelings for Gary. She had no idea what she'd do if he were to die. She knew she loved him. She knew she had fallen hard. "The first man you love will break your little heart," Auntie was fond of saying to her. She wondered whether Auntie's heart had once been broken. Was Uncle just the fill-in for that love? Would Max be her fill-in for Gary if he were to die? Maybe. She felt guilty that the thought even crossed her mind.

She loved them both in their own way. Gary was the man she had dreamed of, the strong one capable of holding her up when she was crumpling. But Max was the damaged one, the brutalized one with a history that could drown her fragile heart. He was another type of boy Auntie had warned her about: the bad boy, the one who could be in trouble with the law. Mind you, Auntie had warned her about all kinds of boys. None of them could muster the goods to charm that old woman, that woman whose own heart had been broken at least once. And who was Uncle? The one who had picked up the pieces and helped her go on, she supposed. The safe one. The sure bet. Who in Jean's life could do that?

She was frightened of the tunnel, the stinking, dark, dank tunnel. But she pushed her way past the barrier and began to walk the length of darkness, her flashlight her only comfort. She heard the rustling of the rats. Some of them were huge, just like she'd heard they were. Were there actual alligators, too? She thought not, but she kept her eyes peeled for any danger. A train roared down the tracks, and she hugged the wall tight as it passed.

"Did you get your errand done?" asked Max when she returned.

"Yes. But now I'm exhausted."

"I fixed up a bed for Gary, and he's more comfortable now. But I haven't fixed ours yet. I'll do it now if you'll take over here."

He had been sitting with Gary and stroking his forehead, his face, his arms, trying to comfort him in his troubled sleep. Gary's bed was set along a crumbling wall inside the recess. The area had little light to see by, so they had to use their flashlights to see properly. Max thought the darkness would afford Gary a more restful sleep, something he desperately needed.

"He woke for just a few moments while you were gone. He asked for you," Max said. He almost seemed saddened by this admission, as though he'd have preferred to be Gary's only comfort. "What time is it, Jean?"

"Four-thirty on the dot. Here, let me take over, Max." Max got up as gently as he could and let Jean sit down so that Gary's head was in her lap.

"I'll have our beds made up in a minute, and then we can all get some sleep. But I think we should take turns keeping watch in case anyone comes."

"Like they do in the movies," Jean whispered to herself. She stroked Gary's forehead. Despite the coolness of the dank air, he was sweating. This was worrisome, but there was so very much to worry about now. Like where was Quinn? Had he been able to follow them? Would he find them here in the dark, where there was nowhere to run? And what about Gus? Would he keep his word and watch the entrance to Canal Street Station? Would he kill Quinn? That would end this nightmare. . . . And most important of all, would Gary live through this?

Max unfolded the wool blankets and lay them one on top of the other. The bottom one would serve as cushioning, while the top would serve as a cover. He grabbed towels, which Jean hadn't noticed until now, and rolled them up and placed them at the top of the blankets as pillows. All in all, the beds looked rather comfortable—as comfortable as they could manage.

"Why don't you take first shift sleeping?" Max suggested.

"But I did while you were up top."

"Not enough. Not nearly enough. And you've been out there in the heat running errands."

"So have you, and you carried all that stuff down here."

"Was there anything else you wanted to eat that I didn't pick up? I mean, anything that's easy to cook?"

"Did you get a pot and silverware and spoons to cook with?"

"Yes, I remembered. But I was in such a hurry to get back down here to you. I was so afraid for you both."

"We can get more stuff tomorrow if we need it. I don't think anyone needs to eat today," she said consolingly.

Max pulled out his six-inch switchblade and placed it under one of the pillows. *How long has he been carrying that knife?* Jean wondered. He'd been on the street since he was thirteen, and she didn't know anything about his life, really. All she really knew were deep, dark and ugly secrets about what happened to him growing up, and not even a lot of them. And yet, she believed that she loved him, this damaged man, this beautiful boy who'd lived through such dreadful beginnings. How could anyone live through what he'd lived through and come out relatively intact on the other side? She would never have been able to survive on the streets like he did. He must have had to turn tricks to get enough money to eat and survive, and possibly even to get protection. She'd read about that in novels she'd purchased—obscure writings on her Kindle that never got published in the mainstream press. He'd told her the smallest number of stories about his past, just the teeniest tip of the iceberg, and it was enough to scare the living hell out of her. What if she'd been raped by Quinn at the age of five? Could she have survived? Could she have gone on fighting her way through life and running as her greatest fear breathed down her very neck? No, she would have crumpled into herself. She would have been utterly destroyed. But that was neither here nor there. It was Max who'd suffered all this. And maybe that was why she loved him: for living through what she'd never be able to live through. For surviving.

"I'm going to take the first shift, Jean."

"You sure?"

"Yes, I'm sure. Lie down now, and get some sleep."

She nestled herself under a blanket, and her head was comforted by the towel he'd provided so kindly. She listened as Max moved his bed around and then settled in, probably in a seated position. She drifted off to sleep quickly, her mind growing dark as the air around her.

In her dreams, Auntie was making breakfast, and Jean could smell the sweet scent of waffles as it drifted across the room. She was seated at the table with a fork in her hand, wearing a child's bib.

"That boy will ruin you, Jean. He's got bad manners," Auntie said.

"But, Auntie, I love him. Don't you know?"

"I do know, and that's why I said he will ruin you."

Then Uncle was there. "That boy will take your heart and crush it beneath his feet," he said. "You'd be better off with Gus. There's a man with stamina, with a purpose, with money."

"But I don't want those things. I want something else."

"You want *love*," Auntie spat. "Where's that going to get you? Where is love going to take you? To the poorhouse in a handbasket."

"Auntie, I'm not you. I don't want second-best. I don't want reruns. I don't want to be safe. I want to be loved."

"It's going to kill you, Jean, this desire of yours."

"No! It will save me! Don't you see, Auntie? My love is what saves me. And Gary. And Max. I love them both, can't you see?"

"I do see," she sneered.

Jean woke with a start. She didn't know how long she'd been sleeping before the nightmare woke her, but she guessed it wasn't long. She felt weak having been stuck in that alarming scene and woken up into this dank, dark place.

Gary was sleeping fitfully beside her, and Max was a few feet away on the other side. She turned over and placed her arm across Gary's chest, hoping for comfort but finding none in his unresponsive arms.

After a while, a long while, she got up, picking up her bedding as she did so, and walked over to Max. He was sitting with his back against the wall, his eyes staring forward and so glazed over that he didn't notice her approach. He seemed lost in his own nightmare. Maybe it was as frightening as hers, but his was probably memories, real memories culled from his hideous past.

"Max?"

She startled him out of his reverie. "Yes?" he said. He looked up at her and was surprised to see her carrying her bedding.

"Gary's no different. . . . Would you hold me?"

"Sure. Come here. Actually, let's move so we don't disturb him." He gathered up his own bedding, and they walked out of the enclosure and into the main area of the station, about thirty feet away. They laid their bedding down side by side. Max helped Jean straighten hers and smooth it flat. Then he laid down on his own bed and opened his arms so she could crawl into them.

"I had a nightmare," she admitted.

"I was having one, too, except I was awake."

"Max?"

"Yes?"

"How do you live? I mean, with what happened to you all those years in that basement. How do you live with the memories and the pain?"

He thought for a long moment before answering.

"I don't know, really. I just keep putting one foot in front of the other. And I try not to think about it."

"But how can you not think about it? Doesn't it just intrude on your thoughts constantly?"

"The nights are the worst. I have trouble getting to sleep. As soon as I lie down, I start remembering. All those men. All those beatings. Some of them liked to beat me as part of their fantasy. They'd tell me, 'You've been a bad boy, Maximilian. You've been a very bad boy.' And then they'd beat me with their fists or their belt before raping me."

"Didn't Cameron ever intervene?"

"He was one of the worst, Jean. He liked to use dildos on us . . . and other things, like the end of wooden spoons and toilet plungers. I could always tell when he was coming. I knew his footsteps on the stairs. He had this way of walking where you could hear his anger in each footfall. And you didn't know which boy he was going to take that night, and you prayed, just prayed that it wouldn't be you. If he stopped outside your door, then you were it. And you'd pray that he'd go away. But he never would."

Max was staring straight up to the ceiling of this unused station, his eyes glassed over again, lost in memories.

"What was it like with Quinn? Why does he love you so much?"

"Quinn was always different with me than the other boys. He usually touched me tenderly, except when I'd done something wrong, like not eaten my dinner. I never liked mashed potatoes, and it was a staple in that damned basement. So if I didn't eat them, he'd storm into the room and say that I'd been a bad boy and I needed to keep my strength up for him, because he didn't want any kind of scrawny boy. Then he'd take his belt and whip my ass so hard that it sometimes bled. But I didn't cry. Ever. Not even that first night, I didn't cry. And he's huge, Jean. He's got a dick that could sink the Titanic. And then he'd whip out his dick without even undressing and push it into me so hard, so painfully. But again, I never cried. I think that's why he loves me so: Because even though all the other boys cried when he fucked them, I never did. And Quinn believed that we liked whatever he did to us. So he'd either take out his rage on us or pet us and stroke us until we were calm. All the other boys were intimidated by him, but because I never cried, I usually got the worst of him. And the best of him, I suppose."

"What do you mean by 'the best of him'?"

"I mean that Quinn used to like to talk to me and tell me secrets, things that he wouldn't dare tell any of the other boys or Cameron. Like, he'd tell me that they were going hunting again to find another boy. Or that he was going to exterminate so and so, a boy who'd gotten too old, and how he was going to do it: by shooting him, knifing him, or setting him on fire with lighter fluid and watching him burn to death.

"I always kept these secrets. Who was I going to tell? I couldn't tell the other boys, especially when I knew that someone was slated to be exterminated. They didn't need to know that. What eleven-year-old wants to know that their death is just days away? I wouldn't have. And besides them, there was no one to tell."

Big, fat tears coursed down his cheeks. Jean wanted to comfort him but had no idea how. How do you shield someone from such horror when that horror lives in their very mind?

"Why did I survive, Jean? Why me and not them? What made me so special that I was given the gift of escape?" His tears were streaming onto his shirt, soaking it wet.

"I don't know, Max. I just don't understand the capacity that we humans have for cruelty. I'll never understand it. I can understand the human heart to be flighty, sedate, curious, harsh or even cruel. But not that kind of cruel. I don't know why this happened to you, Max. There's no reason. There's no explanation. It just happened. We live in a world of chaos, not a world of order, no matter what we might think it to be."

He leaned over and kissed her softly on the forehead. And suddenly, his mouth was finding hers, desperate to erase the images in his mind. Unlike the night before, his kisses were forceful and daring, He licked her mouth, her chin, her neck. He reached under her shirt and cupped her breasts and fondled her nipples in a rough sort of way. She liked it. Oh, how she liked it. She pulled her shirt off and tossed it to the side and held on to him while he pulled down his pants. He was rock-hard already. And then he was on top of her pushing into her—he didn't need her help this time. He rocked into her, in and out, and in and out again until he finished deep inside of her. He collapsed on top of her and nibbled on her ear as he caught his breath.

"Do you need more?" he asked.

"No, Max, I'm good. I'm great."

He rolled off of her, and they slept.

»

"Jean, wake up!" Max called out.

Jean woke suddenly into the dark space. For a moment, she didn't know where she was. Then all of it came crashing in and down on her like bricks.

"What's wrong?" she asked as she sat up. "How long did we sleep?"

"We slept through the night, but I just checked on Gary. He has a fever. And his leg is hot to the touch."

"It must be infected."

"We need to wash him down and keep a cold compress on his forehead to try to bring down his fever," said Max. "We need medicine—fast. But I have no idea what we need, or where to get it." He looked down at Jean, who was chewing on her nails.

"I do. I know where to go. Pass me a flashlight and I'll go. But I think it's going to be expensive, and I don't have that kind of money."

"Here, take this." He handed her the wad of cash from his pocket. "Take what you need. And hurry."

Jean kissed him, not on the cheek as a friend would do but full on his lips, with energy and passion. Only it wasn't driven by desire; it was driven by fear.

"I'll be back as soon as I can."

In moments, the only evidence of her presence was the beam of the flashlight bob-bob-bobbing as she ran as fast as she dared down the dark, stinking tunnel.

»»

Gus had spent the night in a small hotel near the Canal St. Station. Having wanted to be within close distance to the entrance to the Worth St. Station to help protect Jean and her friends, he'd decided that he'd splurge his own money. He knew he wasn't getting paid for this job, but he wanted to do it for Jean. He'd always harboured a special liking for the girl, ever since she began working at her uncle's shop. So he dressed quickly and headed out to the station with his Glock 19 tucked under his shirt as usual.

Outside the station, he stopped at a coffee and bagel stand. He bought three coffees knowing the second and third would be cold by the time he got to them. He also grabbed a bagel with strawberry cream cheese—toasted the way he liked it—and some napkins. He was a messy eater.

As he entered the station and stood on the platform, he saw Jean racing through in the opposite direction on the opposite platform. He had been watching that entrance to the tunnel from here in order to maintain anonymity, so that Quinn would not remark him if he were to come looking for the three. Had something happened? At least Jean was safe. Instead of walking down the tunnel, he took up a spot near its entrance and waited to see whether anyone matching Quinn's description came along. Same as yesterday, no one did. He waited.

»»»

Max and Jean could wait to eat. Gary couldn't. So Max set up the cookstove on the floor and then poured water into the pot to boil. At least he knew how to cook oatmeal.

When he was finished, he set it aside to cool and blew on it for a minute to help the process. He was so frightened for Gary. He wished that Jean would hurry. He knew that she was moving as fast as she could, but the waiting felt like nails being driven into his mind. What if Gary were to die? Was it truly the best choice to bring them here? Or was it a mistake? It was either bring them here or to take Gary to the hospital. At the hospital, they'd ask questions that would lead to Quinn, and eventually to Cameron. Max figured that Cameron didn't even know Quinn had found him. If he had, he might have come after them himself. And if there's one thing Max knew, it was that Cameron would not want to take him back. He would want him dead.

Throughout the years, Max had grown to believe that Cameron must somehow know he was alive. Perhaps the guilt of not following Cameron's directives finally got to Quinn and he admitted to Cameron that he never did kill Max all those years ago. Cameron's information gathering was second to none, and maybe one of his clients told him that he had seen Max working the Meatpacking District in Manhattan. Max had always kept his mouth shut while hiding, and he felt that he and Cameron had an unspoken truce between them. But if the police were to begin asking questions and Max were to begin to talk, then that truce would be ended, and it would only be a matter of time before Cameron had him killed. Or killed him himself. And Gary and Jean wouldn't be spared. Death by fire was only one of his methods. Cameron was a master of cruelty. Max had experienced only some of it in that damned basement so long ago. That basement of lost dreams. That basement of lost lives.

No. No hospitals. He wanted to live. He wanted them all to live.

Finally, the oatmeal was cool enough. He mixed some dried milk with some water, poured it over the oatmeal and sprinkled some sugar on top. He tried to wake Gary, but he didn't seem to want to wake up. He held him in his arms, supporting his upper body, and splashed cool water on his face. He woke slowly and looked up at Max.

"Hey, bro. I've got some food for you."

"I'm not hungry," Gary muttered. He smiled weakly. "Where's Jean?"

"She went out for some medicine. Now don't talk. You have to eat."

With tiny spoonfuls, Max managed to feed some of the oatmeal to Gary. It warmed Max's heart to see his brother eat something, but Gary stopped eating and pushed Max's hand away when he'd eaten far too little. As he dropped his hand back down, he knocked a jug of water over, and it rolled out of Max's reach and spilled onto the smooth tile. His eyelids fluttered a moment, and then his eyeballs rolled back and his eyes were closing again. He was unable and unwilling to eat another mouthful. Max placed the oatmeal aside and held on to him.

»»»»

In Chinatown, Jean hurried along the avenue and turned up a side street. She knew where to go because she'd been here with Auntie on several occasions. The yīzhě was just around the corner. When she found the right building, she climbed the stairs breathlessly and pounded on the door. When no one answered immediately, she pounded again. Finally, the yīzhě opened it just a crack and peeked out.

"No appointment, no help," she said.

"But it's an emergency. Please, yīzhě. Please, help me."

The woman regarded her for a moment and then opened the door and stepped aside to allow her entry into the small flat. She was a tiny woman with long braids hanging down past her shoulders to the middle of her back. With eyes that were slightly crossed, one of them covered with a whitish film, she stared at Jean balefully.

She had always frightened Jean on previous visits with Auntie. They'd come that time Uncle burned himself badly with hot steam at the coffee shop. And the time he had pneumonia, when his chest had a desperate rattle, his breath was shallow and his face was all white and uneasy. The yīzhĕ had come through on both occasions, sending them off with bottles of deeply coloured liquids to administer to Uncle. She eased the awful pain in his hand, brought up the greenish phlegm that had shortened his breath and brought down the fever until he could walk again without trouble. In this moment, the yīzhĕ was all Jean had, and she was putting her faith in the cross-eyed woman's abilities. She didn't know whether it would be enough. Gary was desperately ill.

The yīzhĕ motioned her to sit at a small, wooden table in the centre of the room. Up above, patterns were etched into the ceiling that flowed together to form the Chinese astrological signs. It was a beautiful piece of artwork. Jean had never noticed it before, and she would have appreciated it more if she weren't so distressed.

She looked across the table at the yīzhĕ. "My friend is sick. Very sick. He's been stabbed with a knife."

"What kind of knife?" asked the yīzhĕ, staring at her with her one good eye.

"What do you mean 'what kind of knife'? It was just a normal blade, I think. It looked like a switchblade, but I'm not sure. I didn't get a good look at it."

"Fever?"

"Yes."

"Infection?"

"Yes. Yes, yes, yes! Please help me. I'll pay you what you ask." She'd cried so much these past few days, and it wasn't like her. But the tears began to flow once again.

"You cannot cry. It weakens you. And your friend. You diminish your strength by crying. And you take away his, too."

The yīzhĕ got up from the table and walked through a curtain of beads into the back of the space. Jean occupied her mind by gazing up at the stars etched into the background of the astrological signs. It felt like hours had passed, though it was probably only a few minutes. Finally, the yīzhĕ returned carrying six small vials in her hands.

"One is for the fever. One if for the infection. One is to purify the blood. One is to stop the bleeding. One is for the memories. And one is for your tears. Each one is labelled with what it's for and how many drops to mix in water. Don't give too much, and don't give too little. I'm not charging you for the last two, because you didn't ask for them. But you'll need them."

"What does the one for memories do?"

"It helps to soften bad memories from taking hold in the mind. Your friend will need it before this is all over. The man who is after you hasn't finished damaging him, and you will need to soften those memories to reduce their potency now. There's no way to block them out completely, I'm afraid. I would if I could. God knows they should be blocked, but this will help."

"But how do you know that someone is after us, or that he hasn't finished with Gary?"

"Don't ask questions whose answers you cannot understand, girl. Now go. Go! Your friend needs you. Maybe you'll get back in time. Maybe you won't."

Jean left the flat, ran down the street and turned up the main street toward the subway.

»»»»»»

Gus had to go to the bathroom—badly. The three coffees had traveled right through him. They'd done their magic: He was fully awake now. But he also had to piss.

There had been no action to worry about all through the early morning. The mysterious Quinn guy was nowhere to be seen and so, Gus decided to chance it and find a bathroom in some nearby restaurant. This was always hard to find in New York. Every establishment had a "Bathrooms for Customers Only!" sign. Not the friendliest of cities. He'd probably have to purchase some kind of takeout food for the privilege of using the men's room. Oh well. One of the hazards of the job.

So he unfolded himself from the bench he was sitting on and walked his stiff body toward the exit.

»»»»»»

After Gary had eaten, the next most pressing problem was their water supply. He'd been soaking the end of a towel with water and applying it to Gary's forehead to try and bring down the fever. He wasn't sure it was working, but he had to do something. He hadn't foreseen needing more water for at least another day or so. Gary wasn't going to get any better if Max stayed where he was, and they were all safe down here, at least for the time being, so he decided that now was as good a time as any to go up top and pick up some more.

After waking Gary to drink some last sips of their precious supply, he let him slip back into sleep. Max gently laid his head down onto his pillow, grabbed his duffel bag and flashlight and headed down the long, dank tunnel to Canal St. Station. He listened for signs of movement, but the only sounds came from a couple of trains passing by. With each train's approach, he pressed himself into the wall so as not to be seen by the driver or any of the passengers. But he needn't have worried; no one looked up from their lives to notice the golden-haired man with the camouflage duffel bag slung on his back. When he reached the station, he darted through the gate and headed for the cleaner air beyond.

»»»»»»»»»

The man with the copper hair and purple lips walked quickly toward the end of the platform at Canal Street Station. He pulled a flashlight from his pocket, looked around behind him and then pushed his way through the gate and into the tunnel beyond. As he left the penumbra of light cast by the overhead lights behind him, he flicked on the flashlight.

This had always been Maximilian's last-resort place of refuge, his one true hiding place. Quinn had been to all of his other hiding places, and none of them had panned out. He'd hidden himself—and his brother and that bitch—most completely. This had to be it. He had stabbed Gary good in the leg. What else would Maximilian do if his brother was weak and that bitch was scared? Hide. This had to be it, it just had to be. He was nowhere else in sight.

He began walking toward the abandoned station beyond.

CHAPTER SEVENTEEN

Quinn fumbled his way along the tunnel. Because of his large stature, it was hard to maneuver along the pathway. The pain in his jaw made it even worse. He knew it wasn't broken, because he could still speak. Yet it was bruised and swollen where Maximilian had clocked him. Damn him! He was going to teach him a good lesson when he finally got his hands on him.

Quinn knew all of Maximilian's hiding spots; he had been following the boy for years now, watching him from afar, watching him grow up from the thirteen-year-old boy whom he had set free to the twenty-two-year-old boy he'd become. Sometimes he lost sight of him, or lost track of him for months at a time even, but his sleuthing abilities were second to none, just like Cameron's. With enough questions to the homeless, enough cigarettes given out and enough threats made, he always found the boy again.

This underground station was one of Maximilian's favourite haunts. He would return to it whenever he needed to hide from the world and thought he could get away, or whenever he felt Quinn might have a sniff on his trail. Quinn had always been careful not to come too close to this spot, not to show his hand, because when the boy was down here, however safe he thought himself to be, he was really trapped. Trapped by the darkness. Trapped by the distance from the rest of the world up above. Trapped in a way that only Quinn really knew. And Quinn liked this, this illusion of safety that the boy had created for himself, because then he had him where he really wanted him: trapped.

When he arrived at the end of the tunnel, he could see why Maximilian liked this place so much. It was exceptionally dark, which would provide a bit of cover should Quinn ever emerge from the tunnel. And it was so quiet, so very quiet, that you could hear someone approaching from any direction. But together, these elements only amounted to an ounce of safety, a facade really, as you could hear someone approaching but never tell from which direction they were coming.

He snapped off the flashlight and tried to get his bearings as his eyes adjusted. All he could hear was the sound of someone sleeping: that slow, rhythmic flow of breath in and out that suggests a sense of safety. There were no voices, no movements. Here, right now, Quinn had the advantage. He turned the flashlight back on, climbed the few steps up to the platform and entered the cavernous station, stepping carefully and quietly so as not to wake the slumberer who lay somewhere in the darkness beyond.

He moved gingerly to avoid debris on the tile floor. There was remarkably little garbage for an abandoned space, but graffiti covered every conceivable surface. Some of it was almost beautiful . . . in a post-apocalyptic sort of way. Down here, you would think the world had ended and you were looking at the last scribblings of a corrupted civilization. He liked it. Or maybe he liked the feeling that whomever was sleeping down here was waiting for him, a sitting duck unaware of the gun that had him in its sight. He moved forward.

He could see a recess in the wall up ahead, where the station opened up into more darkness. The soft snores were emanating from there. Quinn moved toward it like a mesmerized moth to a flame. As he went deeper into the space, he saw a figure lying on the ground, a tall figure still undisturbed despite his proximity.

Gary, he thought, *that fucking brother I should have killed yesterday.*

He reached down, grabbed Gary by his shirt and pulled him up toward him. He looked very sick. All the better. Maybe he wouldn't have to kill him himself. It wasn't that he was squeamish about another kill but that he wanted Gary to suffer.

"Gary! Wake the fuck up! Gary!" He slapped him hard across the face.

Gary's eyelids fluttered open. His eyes focused and registered fear when they realized who was staring back.

"Where's Max?! Where's Jean?!" he asked in a scratchy voice. "Why did they leave?"

"You've been a bad boy, Gary. And bad boys get punished." He twisted Gary violently onto his stomach and pulled down his pants.

»

Since when does a men's room have a line? Gus thought. *When it's a single toilet.* He cussed under his breath and waited for the two before him to have their turn.

»»

Why the hell is it taking so long? Jean asked herself. *Someone probably jumped on to the tracks.*

She paced back and forth, back and forth, waiting impatiently for the J train to come.

»»»

Goddamn! How can this place be out of water, too? Max asked himself. *Fucking heat wave! Where else can I go?*

He stormed out the door, letting it slam behind him.

»»»»

Though his mind was still fuzzy, Gary was well aware that he was lying there exposed with Quinn behind him.

Fuck! Quinn! Gary's mind was numb. His heart pounded against his eardrums, and his tongue had a thick paste all over and around it. He tried to think of a way out of this situation, but he was still so sick that he couldn't follow his thoughts properly, couldn't trace their pathways.

How would he ever get out of this? He knew he was too weak to stand, let alone run from him, this monster standing over him. He heard Quinn unzipping his own pants and slowly dropping them around his ankles.

My god. What's he going to do to me? Use his belt on me?

"Yes, you've been a very bad boy, Gary. And you deserve to be punished. You took my Maximilian away from me and filled his head with all kinds of ideas."

"I'm his brother, and I love him. I always have."

"*I'm* the one who's always loved him, Gary! Where were you all those years when Maximilian was in that basement? *I* was there. *I'm* the one who helped him. *I'm* the one who loves him, not you. You're just a dirty little bad boy. And dirty little bad boys deserve what they get."

Quinn dropped to his knees, and Gary felt his weight fall on top of him. Adrenaline pulsed through his body as he realized what was about to happen.

He tried to kick out from under him, to twist himself around, but his damaged leg had poisoned him, and he didn't have the strength. Gary tried to gather everything he could, every ounce of strength, every string he could pull taut to make one strong stand against his attacker. But at the last moment he fumbled, right when Quinn pushed his face into the towel hard, like he was trying to knead bread dough. He just didn't have the courage anymore to fight this man, this huge, hulking thing.

He could feel the heat from Quinn's body. The slimy sweat that coated his chest dripped all over Gary's back, and he pressed his big cock against him. He was rubbing it up and down the crack of Gary's backside. He could feel the thickness of it, the sheer hugeness of it, like some kind of cartoon cock drawn from some adolescent pornographic mind. He tried to reach back and wail on Quinn's face or scratch him, but he was out of reach. He was behind him, on top of him, completely in another world.

And then he was pushing his cock against Gary's sphincter, pushing at him, and Gary felt his masculinity, that curious mix of virility, boldness and courage, which he had carefully built up over the years, begin to crumble.

Then he was inside of Gary, and Gary was screaming— screaming from the pain, from the hurt, from the shame.

This can't be happening! he cried out in his mind, but he knew it was. This pain was too visceral, too real, to be originating from his fevered imagination.

He tried to push Quinn out by clenching his muscles, but he couldn't. He just couldn't. The pain was searing into him, cutting him like a knife twisting and turning deep in his rectum. Quinn pushed deeper, tearing Gary's sphincter open, shredding it as he pushed and pulled in and out, in and out. And some part of his soul, some stained and damaged part, stood at a distance and wailed into his hands as he watched the scene.

Suddenly Quinn was breathing into his ear, his breath hot and sour, and he crooned, "Take it like a man, Gary. Take it like the man I know you are."

Gary tried to quell his fear and his rage, to calm himself and stem the flow of his tears. But he couldn't. He just couldn't. He tried to take it like a man, but he couldn't calm the fear that was pounding him like the waves of a burgeoning sea.

"Stop! P-please stop!" he cried between sobs and tears. But Quinn wouldn't stop. Instead, he began to laugh. He was laughing at Gary and his manhood destroyed, laughing at the fear he was causing, laughing at the sheer pleasure of it all. He refused to pull that monstrous thing out of him. He wouldn't stop fucking him. So Gary screamed until his voice became hoarse and all he could do was cry, cry like only a broken man can cry.

But like every odious thing in life that must come to an end, eventually he did stop. He pulled out, his dick limp and spent, and his breath slowed. Gary felt something trickling down his thighs; he didn't know if it was blood or Quinn's cum.

He was broken, his mind, his body, his safety torn in half. His sphincter ached. His soul felt separate and apart from him. Where was Max? Where was Jean? He wished with all his heart that neither of them would ever return and witness his anguish, that they would leave him there to die in his own private shame.

"How was that for you, boy?" Quinn asked. Between his sobs, Gary could hear him pulling on his pants, zipping them up and putting on his shirt.

"How was that for you, you bad little boy? It sure was good for me. I've always liked a tight virgin ass. That's one of the things I've always liked about your brother: No matter how many times I fucked him, he was always like a tight, little virgin boy." He pat his stomach, satiated. Cruel laughter rang through the dark.

"That's what happens to bad little boys who cross my path—they get punished. We should do this again."

"Let me tell you what happens to big, bad monsters, you motherfucking prick!" Jean screamed from the darkness, from somewhere within this hell. And she was angry, oh so angry.

Quinn froze and swivelled around to find her voice. His flashlight caught one sight of her before she disappeared from his view. Her long black hair was tangled and knotted from running as fast as she could through the darkened tunnel, listening all the while to Gary's distant screams. Her cheeks were flushed, and sweat dripped down her neck and temples. Her eyes flashed ferociously, and even in that split second he caught her in the light, he could see that they were as hard as diamonds.

"Where the fuck are you, you nasty little whore? Come out where I can see you!"

He grabbed his flashlight and waved it around the room. Max was caught in the beam as he ran to Gary, whose loud, racked sobs continued like they'd never stop. Max was crying, too, great sobs that were tearing from his throat like he'd also never stop, and the pain would never end, and this hellfire would never be doused. He dropped his duffel bag and slid the last few feet on his knees.

"I'm going to kill you, you fucker," Jean said. "I'm going to kill you for what you've just done to Gary. And what you did to Max all his life."

"Your boyfriend deserved what he got, you little Chink. It's just like I told him: He's been a bad boy, and bad boys get what's coming to them. And I'm going to do the same to you as soon as I catch you, you little fucking bitch."

"Come catch me then!" she screamed.

He panned his flashlight right and then left again, and then there she was: caught in the only light that pierced this grisly scene. At her feet was an open small red handbag, and in her hands was a sleek black handgun levelled straight at his head. Quinn hadn't expected this. Surely the girl couldn't shoot worth a damn. But with the gun pointed straight at him, a small doubt crept into his mind. He took a tentative step forward toward Jean, but she stayed her ground. He took another step, and then another. Though she held her spot, now there was a certain hesitancy about her stance, something in the way she held her shoulders and arms, as though she were deciding how far to take this scene. Quinn kept moving slowly toward her. She seemed not to notice the shortening space between them.

She took a deep breath and said, "You tortured Max all his life. You stole his innocence. You stole his imagination. You stole his life. I'm going to take yours right now, Quinn. I'm going to put a bullet straight through your brain. And you'll never hurt anyone again. Not me, not Gary, and not Max. No one."

In two quick movements he was on her. He ran quick as he could toward her. Then he shot his huge hand out at her, aiming for the gun, and it circled her wrist and twisted. A gunshot rang out and echoed off the walls. Then another.

Quinn crumpled to the floor.

Jean knelt to Quinn in the dark. Only his flashlight gave any sense of where he lay. She picked it up, stared at him and stood up. She turned his head with her foot. Two bullet holes were evident. Two bullet holes, their bullets lodged in his brain. His unseeing eyes were open, but she didn't even think to close them. There would be no comforting this man, even in death.

Footsteps were approaching from the direction of the tunnel. *What now?* was all Jean could think.

"He's dead?" asked Gus as he came into the light.

"Very. Thank you, Gus, for helping."

"I didn't do much. I'm only sorry I couldn't get to him before he attacked your friend. Is he your boyfriend?"

"Yes."

"Go to him. He needs you both now. He's got a long road to travel, I expect."

"I'm sure he does." She turned from the lifeless Quinn and walked to pick up the paper bag full of medicine she'd left on the floor out of sight. When she turned again, Gus was gone.

In the melee, Jean had completely forgotten that she had even asked Gus to help them. And truthfully, she hadn't expected him to do much. In the final tally, he hadn't saved them from Quinn at all, but the fact that he had even shown up was something to be thankful for. It meant they had a friend in all this, an ally.

As she approached Gary, Max was hanging on to him as though his world were on fire. He sobbed into Max's chest. She dropped to her knees and then froze, not knowing what to do. Finally, she reached down and took his hand. She stroked it gently, trying to imbue him with as much of her love as she could. But he snatched his hand away, as if her very touch were burning his skin. His trousers were still off, so she covered him with a blanket.

She remembered the medicine bottles, reached for the bag and tore it half open. She grabbed a Styrofoam cup from one of the bags of supplies that Max had purchased and poured some water in it. One by one, she opened the bottles and squeezed drops of the medicines, all of which were different colours—dark blue, red, amber, azure, pink, reddish brown—into the mix with a dropper that the yīzhĕ had provided.

The yīzhĕ's words came back to her. 'What does the one for memories do?' 'It helps to soften bad memories from taking hold of the mind. Your friend will be needing it before this is all over.' She had thought it was for Max, but now she realized it was intended for Gary after all.

She handed the cup to Max, who made Gary drink it down.

Eventually, he drifted off to sleep.

»»»»»

They were sitting together, with Gary's head in Max's lap. It had been two days since Quinn's death, and his body was beginning to smell even though Max had dragged it by its feet into a far corner of the station. Sometimes Jean thought she could hear rustlings from over there, as though he were somehow still moving, slithering across the floor toward them. Though she knew it was only her imagination, she had a hard time dispelling these thoughts. It was worse when Max was sleeping. When he was awake, she would just sit beside him knowing that if anymore danger were to arise, they would protect each other. But when he was sleeping she had a difficult time dispelling the images that crept into her mind and sunk their nails into her brain. She wasn't all that used to fear, for she'd never been a fearful girl and certainly was not a frightened woman. She was a New Yorker—and proud of it—despite its trappings of false security. She didn't like this newly found fear; it made her uncomfortable. Perhaps after Gary was well enough to move and they'd crept back up top, the late-summer sunlight would melt these fears and push them to the shadows where they belonged. . . . Right now, though, she wasn't sure that would ever happen.

Gary's fever still hadn't broken, though it had come down significantly. He slept a lot, but Jean had the feeling he sometimes feigned sleep so he wouldn't have to face them, as she thought she'd caught him with his eyes open several times as she prepared his medicine. He closed them quick as a wink, and she wondered whether she'd imagined them ever being open.

He took his medicine willingly and without a murmur, somehow knowing that everything they were doing was for his better welfare. The medicine seemed to be helping as much as it could. The fever that had risen in his leg indicated an infection had been caused by Quinn's blade, but that was coming down as well. The puffiness and the redness surrounding the wound were abating somewhat as well. The skin around the gash was still taut, but it, too, seemed to be healing. All in all, Gary seemed to be on the mend, but even though the worst of it seemed over, both she and Max knew that he wasn't out of the woods yet.

The memories of his rape had to heal, and Jean had no idea whether they ever would.

Every time she tried to touch him, he pushed her away, however feebly. He was tortured by the memories of Quinn's retribution. His sphincter had finally stopped bleeding, Max had told her earlier that day. It had bled for quite some time. Gary only let Max tend to this wound, but Max showed it to her once while Gary slept. She couldn't believe the damage that had been done to him, her love, her man. But was he her man anymore? She didn't know. Since Quinn's damage was done, he couldn't look her in the eye. It was as though his very core had been torn asunder, shredded, cast aside like some forgotten toy.

Quinn's rape did not make Gary any less of a man in her eyes. He was still Gary, though he was a different Gary, a damaged Gary who had to heal. But how would he ever heal from this? Were there groups for adult men who had been raped, with meetings he could attend? Maybe, but she doubted Gary would take well to something like that; in some ways, he was a very private man, a man who liked to heal the world, not have the world heal him. Then there was therapy. He'd probably need years of it. How unfair it was that one event in a man's life could damage him so badly, so completely, that it would take years to recover. But that's what it would take. She wanted to be there for it. She wanted to share his life so badly. Not Max's. She knew that now. It wasn't Max she loved. She did love him in some way, but not that way. It was Gary she wanted: his touch; his arms around her, loving her, protecting her, providing for her; his laughter rolling throughout the days ahead; his eyes watching her in the morning, taking all of her in. It was Gary she wanted.

She loved Max's badness. She loved his danger. She loved his adamant desire to survive at all costs. But that wasn't the kind of man she wanted to spend her nights with. That wasn't the kind of man she wanted to complete her days. But she was sure Max would find love before he was finished walking through this world. There was some woman out there capable of taming him. She just wasn't it.

"Will he ever heal, Max?" Jean asked.

"I'm not sure, Jean. What Quinn did to him . . . it's hard enough for a child, but children are resilient. At least I was. I don't know about the others, because none of them lived past the age of eleven. None of them ever had a chance to heal. But I did. And I seem to be healing . . . in my own way."

She took his hand and just held it.

Max continued. "Gary's an adult. His ego is already intact, but it's been broken now by Quinn, by all that's happened. His very sense of self has been damaged, do you know what I mean? He's been damaged to the core, and I'm not sure if anyone can heal from that. I don't think you ever get over it. Men are fragile beings in a way: They only ever let small amounts of themselves be seen. They try to be strong, and they are in some ways, just like women are strong in some ways. But we all are just trying to hold ourselves together against the world, against the horrors of life itself."

She thought for a moment and then said, "The yīzhě I went to knew this would happen. That's why she gave me the serum for Gary's memories. At the time, I thought it was meant for you. But now I realize it was always for Gary. She said they'd soften them, make them easier to deal with. But I'm not sure whether it's working for him. Sometimes I hear him crying when he thinks we don't hear, and it's so pitiable, so bitter, as though nothing will ever help take those memories away, nothing will ever take that pain away."

"They'll fade . . . after a time. They'll become hazy and softer around the edges. But nothing will ever take them away. That's impossible."

"That's what the yīzhě said."

»»»»»»

On the third day, when Quinn was really starting to smell, Gary's fever broke. He woke hungry, though he still had trouble sitting up. Max gave him some weak tea while Jean made him some oatmeal. When she finished, Max went to retrieve it from her.

"Please, let me do it, Max," Jean implored. These days of not touching him, of not being able to help him, had hurt her more than she was willing to admit. As she sat down beside Gary, she saw reluctance in his eyes.

Throughout the feeding, he avoided looking into her eyes. Jean propped his head up a bit by placing her shoes under the towel that his head rested on. He still wasn't able to hold his arms up long enough to feed himself, so he let her do it. Once finished, Jean removed her shoes and he laid back down, turned away from her and feigned sleep.

"I know you're not sleeping, Gary," she said to him with love. "If you won't talk to me, then I'll talk to you." There were so many things to say that she didn't know where to begin. After sorting through her thoughts, she decided with the simple truth.

"This wasn't your fault . . . what happened with Quinn. It wasn't your fault. This is something he did to you. This is something you couldn't control, you couldn't stop, you couldn't prevent. You were weak from the infection in your leg, and Max and I had left you thinking you were safe down here, that Quinn wouldn't—couldn't—get to you. But we were wrong. God, we were so wrong. If anyone were at fault, it's us. You trusted us to keep you safe, and we all trusted in this god-awful place to keep us safe. But we were wrong, and you paid the price. It's not your fault, Gary. It's not your fault, and you are no less of a man because this happened. You're no less of a man, Gary. Do you think that Max is any less of a man for how Quinn raped him? Of course not. I know you don't. So you mustn't blame yourself for what happened to you. Max was a child, weak and frightened and unable to run. And you were sick, as weak and frightened as a child, and also unable to run. You cannot blame yourself.

"Please let me in, Gary. Please let me back in. I love you. And what Quinn did makes no difference in my eyes. You're still the man you always were, and I love that man, Gary. I love you. No matter what happened, no matter what happens, I'll always be here beside you, inside you. I'll always be with you."

As she spoke the last of her words so laden with sadness and desperation, tears sprang forward and fell from the corners of her eyes. How else could she put it? How simply could she say it? He needed to know that she loved him, and that his worth was not diminished in her eyes.

Jean waited, but Gary refused to open his eyes. Was he really sleeping? She was sure he wasn't. Then why wouldn't he engage with her? Why wouldn't he talk to her? Why wouldn't he let her in?

Finally, she turned away, wiped the tears from her cheeks and turned off the flashlight.

»»»»»»»

By the fourth day, they were all beginning to smell (though Quinn smelled decidedly worse than any of them). Gary woke with his fever completely gone, and he was ravenous. Max made him another cup of weak tea, and Jean fixed him two packages of instant oatmeal. Jean sat beside him holding the flashlight as he devoured his whole meal while holding the spoon himself. As Gary neared the end of it, Jean went to Max and whispered a request to leave her and Gary alone for a few minutes to talk. Max went off to another part of the station by himself.

"Gary?" she asked.

"Hmmm?" he murmured between mouthfuls.

"You heard what I said the yesterday after I fed you, right?"

Seconds passed. They seemed like hours to Jean as she waited for Gary to answer.

"Yes."

"So you understand that I love you? You know that I want to be with you?"

"Yes, I do." He put down the empty bowl. "But I don't understand why. Or how. How could you ever want me again?" A single tear formed at the corner of one of Gary's eyes and threatened to drip down the side of his face, but it remained there, caught in the folds of skin and glistening in the glow of the flashlight.

"Because it doesn't change anything. It doesn't affect our love for each other. It doesn't make me want you any less. Can't you see that I love you and always will?"

"Jean," he said. He turned to look up at her. "How could you love me now? How could you ever love a man who's been so debased, so torn, so . . . so infantilized? How could you ever forget what's happened to me? When you look at me from now on, you'll see Quinn and what he's done to me. You'll see rape." He barely spoke above a whisper when he said the word. But he continued.

"It's damaged me . . . more than I can say. Quinn took more than my ass the other day; he took my innocence. Even though I'm twenty-five years old, I guess I still had some innocence. Like . . . there were things I believed in about right and wrong, about what happens to bad people and what happens to good people. Quinn infantilized me that day. He told me I'd been a bad boy and that I needed punishing. But he also stole my maleness, something that every man prizes. He ripped that right out of me. He tore into me like he was a raging bull and I was his cow. What man deserves that? Tell me, what man deserves that?" His eyes were on fire, and Jean could sense his rage oozing out through his very pores.

"No man deserves what happened to you, Gary. No man."

"Then why did it happen, Jean? Why me?"

"I don't know, my love. There's no sense to be made of it. There's no justification for what Quinn did to you . . . this brutality . . . this rape of your very soul."

Gary closed his eyes tightly, squeezing more tears from them. "I don't think I can live with this, Jean. And if I can't live with it, how can I expect you to?"

"Gary, I'm a strong woman. You know I am. I can live with just about anything. And you're the one I want to spend my life with. Don't you know that? Can't you hear me? Please listen. . . . I don't know how else to say it."

The dark silence closed in around the end of Jean's words, but still Gary did not speak. After a long while, he opened his mouth as though he were about to break the silence but then closed it again.

"Yes, love? Were you going to say something?"

"I was going to ask you to marry me," Gary admitted. Jean reached out and took his hand from where it lay on the blanket covering him.

He went on. "I know we've only known each other a short time, but I know I love you. And I believed you loved me, too."

Jean was surprised by this admission but not wholly. She'd always believed she'd marry a man she loved, and Gary was obviously that man. Would she have accepted? Yes, she would have.

"I still love you, Gary. And if you had asked, I would have said yes." She let that sink in for a few minutes. As she waited, she thought she could hear the sound of Max's breathing just beyond the edge of the darkness, but she knew she must be imagining it. Max would never eavesdrop on their conversation. Gary finally spoke again.

"Would you still? Would you still say yes if I asked?"

Was it real? Was it true? Was a man really asking her to marry him? Not just any man but the man of her heart's desire, the man she craved, the man she wanted to spend the rest of her life with? That man? She looked down at Gary's face. It was traced in the shadows of her flashlight. What was it she saw there, etched in the lines that had grown over the past few days? Fear. Of her? No, not of her but of her answer.

"Yes!" she said enthusiastically.

"Jean," he said, looking up at her again with tears in his eyes. "Will you marry me?"

"Yes! Oh, yes, my love! A thousand times yes! As soon as we get out of this hellhole, if that's what you want. We can even go to a justice of the peace. I don't care what I look like; I'll go like this."

"But what if I care? I've always wanted a bride in white. And a wedding by the sea. It doesn't have to be big or fancy, but I want it to be nice—for both of us. Because we deserve it, Jean," he added, squeezing down on her hand. "Maybe now more than ever, we deserve to be happy, Jean. You deserve to be happy. And we'll get you on my insurance plan right away so that you can go to a doctor to see what's wrong with you—why you can't keep food down and why you're losing so much weight. We deserve it, Jean." He looked almost desperate as he uttered his last words. Then he relaxed, all his muscles losing tension, loosening up as he paused momentarily.

Then he said, "We can probably go to a justice, because I've never been religious, but it shouldn't just be in some government office downtown. It should be something pretty that'll complement your beauty, something just for the two of us."

He lifted his hand to her cheek, held it and then brought her face down to his. They kissed softly, gently, with all the love their shattered hearts could muster.

EPILOGUE

"I want to get married soon. How does that sound to you?" Gary asked.

Jean paused as she wondered about Auntie and Uncle. What would their wishes be? Auntie would want a big wedding. It was traditional in Asian cultures to show off as much as you could when you host a wedding. Jean knew that if Auntie were a part of the wedding, then she would likely try to plan a big wedding. But they couldn't do that. For one thing, there was the money. Beyond that, Cameron was still out there, and if he were to somehow catch wind of the Aldertree name floating around town in the wedding announcement, then none of them would be safe.

Jean found her voice, having lost it momentarily when a lump formed in her throat, and she replied, "Anytime. Now. Later. Whenever. I just want to be Mrs. Aldertree, for the rest of my life." She leaned over and kissed him short and sweet.

The morning light crept into Gary's bedroom in great swaths of warmth. It was going to be a fine September morning, and he was looking forward to heading out to the farmers market with Jean and Max.

Jean swiftly hopped up and out of bed. "C'mon, lazybones. We've got to get moving."

"Hang on a minute. You know that once we're married, you'll be on my medical insurance, right?"

She hadn't thought of it before now.

He added, "And once you're on my insurance, I want you to go to a doctor. Right away."

"Okay. But are you marrying me just so that I can have medical insurance, my love?"

"I'm marrying you because I love you, silly. I'm marrying you because I want you to be my wife, and because I want to change your name from Jean Choi to Mrs. Jean Aldertree. The medical insurance is just a side benefit. I'm sure you realize that."

"Yes, I do."

"No, you say that later, not now." They chuckled, Jean letting out her beautiful, intriguing horsey laugh he found so endearing.

Gary got up slowly and reached for the cane next to the bed. His leg had healed by now, but the injury still troubled him somewhat, and he still found it hard to walk unaided. He had a nasty scar down his calf, too, one that looked like it would be there for life always reminding him of that awful morning. But it wasn't as awful as the scars in his mind; they would always remind him of Quinn and the ghastly thing he did to him in that darkened subway station that day he'd been left alone and thought to be safe.

Every night he had nightmares about being raped by Quinn in the dark. He wondered whether they would ever go away, these nightly visitations. And would he ever be free of his fear and loathing of the man?

Sometimes he would wake with an excruciating pain in his rectum, like that knife was twisting and turning inside him again.

And sometimes he still bled from his rectum after using the bathroom before going to bed. Though the doctor told him there would be no lasting damage, Gary sometimes wondered whether she was wrong. She wanted to put a scope up inside him to better see what was there, but he couldn't let her. He couldn't allow anything up there, any kind of probe that would provide a better view of his inner workings. It just hurt too much, even though she was trying to be gentle and kind. The two times she did try, sharp, stabbing pains reminiscent of Quinn's lust ripped at his nerve endings. He'd gone to see a female doctor because the thought of allowing a man to view him, to poke and prod and scope him, was unthinkable. He just couldn't allow another man to get at him despite professional training.

He grieved heavily sometimes, and then the tears would come—deep, dark tears born of inner demons that Gary just couldn't dispel. If he could have bled tears, he would have, and they would still feel like they were doing damage inside. Intellectually, he understood it; he'd been raped by a man. It was the emotional understanding that he couldn't get to. And when these tears came, they wouldn't stop. He just cried and cried. His moods were dark and taciturn, and he wondered whether they would ever leave him, ever release him from their grip.

Jean would try to comfort him. She would put her arms around him, her own tears coming hard and fast, and try to speak soothing words to ease him, to bring his mind back to the here and now. But he was trapped in his place of gloom, a place unknown to her where he was alone and desperate and lost. She could not follow him there, this place where night terrors were born of need and longing: a private need to heal and a longing to be rid of the past and be whole again. It was his place, a place that maybe only Gary himself could know, a place where maybe no one could follow. He hadn't talked to Max yet about what had happened or how he was feeling.

He hadn't confided in him, because Max didn't seem to go to this place in his own mind very much at all. Max had his own fears, his own private places that he went to, but they were different from Gary's and expressed themselves differently.

"Come on, love," urged Jean. "Let's get moving, or all the good stuff will be gone."

Gary reached for a pair of shorts and a T-shirt.

"I think you'll be cold with just that on. It's supposed to be a chilly autumn day," she noted.

Gary was thankful for the break in the heat. He exchanged his shorts for a pair of pants.

"One of these days, I'm going to stuff those things in the garbage chute."

"But I like them."

"They're completely out of style, my love."

Gary liked it when she called him that. It reminded him of warm nights and warmer days, of falling in love for the first time in his life—the last time in his life.

"We have to stop by Auntie and Uncle's house. I promised them I'd take you to meet them. They want to meet my fiancé, and it's high time they did."

»

After the events in the subway station, Jean had gone back home to visit them later that morning and walked in to the smell of waffles cooking on the stove.

"Jean?" Auntie called out.

"Yes, Auntie. It's me."

"Finally."

"I'm sorry it's been so long, Auntie." She entered the kitchen with trepidation. "Your waffles smell great."

She stirred the waffle batter with strong vigour.

"I'm sorry, Auntie. A lot's been happening."

"I know."

"How could you know?"

"The yīzhě has been calling and keeping me up to date." She placed the bowl on the counter and turned to face Jean with her hands on her hips, a signal that usually meant something was wrong. "But you're safe now."

"I'm sorry, Auntie. I'm so sorry." Fat, ripe tears gathered at the corners of her eyes. She ran toward Auntie but stopped short in front of her and just stood there.

Auntie held out her arms. "Come here, Jean."

She enfolded her in them and held her tight. Big, full tears began to course down her cheeks.

"Oh, Jean. My child. My dear, sweet child with a heart that loves with wonder. I had no idea whether you would come home. I was so scared. This is your home, Jean—whatever happens. And you are the daughter I could never have. You know I love you, don't you, and that I would do anything for you? Your Uncle and I, the both of us, would walk through fire to help you and ensure your safety."

She cupped Jean's face in her hands and then held her to her body, protecting her from the assault of the world. She said, "Your uncle and I both love you, Jean. We both love you so much, and you've been so hurt by grief. I was so worried for you, and for your man and his brother."

Jean pulled her head up to look at Auntie. "But how do you know? How do you know about Gary and Max?"

"The yīzhě told me. She always knows more than she lets on . . . more that I ever think she does."

"I'm getting married, Auntie." She put her head back on Auntie's shoulder. "I'm getting married to a man I love. I love him more than words can say."

"I know you do, Jean. You love like the world is ending. And I'm happy for you, my child. I'm so happy you've found love that can hold you. You love a man more than I ever could when I was your age. I tried to love like that once, but I just couldn't hold it in. I couldn't control it. I just couldn't love like you do. And I'm so damned happy for you, for Gary and for Max. Your man can help heal you. He will bring peace to you one day. And I'm so thankful for that."

"He's the one who needs to heal now, Auntie. He's the damaged one."

"We'll heal him together—our family will. He needs love and kindness, and that is something that Uncle and I can provide. We'll heal him together."

"Thank you, Auntie. Thank you so much for loving us both." She paused a moment, this courageous and impulsive woman and then said, "Will you be my bridesmaid, Auntie? I want you to be my bridesmaid at my wedding."

A smile erupted on Auntie's face. "Yes, my little one. Of course, I will."

"Good morning, Jean. I thought I heard the sound of your voice," Uncle said gently. His limp was gone, and he strode into the room thrilled to see her.

"Uncle!" She let go of Auntie and crossed the room to hug him.

"Hey, what did you do to Gus?" he asked.

"What do you mean?"

"He came into the shop the other day and told me he was releasing me from our agreement. And then, he shook my hand and walked out." Uncle looked almost comical. His mouth was open in surprise, and he turned from side to side, looking first at

Jean and then at Auntie. The shock on Jean's face was evident to anyone looking, and no one was more surprised by this admission than she.

"I have no idea what's up with him. I didn't do anything to him," said Jean, though she was thinking of that morning when they heard Gary's haunting screams from down the tunnel. That must account for Gus's change of heart. "I suppose he just likes you more than you thought."

"Well, whatever you did, thank you."

»»

Once they were dressed, Jean opened the bedroom door and walked down the hall to the living room.

"Hey, sleepyhead," she said to Max. "Up and at 'em."

"Rise and shine, sunshine!" Gary added.

Max sat up slowly and rubbed the sleep from his eyes. "Do you two always have to be so chipper in the morning?"

"The early bird gets the salami, bro," added Gary as he walked in behind Jean. "And we've got a farmers market date. Or did you forget?"

"I didn't forget. I was just enjoying my sleep."

Gary noticed that Max's brows were furrowed and his shoulders looked tense, as though he were struggling to overcome bad posture.

"How are you this morning?" Gary asked him.

"I've made a decision."

"This sounds important."

"It is." He paused, letting the weight of the moment sink in.

"Well, are you going to tell us what it is?" asked Jean. "You're not going back to the streets. Not now that Quinn is out of our lives forever. Are you?"

"No, it's not that. It's nothing like that." He looked up and out the balcony window at the sky beyond.

"Okay," said Gary, "enough making us wait, tough guy. What have you decided to do?"

"I'm going after Cameron." Max watched their faces for their reactions. Gary seemed to melt in front of him, while Jean's eyes looked almost crazy with fear.

"You're what?!" Gary said.

"Are you crazy, Max?" added Jean.

"I'm going after Cameron. He's still out there stealing children, raping them, selling them to high bidders who rape them over and over and over again. When I lived in that basement for all those years, I dreamed of someday bringing an end to Cameron and his empire. I dreamed of the day I would murder Cameron in cold blood and release all those kids in that cursed basement.

"We got past Quinn a little worse for the wear, but we got past him. He's dead, rotting in a corner of Worth St. Station. Now it's Cameron's turn. It's time someone challenged him and stole his little business enterprise out from under him and destroyed it. *I* want to do that. *I* want to be the one who looks into his eyes and cuts his jugular clean so his blood spills on the ground—all that blood to cleanse all the dirty deeds he's done over the years."

"Do you realize what you're proposing to do, Max?" asked Gary.

"Yes. I fully understand the road ahead of me, and how hard it will be for me to do this."

"What do you mean 'you,' Max?" asked Jean. "Don't you mean 'we'?"

"I definitely do not mean the three of us. This is my job. This is something I have to do. I've put you both through enough hell with Quinn. This is my responsibility, not yours."

"Max," said Gary, "you know we don't think of it like that. We dealt with Quinn together, the three of us. And that's how we'll deal with Cameron. Safety in numbers, remember?"

"The three amigos ride again," said Jean, trying to find some humour in the situation.

Max decided to concede the argument. But as far as he was concerned, Gary and Jean would be kept at a long distance from what he would do to trap Cameron. He would never endanger them in his affairs again. Too much had happened this time with Quinn, and Gary had almost died as a result. It would never happen like that again.

"So, what godforsaken time of the morning is it, anyway?" asked Max.

"Eight o'clock on the nose."

"Hey, buddy," Jean said to Max. "You remember we have our own date tonight, right?"

"I do. Classes begin tonight. Tutoring with my teacher, Ms Choi."

"Don't get too familiar with that name. Soon it'll be Jean Aldertree—*Mrs.* Jean Aldertree. And don't you forget it, Mr. Max Soon-to-Be-Best-Man Aldertree," she said with a truly radiant grin.

»»»

Gus put one foot in front of the other, higher than the last and then higher again. The trees were different than he'd ever seen before here in the Andean jungle, and he liked it.

Earlier that morning when the group set out, the air was cool and dry. But the day was slowly warming up, and the humidity was growing. Large, rough stones were lodged deep into the ground to form a path, leading the group up and up the mountain at an incredible incline, the likes of which he'd also never known before.

They'd been placed God knows how long ago, though he was sure that if he were to ask their guide, Jose, he would tell them.

Jose was a short, wiry man with a close crop of richly coloured dark hair, and he seemed to know everything—at least everything about Machu Picchu and the mountainside trail leading up to it. He seemed like an okay sort of man; he was always ready with a joke or a story about another hiker who hadn't fared so well.

Gus was wearing the new hiking boots he'd bought in Cusco before catching the train that dropped him at the base of the trail. Once there, he signed up with a touring company that specialized in bringing tourists on the four-day hike up the mountain. You weren't allowed to hike the trail without either a guide or extensive training under your belt.

At the end of the day, Jose led them to sleeping villas that served impeccable food and had water supplies.

"This next part of the trail is flat—Inca flat," he joked, and they all knew this to mean that it was still incredibly steep, though maybe not as steep as earlier portions of the trail.

Gus was happy here. For the first time in his life, he wasn't looking back over his shoulder to see whether a stranger's gun was pointed at him. And for the first time in his life, he didn't have anyone to kill.

Quinn's death had taken its toll on him. He'd been so frightened in that tunnel as he raced against time knowing that Gary's screams meant he was being attacked. Quinn had made his move, and a god-awful move it had been. He had raped Gary, and it was all his fault. He knew better than to put a protection job like that on hold just because he had to piss. He shouldn't have been drinking coffee, but some part of him didn't really believe that Jean and her friends had much to worry about. Weren't they just a couple of kids overreacting? When he heard the screams of pain coming through the dark to him, though, he finally understood that

Jean wasn't exaggerating the danger, and that whomever was after them must really be deadly.

Gary was screaming out, crying for help, and Gus was still minutes away, running in the dark. It was treacherous, that run. The pathway was narrow, and he had trouble seeing where the tracks ended and it began. He couldn't help Gary from where he was. He could only run and listen to the screams and sobbing that echoed along the tunnel. And it wasn't the kind of sound he ever wanted to hear again. Maybe he would be able to save him from death, but what kind of death was Gary already experiencing? The death of his manhood. The death of his very being.

They'd each run in on Quinn only moments apart from each other, Jean first, Max second and Gus last. From his perch, he'd seen Jean running into the station and down into the tunnel. So he scurried through the crowds up and over to the other side of the platform to follow. Max must have seen Jean rushing through the station and followed at a similar pace to be there to help her administer the medication to Gary. As Gus arrived, he understood better why Gary was screaming for his life.

Gus had listened to a great deal of sobbing in his life: people pleading for their lives, begging him to renege his contract and let them live to see another day, so they could put their affairs in order, better their lives, and look the one who had hired him in the face again and demand why. But none of that sobbing, none of those tears, none of that pleading sounded as anguished to Gus as it did here. Rage soared through his body, his mind, his very soul—if he were to admit he even had one. What sick, twisted human being would do such a thing? What kind of man rapes another man? When his eyes laid on the scene, it was all he could do not to run through the dark and grab him and bash his brains out on to the tiles with his bare hands.

"Okay, we're coming to our sleeping spot for the night. Everybody can rest up really good here. They make great Peruvian food and have some very good German beer," said Jose.

Gus was thankful for the reprieve. He was more than winded by this third day; he was exhausted. But tomorrow they would arrive at Machu Picchu, the place he'd longed to see for most of his adult life.

He ate that night with the rest of his cadre, something that was foreign to him. He had been a loner all his life . . . a man who ate alone, a man who lived alone, a man who slept alone. The three German girls sat apart from the group, drinking copious amounts of German beer. So did the rest of them. But Gus refrained. He knew too well how drinking in excess hampered your senses the next morning, and he didn't want to miss a moment of this wonderful ride. He slept fitfully that night, tired from the day's exercise. Images of men came to him in the dark—bigger, stronger men who were laying on top of him and ripping him to shreds. At one point, he woke sweating with a scream caught in his upper throat.

They set out while it was still dark the next morning, earlier than they had on the previous three days. Jose said it was because he wanted to show them something special. So they trudged out, one after the other, the last remnants of sleep causing their bodies to move slowly. Most of the group was hungover, but Gus was alert and anxious to complete their journey. Jose hurried them on and picked up the pace until their blood was pumping in their ears.

It was already hot and humid by the time the sun came up. The jungle was thick around them, and Gus wondered how anything could be so beautiful. They rounded a corner, and at the end of a short stretch of trail was a huge rock with a large crevice in the middle. The crevice began almost at the bottom of the rock and opened up and out to about seven inches wide at the top of the rock.

"Quickly. Hurry," ushered Jose. "Gather around the rock!" They shuffled together, and he urged them to look through the crevice.

Gus saw it at once. Below him, spread out across the top of a large platform of hard rock, was the ancient city of Machu Picchu. In the east, the sun was just rising on it. From nowhere else could the whole of the city be seen like this. The red rock was absolutely glowing in the early-morning sunrise, flickering with some kind of inner flame. And as he watched, the city seemed to catch fire, to veritably smoulder before him.

Gus sat down on a rock and watched the burning city below him through the crevice. He thought of Jean and Max and poor Gary. He wondered how they were faring. Had Gary come through the infection without dying? Would he ever come through what had happened to him that day, that awful day in the dark? And what about Max? He remembered what Jean had explained about Max's past.

In his mind, he gave all three of them a blessing. They all needed to heal now. They all needed to be safe and keep each other safe. He hoped with all his heart that they could be more than just safe, that they would thrive. Like his own heart had, he hoped against hope that those three young people could catch a healing flame that would burn a hole right through their pain-filled memories. They were strong enough. They were blessed with a healthy combustion that could devour them. But more likely it would flare up and blaze hot and burn the pain right out of their souls. They were blessed with each other.

He smiled to himself, got up and walked down the hill into the burnishing city below.

ACKNOWLEDGEMENTS

There are so many people to thank when it comes down to writing a book. An overenthusiastic young writer is often caught filling the acknowledgement page with thanks for his third-grade teacher, and the old widow who used to babysit him and always read him a bedtime story.

Well, this isn't the Academy Awards.

I have three siblings, Donna Jorgensen, Suzanne Gero and Dustyn Rutherford. They have each supported me to their own capacity and in their own way over the years. For all their support and all their love, I thank them.

I also have my own little Betty, who helps me make it through each and every day. Thanks, Dollface.

I think one of my biggest thank-yous goes out to Brown University for accepting this frightened, soul-searching, far-too-old-to-be-doing-this thirty-year-old into its undergraduate halls of learning. While enfolded into this vibrant, fascinating and thrilling school, I learned to become myself, rather than all those personas I had been living. I'm still grateful for everything you gave me, Brown.

To the memory of Douglas Grass, a friend like no other. Look, Dougie! Twenty-five years later and your premonition has come true—I'm getting published! And guess what. Working with an editor wasn't nearly so painful as you predicted. See? I'm not as stubborn as you always thought.

Okay. Thank-yous in earnest now:

To Elizabeth Raible for being the greatest friend a man could ask for. Liz, my deep respect and love for you only grow with each passing day.

To Beatriz Arantes for always knowing the right thing to say. To Amanda Doster for always knowing the right thing to do. To Sarah Bowman for always knowing the right way to reach out. To Greg Machlin for always knowing when to laugh. To Gilles Choquette for always knowing when to play. To Auntie Alvina for the comforts of home. To Albano Magrin for the smile he so freely gives. To Audrey Rollins for reading so closely. To Karen Tchir for being so enthusiastic. To Colin, for having been there. To B.J. Laschowski for just being my friend. To Heather Laschowski for everything you do. To James Candy and a burgeoning friendship cut loose too soon. I hope you are finally getting to read this book, wherever you are. To Sharon Candy for being so supportive. To Anthony Cokes for being the best friend a student could ever find in an Ivy League professor. To Leslie Bostrom for being the *other* best friend a student could ever find in an Ivy League professor. You both taught me more than you know in ways you'll never dream of, and I thank you for it.

To the Alice Melnyk Public Library in Two Hills, Alberta, Canada. It supports the life of this tiny town of about 1,440 people and is a central part of it as a result.

To the members of my book club, who collectively provide a place to go and are the kind of people you'd want to chat literature with on the third Thursday of every month.

To the staff and members of Potential Place, Progress Place and all the International Center for Clubhouse Development Clubhouses worldwide. Your strength and courage shines forth in all you undertake. And a special thanks to Frank Kelton. A finer supporter and friend could be found nowhere.

To Maria Elkow for her unfailing faith in God above and her belief that He can heal the soul. I may not believe hook, line and sinker, but Maria, you make the world a better people of us all. Thank you for your unshakeable love. I love you back.

To the Editorial team at Creators: Thank you, from the bottom, for your belief in *Finding Max*.

And to the creative team at Creators (and I include the marketing team here), thank you for making *Finding Max* special, from its typeface to its cover imagery to its particular feel.

A special thank you to Simone Slykhous, Managing Editor at Creators, for being so enthusiastic about *Finding Max* from the moment I first opened her email informing me of the company's interest in the book. Was I still willing to publish my book with them? (Was I still willing to publish my novel? And was I still in the market for a publisher? Was I ever!) I often think back on our first conversation, when you thanked me for my "eagerness." Did I really sound that naive? I must have been.

And there is one editor at Creators who deserves special, deserved thanks: my own editor, Alissa Stevens. Thank you for excising my all too many commas that I litter around haphazardly; for taking a complex structured paragraph, awkward in its execution, and simplifying it beautifully; for beating me over the head and shoulders with the Chicago Manual of Style until I was black and blue and unrecognizable even to close relatives. Well, maybe she didn't really do THAT, but sometimes it sure felt like it. Alissa, you are a writer's dream come true. You edit with style, grace, surefootedness and sound judgement. And all this you do while making your writers feel on top of their game. Always willing to adapt your own processes to the needs of others, you make your writers feel at home. Thank you, Alissa, for everything you've done for *Finding Max*, but also everything you've done for me.

And, last but not least, two of the most grateful beings in my world: Molly and Dobby. Molly is my gentle force of nature, doling out butterfly kisses only as she sees fit. She's always game for a brushing followed by a tummy rub, all fours splayed in the air. Dobby is a little more rambunctious, a lot more energetic and scads more mischievous. Her kisses are more like the travesty left behind in the wake of a storm, and nothing gives her greater pleasure than to slobber all over you with as many kisses as she can get in before you indignantly shove her off for the night. Molly, you are my gentle being. Dobby, you are my touchstone. Molly, you remind me how far I've come. Dobby, you remind me how far I still have to go. You two constantly show me how much I've grown these past ten years or so. I will never forget you, or stop loving you, as long as I live.

ABOUT THE AUTHOR

Darren M. Jorgensen grew up among the fields and forests of Alberta, Canada. At seventeen, he left home for greener pastures. He settled in various cities, including Toronto, Montreal, Stratford and New York City. While in New York, Jorgensen worked at the United Nations in various capacities, even spending a year in Baghdad to help dismantle Iraq's weapons of mass destruction programs. After returning to the States, he matriculated at Brown University at 30 years old, one of only six adults older than traditional college age granted admission that year.

While at Brown, Jorgensen garnered several awards, all in the area of video and film production. Later, at the University of Michigan School of Art & Design, he directed, produced and shot the film *At the Hands of Another: When Someone You Love Is Murdered*, a documentary that incorporated personal interviews with family members of murder victims.

Jorgensen has studied law, society, art, theatre and professional photography. But it became too clear during his years of higher education that his first love was writing. He has always fed his passions through involvement in book clubs and writing groups. Writing has served as the best vehicle for Jorgensen to explore the trauma of homelessness, hunger, extreme poverty and illness, issues he's faced throughout his adult life. He wrote his debut novel, *Finding Max*, in just 12 days.

Jorgensen now lives back in his native province, on a farm east of Edmonton, with his wonderful wife, Ginette, and two extraordinary dogs, Dobby and Molly, who march to the beat of their own drum. He loves to walk with his dogs through the fields while watching the sun rise on the eastern horizon.

Finding Max
is also available as an e-book
for Kindle, Amazon Fire, iPad, Nook and Android
e-readers. Visit creatorspublishing.com to learn
more.

○ ○ ○

CREATORS PUBLISHING

We find compelling storytellers and
help them craft their narrative,
distributing their novels and collections
worldwide.

○ ○ ○

88991891R00211

Made in the USA
Lexington, KY
22 May 2018